DUKE WITH A REPUTATION
WICKED DUKES SOCIETY
BOOK ONE

SCARLETT SCOTT

Duke with a Reputation

Wicked Dukes Society Book 1

All rights reserved.

Copyright © 2024 by Scarlett Scott™

Published by Happily Ever After Books, LLC

Edited by Grace Bradley and Lisa Hollett, Silently Correcting Your Grammar

Cover Design by Wicked Smart Designs

This book or any portion thereof may not be reproduced or used in any manner whatsoever without the express written permission of the publisher except for the use of brief quotations in a book review.

The unauthorized reproduction or distribution of this copyrighted work is illegal. No part of this book may be scanned, uploaded, or distributed via the Internet or any other means, electronic or print, without the publisher's permission. Criminal copyright infringement, including infringement without monetary gain, is punishable by law.

This book is a work of fiction and any resemblance to persons, living or dead, or places, events, or locales, is purely coincidental. The characters are productions of the author's imagination and used fictitiously.

Scarlett Scott is a registered trademark of Happily Ever After Books LLC.

For more information, contact author Scarlett Scott.

https://scarlettscottauthor.com/

*For my incredible team, who works so hard behind the scenes to make my books (and me) shine in every way: Estela, Grace, Heather, Lisa, Pam, and Tatyana
Thank you!*

PROLOGUE

HERTFORDSHIRE, 1872

The scene in the Wingfield Hall dining room would have put a Roman Bacchanalia to shame. The Duke of Brandon smirked as he surveyed the tableau before him from his vantage point at the head of the table.

No fewer than three dozen bottles of the fine French Bordeaux he had procured on his most recent trip abroad—*Chateau Margaux*, vintage 1864, truly *une grande année*—decanted and in various states of consumption.

To say nothing of the women in a debauched array of scandalous dishabille. There was a thoroughly sotted brunette with her breasts fully exposed above her bodice like ripe offerings, her nipples rouged to enhance their obscenely glorious display. Then there was the incomparable actress, Mrs. Helena Darby—not to be outdone by a rival—who launched suddenly from her seat, spun about, and flipped up her skirts to expose her full ivory bottom for anyone who cared to look.

Most of the room, as it happened.

For Helena possessed one of the finest arses Brandon had ever been fortunate enough to see. Or spank. Or…

Well, never mind *that*. Brandon gave his trousers a furtive tug beneath the table at the unfinished thought. Ah, lewd reminiscences. He might fully indulge in another bout of memory-making later, should this evening progress as he intended.

Or perhaps, he would take his pleasure from another of the bevy of beauties in attendance, or two—or even three at once. Helena had never liked to share, which was deadly dull. Even if she had a mouth skilled enough to suck the silver plating off a vicar's spoon. Why limit himself when the possibilities were endless?

Brandon sipped idly at his Bordeaux, a pleasant haze enveloping him that likely had something to do with the latest potion Kingham—King, as his familiars knew him—had insisted he drink. Had it contained opium? Who gave a bloody damn? This night was the culmination of his efforts—a celebration, of sorts. And he intended to savor each moment with every woman he could.

Hairpins had long since been dropped from all the demimondaines in attendance, along with the initial pretense of decorum. Tapes and hooks and laces had come undone. Neckties and coats and any hint of formality had been dispensed with at the door to the grand dining hall, where a pile of discarded garments had been discreetly carried away by circumspect servants, who were trained and paid well enough to avert their gazes and hold their tongues.

The vignette before him was as pleasing as it was rousing. Oh yes, indeed. Brandon's coterie of friends, summoned for this inaugural fête of sin, were indulging in every vice he had presented for their delectation. They had come up together at Eton, and they were united by two common goals.

Common Goal the First: their mutual disdain for the wretches who had sired them and their desire to show it at every opportunity, in whatever manner possible, regardless of the ensuing scandal.

Common Goal the Second: their desire to pursue pleasure at any and all costs.

It was the latter, rather than the former, that currently preoccupied his friends most. Riverdale had a woman on each knee. Camden had his face buried between the bountiful bubbies of a black-haired beauty. Richford was whispering in a fetching redheaded lady's ear. Whitby had his arm around a blonde's bare shoulders, whilst his other hand appeared to be in a lovely brunette's lap. King's face was pressed to the ivory throat of an opera singer.

And then there was the *pièce de résistance*, a naked wench in repose amongst the feast served *à la française*, covered in an assortment of tarts—the dessert course. No one had taken the cherry tart resting disproportionately on the peak of her left nipple, even if someone had already scooped the gooseberry galette from her cunt; Brandon had his heart quite set upon that cherry tart. He so despised incongruity of any form, and her right nipple bore only the faintest hint of blueberry.

Rising from his chair and swaying on his feet as he reached for the dessert—the bloody Bordeaux had gone to his head, as well as King's sweet brew—Brandon snagged the lonely tart and deposited it on his plate. Now that his guests had consumed their feast and the true revelry of the evening had begun, it was time for a small matter of business.

He raised a glass, tapping it with his fork to draw everyone's attention to him.

When glassy-eyed stares settled upon him, the tittering and naughty murmurings dying down, he spoke loudly enough that his voice would carry through the cavernous Wingfield Hall chamber. The majestic maternal ancestral estate was an excellent place to host his revelries, for although it belonged to his grandmother, she had not entered its walls since his grandfather's passing some years before. Instead, she kept to London or paid calls upon friends in the country, giving Brandon the reins since he would one day inherit the massive manor house and grounds as her heir. He had given Grandmother's domestics a few days of paid leave, and he had brought his own discreet servants, all paid handsomely for their silence.

"I call to order this first meeting of the Wicked Dukes Society," he said now, his voice echoing through the centuries-old dining room.

It was the silly, bombastic name they had agreed upon after a three-day party at King's country seat, during which they had raided and consumed nearly the entire impressive alcohol stores of Dukes of Kinghams past.

A chorus of enthusiastic agreement sprang up. "Hear, hear!"

Camden's inamorata raised her wineglass with so much sudden force that her Bordeaux splashed all over her silk bodice and bare breasts, leaving Camden with no choice but to lick up the mess.

"We are gathered here this evening," he continued, "united in a common cause—the pursuit of pleasure. What happens within the walls of Wingfield Hall stays within the walls of Wingfield Hall."

King removed his lips from the opera singer's neck long enough to raise his own glass in toast. "We should all speak a vow of secrecy."

Brandon hadn't thought of that, and he was rather put out with himself for the failure. "Excellent idea, old chap. Have you a vow in mind?"

"Camden has always had a head for poetry," King offered. "Cam, what say you?"

Their friend was still drowning in bubbies, but he raised a

bleary-eyed stare at his name. "What say I? What are we speaking about?"

"A vow for the Wicked Dukes Society," Brandon intervened. "King thinks we ought to make one, and he nominated you for the sorry task on account of your poetical heart."

Cam issued an indelicate snort. "The only part of my body that is poetical is inside my trousers."

The room burst into guffaws and snickers.

"But I seem to distinctly recall the poem you wrote for Lady Flora Seaton," King prodded. "A beautiful sonnet, if I'm not mistaken."

Cam was usually imperturbable, but now his face flamed. Lady Flora was a delicate subject, one which he preferred to avoid. King always knew how to cut a man to his marrow, friend or foe alike, and he was more perceptive than anyone Brandon had ever met.

Cam's eyes narrowed. "Indeed, I did. But I find I'm not nearly as eloquent as Riverdale. Perhaps he ought to write the vows."

"If King thinks we should have one, then King can bloody well write it," Riverdale said, before whispering something into the ear of one of the ladies on his lap and earning a sultry chuckle in response.

"Not terribly sporting of you," King grumbled with a sigh before raising his Bordeaux. "Very well, then. I surrender. You shall have a simple vow from a simple man."

Ha! Brandon couldn't stifle his chortle at his friend's claim. There was nothing simple about the Duke of Kingham. Indeed, King was the most complex person he had ever met.

King raised a brow at him. "Brandon, is there something which amuses you? Perhaps you'd care to share with the rest of the company."

Brandon wiggled his fingers in a dismissive gesture. "Carry on with your simple vow, old chap, before we all grow old and gray."

"Old and gray?" Whitby shuddered dramatically. "I hope I meet my ignominious end well before that day."

"Oh, do stubble it, Whit," Richford said congenially as he gave the redhead's breast an indolent fondle. "We all know that you've the devil's own luck. You'll likely be hearty as a stallion at five-and-ninety, quite unlike some of us."

Whitby grinned. "Am I to blame for my own good fortune?"

"Enough," King interrupted in a lighthearted tone. "I've settled upon a vow."

Brandon inclined his head in his friend's direction. "Carry on then, old chap."

King frowned. "We should have a bible to swear upon."

"I haven't got one." Brandon thought for a moment, frowning. "We'll have to swear upon the *Chateau Margaux*. Raise your glasses."

All six incipient members of the Wicked Dukes Society did as he bid.

"Repeat after me," King ordered. "From this moment on, I solemnly devote myself to the pursuit of pleasure and to the utter destruction of my father's legacies."

The friends repeated King's vow, followed by the clinking of glasses and a resounding cry of, "Hear, hear!"

"May he rot in Hades where he belongs," added Riverdale grimly.

In that moment, the Wicked Dukes Society was born, steeped in sin and fine French wine.

CHAPTER 1

LONDON, 1878

*B*randon was having a nightmare.

That was the only explanation for the sight opposite him, he was certain of it. Either that, or he had imbibed one of King's ingenious brews and was now suffering the delusional aftereffects of the dubious elixir.

"Have you nothing to say for yourself, Brandon?"

The sharp, censorious voice, however, was disturbingly real. As was the glacial green-eyed glare so similar to his own. And the massive, billowing silk gown, beneath which hid a crinoline more suited to the fashions of thirty years ago than now.

He blinked, hoping the action would dispel the image before him. Pull him from the throes of sleep. Cast away the demons brought about by one of King's inspired concoctions.

But no.

His grandmother remained.

Hellfire. Perhaps she was real after all.

Brandon cleared his throat. "I do beg your pardon,

Grandmother, but I have no notion of what I ought to be saying for myself."

"Have you not heard a word I have just spoken?"

Admittedly, he had been wool-gathering. Hoping he had found himself thrown into some slumberous alternate reality.

"I'm afraid not," he conceded.

Her nostrils flared, and for a fanciful moment, he imagined her breathing fire like a mythical dragon swooping in to scorch him and other unsuspecting mortals in her path.

"I will begin again, Brandon," she said succinctly, as if she feared very much he lacked the mental acuity to comprehend. "Do try to heed me this time."

Her scolding was nothing new; Grandmother had always been harder than granite. Although her dark hair had long since turned snowy and the face that had made her the most-sought-after debutante of her day was now lined, nary a hint of infirmity surrounded her. She was a tiny wren of a woman, but sturdy of form.

Now, as ever, she terrified him.

Brandon shifted on his dashed uncomfortable chair, wishing he'd had the forethought to have Grandmother await him somewhere other than the drawing room, a chamber he scarcely used for its fervent *Louis Quinze* devotion. "Of course. Pray, proceed."

She inclined her head and, with a regal air, continued. "As I was saying, a visitor most unexpected and uninvited paid a call upon me yesterday. I am told she was turned away by your domestics. Ordinarily, I would have no desire to concern myself with such matters. Indeed, it is most unseemly. However, the child has your eyes and nose."

Surely he must have misheard.

"The child?" he repeated, feeling as if the world had suddenly turned on its head.

Everything before him was unrecognizable.

"The girl child," Grandmother elaborated, disapproval dripping from her voice.

Brandon was still struggling to understand. Was there wine to be had? A cursory glance about the drawing room suggested only tea that Grandmother must have requested. He needed something far less tepid.

"Are you attending me, Brandon?" she asked, her voice sharp.

He wrested his gaze from the tea and pinned it back upon his grandmother. "What girl child?"

"The one who was delivered, much to my butler's horror, to my door yesterday afternoon by her mother, just before the woman ran off with her lover."

"Who was the girl's mother?" he managed, his necktie feeling more like a noose by the moment, growing tighter and tighter.

"She said her name was Mrs. Helena Darby-Booth." Grandmother's lip curled as if she had just tasted something spoiled. "A woman of ill repute, to be sure. She was dressed like a harlot, and it is to my everlasting shame that such a sinful creature should have had cause to arrive at my door after having been refused from yours. Have you any notion of the tongues that will gleefully wag? No, I daresay you do not. You are too busy cavorting with your lemans to save a thought for anyone other than yourself. Just like your father. I warned my darling Diana not to wed that scurrilous scoundrel. I didn't care that he was a duke."

His grandmother shook her head, caught in the throes of the past and temporarily distracted from her diatribe. Brandon was in shock. Helena had been his lover off and on over the years until she had abruptly married and left the stage some time ago. Had not that man been called Booth? Brandon searched the dim recesses of his mind for the name and the particulars. He had not seen her since, nor had he heard from her. What cause had she to call upon his grandmother, bringing a girl child?

One with his eyes and nose?

He swallowed against a rising sea of bile. "The sins of the father, madam. Tell me, if you please, why Mrs. Darby-Booth should have called upon you, bringing a child."

"Because Mrs. Darby-Booth is following her new gentleman friend to America, and according to the letter she left with the girl, the man in question could only afford passage for two." His grandmother's green eyes, assessing and bright, narrowed. "She was required to leave the child behind, and she therefore deemed it better to leave the child in the care of her father's family rather than an orphanage."

No, no, no.

He heard the words Grandmother was speaking, but he didn't wish to understand them. Surely this was all a dreadful mistake. Some manner of ploy Helena had concocted. He had always taken care with his lovers. He used a sheath. Unless… There had been occasions, particularly in times of drunken revelry at Wingfield Hall or in St John's Wood, when he may have been too sotted to take care…

Dread seized him, a fist choking his lungs.

"In the care of her…father's family?" he repeated.

"Yes, since the father himself refused to see her. There was a ship leaving, and our Mrs. Darby-Booth only had so much time in which to complete the task of abandoning her bastard child."

His grandmother was forbidding.

Bastard child.

The father.

Eyes and nose like his.

A daughter.

Fucking hell, could it be possible he had a daughter he

hadn't known existed? That when Helena had left London, she had been carrying his child?

"How old is she?" he asked hoarsely. "The girl."

"She tells me that she is four years of age, nearly five."

It was as if Brandon had been dealt a vicious punch directly to the gut. The breath left him. He gasped for a moment, trying to suck in air, to make sense of everything he had just learned. The timing certainly suggested, along with Grandmother's description, that he was indeed the father of the girl who had been deposited at her house yesterday.

Oh God, oh God, oh God.

Surely not.

Surely it was impossible.

Surely he could not be anyone's father.

"You…you spoke with the child." He swallowed hard.

"Of course I spoke with the child." Again, his grandmother's lip curled. "Despite her rude origins, the girl appears to possess reasonable intelligence. But I will warn you, Brandon, that I will not lower myself to playing hostess to your illegitimate children. You must tend to your responsibilities as you see fit. I'll not concern myself with them."

The world was spinning madly about him. How much wine had he consumed last night? Was it the news or was it the despicable aftereffects of too much indulgence that had him feeling as if he were about to cast up his accounts?

"Her name," he managed. "What is her name?"

Not that it mattered one way or the other. But if he was to be a father, then he might as well know what to call the child. Somehow, that seemed of grave importance.

"Her name is Pandora," Grandmother informed him archly. "It seems uniquely appropriate."

Pandora.

He had a daughter. Quite possibly. An illegitimate one.

And she had a name and his eyes and nose.

He patted his nose absently, thinking it perhaps a bit too sharp for a girl. "Where is she now?"

"In the absence of a proper nurse for the child, I've left her under the care of my companion, Miss Heale, at my town house," she informed him icily.

He nodded, wondering what the devil he was meant to do with a child. "I suppose I must have her collected, then."

"Yes, you must," Grandmother said, stern. "I'll not be responsible for her. It is time you bore some duty upon those strapping shoulders of yours."

He stiffened at the judgment in her tone. "I *do* have a great deal of responsibility."

And by that, he meant that he put rather a tremendous amount of effort into being an excellent host. His social gatherings were the stuff of legend. As the founding member of the Wicked Dukes Society, he took pride in his prowess.

As if hearing his thoughts spoken aloud, his grandmother clicked her tongue. "Hosting scandalous routs is not a responsibility, Brandon. When have you seen to any of your estates recently?"

"I correspond with my steward regularly," he defended, even if that was an exaggeration.

In truth, the more recent letters he had received from the man remained stacked and unopened somewhere in the clutter of his study desk. He was far more concerned with Wingfield Hall than the entail.

"How regularly?" she demanded.

"It is none of your concern," he countered. "With all your disdain for the former Duke of Brandon, I wouldn't think you should worry yourself over the present one."

"I do when the present one is my grandson and appears to be intent upon beggaring himself."

He took umbrage at that. "I am hardly beggaring myself."

"You depend upon the vast fortune you will receive from me when I die."

God, she was too damned clever. It wasn't that he anticipated Grandmother's demise. For all that she was as hard-shelled as a tortoise, she was a part of his mother. And Brandon had adored his mother, who had died in childbirth when he had been but a lad of eight.

"I do nothing of the sort," he said, shifting again on his chair.

"Has it ever occurred to you that I need not direct my funds or Wingfield Hall to you, Brandon?"

"No." His answer was swift and honest. "It has not."

Brandon was his grandmother's sole heir, and his mother's side of the family had been hideously wealthy from decades of building a fortune in manufacturing and trade. His father had never allowed his mother to forget her lack of noble forebears, though he'd had no compunction about availing himself of her immense dowry.

"Then perhaps it should." Grandmother's eyes narrowed. "I will not leave my fortune and my family's lands to be pilfered by you as you abandon a string of illegitimate children about London in your wake like your father before you. Wingfield Hall is sacred to me, as you know. I would sooner consign it to Hades than leave it to a profligate to plunder like some sort of modern-day pirate."

Wingfield Hall had become Brandon's most exclusive den of pleasure. Vast and sprawling in the Hertfordshire countryside, it had been the site of the inaugural meeting of the Wicked Dukes Society for its convenience to London and verdant privacy. It had, for those same reasons, been the host of each meeting thereafter. It was also a desperately lucrative —and intensely secret—business. One he had taken great care to make certain his grandmother would never discover. Losing it had never seemed a possibility.

"You would deny your only flesh and blood his birthright?" he asked with deceptive calm, hoping she would see reason in such folly.

But Grandmother's pointed chin went stubbornly up. "I had hoped it wouldn't come to that, but I will do whatever I must to save Wingfield Hall—and you—from ruin. I would sooner see Cousin Horace have it."

"Ruin?" He might have laughed, were he not still so shattered at the prospect that he had somehow been a father for *four bloody years* without knowing, and had his grandmother not just threatened to give the shining jewel of his estates to a country booby distant cousin who smelled like sheep.

Grandmother sighed. "I have heard rumors you are a member of some infernal society devoted to iniquity. I needed my hartshorn when Theodosia Dowling told me she had heard it from Lady Agnes Bryson. I never could abide by Lady Agnes—she has hated me for years, ever since I won your grandfather after she had set her cap at him. It goes without saying that I disapprove wholeheartedly of any such scandalous claptrap. I thought better of you, Brandon. *Truly,* I did."

She extracted a fan and, despite the relative chill in the air, began fanning herself. Brandon stared at her, everything he had just heard making no more sense than it had when she had first uttered it.

His mind whirled.

Grandmother had heard about the Wicked Dukes Society? But how? Years had passed since that Bordeaux-soaked night when he and five of his old Eton chums had first settled upon the notion. He had not supposed word would ever reach anyone, let alone her. After all, it was meant to be a *secret* society. Not that it was much of a society. More than anything, it was a friendship—a brotherly bond that each of them had found absent in their lives previously, whether by lack of blood brothers or lack of blood brothers who weren't arseholes. It was also making them sinfully rich, even if some of them needed those funds more than others.

"Grandmother, I can assure you that I do not belong to any such society, infernal or otherwise," he said smoothly, "and that Mrs. Dowling and Lady Agnes are indulging in scandal broth. It is idle gossip, nothing more."

"Do not lie to me, Brandon."

He held her gaze. "I would never lie to you, Grandmother."

Unless I have no other option, he added internally.

"I'll not be cozened," she snapped. "Do you think me an imbecile? I've been hearing whispers about you for years, but I have refused to indulge in rumors. Look at where my forbearance has led—to your natural child being delivered to my door."

Blast. This interview was not going well. His head was beginning to ache, and not just because Grandmother had been peppering him with a volley of unpleasant questions and revelations. But also because he was a father, and suddenly, his world had been not just upended, but burned to ash.

He had to concentrate upon what was truly important in this moment. It didn't matter if Grandmother had heard the whispers, or that every man or woman who entered the hallowed walls of Wingfield Hall did so under a vow of strictest silence some had clearly broken. What *did* matter was the child—Pandora, he reminded himself.

She had a name. Dear God, what was a voluptuary like him going to do with a child? He'd need to hire a nursemaid. Could he send the girl away somewhere? So many details to sort through, and the lingering effects of the previous evening's merriments still fogged his poor mind. It was too early in the afternoon for such dire news.

"Brandon, are you attending me at all?"

At the shrill tone entering Grandmother's voice, he jolted from his musings.

"Of course, my dear," he reassured her grimly. "It is impossible not to attend you when you are shouting at me."

"I am *not* shouting!"

The echo of her voice in the chamber was a stark rebuttal.

He had never seen his otherwise impassive grandmother exhibit such a frenzy of emotion. She was in fine dudgeon now, twin patches of angry color on her cheeks, eyes sparking with fire.

"I apologize for the child's unexpected arrival," he said. "I'll send someone to fetch her now if you'd prefer it."

"She is a child, not a parcel."

There was no pleasing his grandmother today.

And unfortunately, at that moment, the strains of the final aria from *La sonnambula* pierced the vexed silence that had fallen. Brandon winced, quite having forgotten that the famed soprano, Madame Auclair, had accompanied him home the previous evening. Any hopes he'd harbored of bedding her had died when she had begun to snore on the short carriage ride, the chanteuse having apparently consumed far more champagne than he had realized. He had seen her to a guest chamber.

Grandmother's eyebrows rose. "What is that *sound*?"

Dear God. What was Marie doing? The singing—whilst beautiful—was growing nearer. Where was Shilling, damn it? He relied on his butler to save him from such unfortunate circumstances.

Brandon tugged at his necktie. "Ah, opera, I believe."

"Ah! non credea mirarti," Marie sang.

The horror etched on his grandmother's face would have been comical had the situation not been so disastrous. "There is an *opera singer* in your house?"

She may as well have said there was a rat in his house, so thorough was her disgust.

"Perhaps," he offered noncommittally just as the drawing room door burst open.

"*Sì presto estinto, o fiore.*"

Marie was wearing one of his dressing gowns, her long, dark hair flowing in waves down her back. Judging by the swaying of her full breasts and her bare feet and ankles, it would appear she was completely nude beneath it. Her voice warbled at the sight that presented her—an august white-haired woman and Brandon fully dressed, a tea service between them—and then her song died entirely.

"Forgive me," she said in heavily accented English. "I didn't realize you had a guest."

Grandmother's tea fell to the floor, the delicate porcelain breaking into shards.

CHAPTER 2

"I'm afraid I must decline the generous invitation to your home, Lady Grenfell."

Lottie stared at the Duke of Brandon, certain she had misheard him in the noise of the ballroom crush. Tonight was *the* night, she had told herself as she had prepared her *toilette* earlier that evening. The night she persuaded London's greatest lover to accompany her home so that she might experience his legendary bedroom prowess herself. They had been dancing about each other, traveling in the same circles, Lottie having been invited to not one but *two* of Brandon's balls.

The time had come for more.

She moved subtly nearer to him, knowing all too well the way her latest corset from Mrs. Loveton put her ample breasts on display in her daring evening gown. "I must have misheard you, Your Grace. The ballroom is so dreadfully loud. What did you say?"

His startling green gaze dropped to her decolletage for only a moment before meeting her eyes again. "I said I must regretfully decline."

She felt like a sail ship in the absence of wind.

"Decline," she repeated stupidly, heat creeping up her throat to her cheeks.

Oh, blast her red hair. Nothing made her more cross than her uncontrollable propensity for blushing whenever she was embarrassed.

But then, this went beyond mere embarrassment. Utter humiliation, she thought with grim self-loathing, would be a far more apt description of her present state.

"Indeed, I fear I have other engagements this evening that preclude me from joining you later." Brandon smiled, and the effect was as devastating as ever, despite his easy dismissal.

The duke's hair was a rich shade of mahogany, worn in carefully tousled waves that perpetually looked as if a woman's fingers had just run through them in ecstasy. And likely, they had. He possessed the sort of astonishing good looks that made women all but swoon over him. Firm jaw, cleft chin, the most sensual mouth she had ever beheld on a man—certainly, a mouth made for kissing—sharp cheekbones, a straight, elegant blade of a nose, and a brooding stare that felt like a caress.

Had she misread the signs that he was interested in her? Since her period of mourning for Grenfell had ended, Lottie had indulged in several flirtations. She was no novice. Surely she had not been wrong about the heated stare she had caught trained on her so many times recently. That, coupled with his association with her dear friend Hyacinth's lover, Viscount Sidmouth, had made Lottie quite certain of herself.

But now, she had offered a blunt invitation to her bed, and he had refused, quite as if it were of no consequence at all. As if the notion were neither tempting nor even remotely of interest to him.

"Of course," she murmured, wishing the floor would open up and provide her with a place to hide and forget she had so mortified herself. "There will no doubt be scores of other gentlemen happy to take your place."

That much was true. Lottie was indeed quite sought-after. But she was also extraordinarily selective.

Brandon's grin turned self-deprecating as he inclined his head. "No doubt."

There was nothing more to say, and the floorboards had not obligingly opened to swallow her.

She forced a smile for her pride's sake. "I'll bid you good evening, then, Your Grace."

She moved to skirt past him when he stopped her.

"Wait."

Lottie paused, angling her head at him even as her wounded pride said she should carry on and forget this dreadful humiliation had ever happened. He watched her with a hooded stare, his eyes intense and brilliant as emeralds.

She steeled herself against the effect he had on her, making her tone impersonal and cool. "Yes?"

Brandon startled her by reaching for her hand, their positioning such that none of their fellow revelers could see what he was about. His hold was gentle, his thumb swirling over her inner wrist in a slow, maddening caress. She wondered if he could feel her leaping pulse and cursed herself for her weakness.

Lottie had been touched before, and far more intimately. There was no reason for her body to catch flame as it did now—her nipples pebbling under her corset, a frisson of awareness stealing through her as quick as lightning, desire pooling low in her belly. And yet, she could not seem to stay her own maddening reaction.

"There's a salon just out of the ballroom, down the hall," he said softly, still stroking her sensitive inner wrist with delicate deliberation. "The third door to your right. I'll meet you there in ten minutes."

An assignation?

He hadn't refused her, then.

"Ten minutes, and make sure no one sees you," he repeated softly, giving her wrist a light squeeze.

Releasing her, he took a step back and then swept into an elegant bow.

Lottie watched him as he moved away, his long-limbed strides containing the casual confidence of a duke who knew his place in the world. He was a breathtaking man. It was impossible not to take note of the way the gazes of other women at the ball strayed to him. The Duke of Brandon had a reputation. A wicked one. And soon, she would be experiencing it firsthand.

A shiver of anticipation went down Lottie's spine, but not without the accompanying surge of nervousness. She had taken lovers in the wake of Grenfell's death, but they had been a few, discreet affairs conducted in privacy, with no chance of prying eyes or ears. She had never, in all her days, indulged in a hasty tryst during a ball.

But she was going to now.

Wasn't she?

Oh good heavens, what if this was a dreadful mistake? She had told herself that being bold and brash and wild was the best revenge she could possibly have upon Grenfell for breaking her heart and then dying, leaving her alone. But she couldn't lie. Some days, playing the role of merry widow—burying her sadness in diversions that never lasted or satisfied—was naught but cold comfort. Her husband was gone, and despite Lottie having been deeply in love with him, he had never returned her love, instead spending the entirety of their marriage bedding a string of mistresses. She had no children. And the lovers she'd taken had not made the emptiness inside her any less.

Would Brandon?

Oh, if only Hyacinth were here. The widowed Lady Southwick was one of Lottie's oldest and dearest friends. Hyacinth often understood Lottie better than she understood herself. However, Hyacinth had also been eschewing polite society recently, claiming she was ill. Lottie was going to have to seek her out at the first available opportunity and force her from her doldrums. Ending her affair with Sidmouth had left Hyacinth desperately melancholy, and Lottie knew all too well the pain a broken heart could cause.

"Lottie!"

She turned at the familiar sound of another, different friend's voice, relieved to banish her concerns for a few moments as genuine pleasure shot through her. "My dear. I didn't expect to see you this evening."

Miss Rosamund Payne was particularly resplendent this evening in a silk gown of shimmering gold and pale lavender silk that complemented her gold-red hair, ivory skin, and dark eyes. An heiress in her own right, Rosamund was renowned for her sharp intellect, sharper tongue, and for her beloved parrot, Megs, who often accompanied her to social engagements. The bird was not with her this evening, however.

"I wasn't intending to come to the ball," Rosamund confided in conspiratorial fashion, "but then I decided I had to see whether Camden would be in attendance."

The revelation piqued Lottie's interest. The Duke of Camden, like the Duke of Brandon, was a rake with a certain reputation. He was also the elder brother of Rosamund's former betrothed.

The Duke of Camden's scapegrace younger brother, Lord Wesley Gilden, a second son with a need for Rosamund's fortune, had broken her heart. He had committed the egregious sin of asking for Rosamund's hand and pretending he loved her, all whilst carrying on with an actress in St John's Wood. When Rosamund had inadvertently discovered his treachery—the actress had sent her a letter to inform her that she was expecting a child with Lord Wesley—she had been devastated, throwing Lord Wesley over.

"Why should you wish to know if Camden is here?" Lottie asked, curious beyond measure.

She *adored* gossip. It was one of her only vices. Well, that and fine Bordeaux. And handsome men.

"Because I need to speak to him," Rosamund answered with a heavy sigh. "He has presented me with a proposition that I find...*interesting*, despite my better judgment."

Lottie's mouth fell open. "Oh?"

Something salacious, she was sure. The Duke of Camden was a bounder. An unapologetic cad. He would never make a proper offer to anyone, regardless of how desperate his circumstances had become, having had a father who had beggared not just himself, but all the estates in the entail as well. He was a rogue to the rotten core, scarcely any different from his brother.

"Don't look at me so," Rosamund chided. "It is not *that* sort of proposition, if you must know."

Lottie bit her lip. "What sort?"

"The indecent sort," Rosamund elaborated, looking distinctly uncomfortable now. "Rather, it was quite proper. He offered me marriage."

Lottie could have been knocked off her feet with nothing more than a feather, so great was her shock.

"He did?" she managed at last past her own incredulousness.

"In return for something I want very much," Rosamund explained, taking care to keep her voice from traveling.

"What is that, my dear?"

Rosamund smiled. "Revenge."

∽

BRANDON CONSULTED his pocket watch for the fifth time as he paced the Axminster in the emerald salon—so named for its abject fidelity to the color green—where he had arranged to meet with the Countess of Grenfell. She was late. Perhaps she had changed her mind. Ordinarily, Brandon was the sort of man who waited for no one. But this evening was different, and he was willing to exert his limited patience for one reason alone.

He needed a wife.

Needed one with as much haste as he could muster, and the very notion of courting made him want to stab his eyes out with a pair of dull pickle forks. Grandmother had made herself clear, however. If he didn't marry within the next *three bloody months*, she had every intention of changing her will, leaving Wingfield Hall and the rest of her fortune to his dreadful cousin Horace.

The redheaded beauty who had been sending him take-me-to-bed glances for weeks seemed as good a choice as any, particularly after she had issued a brazen invitation to her bed. As a widow, she was experienced enough not to have the missish sensibilities of a virgin. She was friends with Lady Southwick, whom his good chum Sidmouth had recently been in lust with—small world, et cetera, et cetera. Her family was respected and well-known, and Grandmother could find no fault in it, even if Lady Grenfell's own reputation was a trifle scandalous.

Brandon didn't give a damn how many lovers she'd taken

in the past. Hell, he didn't care if she took lovers again after they were married. All he *did* care about was placating Grandmother and securing Wingfield Hall forever. Besides, he told himself as he stalked the length of the chamber once more, feeling like a lion trapped in a cage, he would need someone to look after Pandora. Oh, he knew it wasn't done to ask one's wife to tend to a child born on the wrong side of the blanket. However, he wasn't inclined to send his poppet away now that he had her.

One look at her heart-shaped face and dark ringlets, and he had been irrevocably changed. She had slipped her hand into his, the gesture so trusting and guileless that he had been left speechless. Until she had later upended his inkwell, allowed a bird into the house from the gardens which had promptly shat all over the carpets—*but Duke, her name's Emily, 'n we're friends*—and wetted herself whilst sitting on his lap. Then, Brandon had found words, along with the realization that he required assistance when it came to the little imp beyond the nursemaid he had hastily hired.

Yes, the timing would be excellent in all ways.

He knew what he had to do.

As if on cue, the door to the salon clicked open, and the Countess of Grenfell slipped over the threshold, closing it at her back. Their gazes met and held, and for a heartbeat, something coursed through him—a deep, elemental acknowledgment of her as a woman. She was astoundingly lovely, and it couldn't be denied.

Lady Grenfell hesitated as he took a moment to admire her. She was lush of form with a mouth any courtesan would covet, fiery tresses, and sea-blue eyes. Her skin was pale, dusted with a delightful smattering of freckles he wouldn't mind exploring with his tongue. He wondered if her breasts were dusted with freckles as well. Tiny flecks of gold to contrast with ivory mounds and sweet pink nipples.

His cock went rigid at the thought of exploring her.

Not now, old chap. We have more important matters to attend to just now.

Matters such as marriage.

The reminder made his rampaging prick wilt enough to render forward locomotion less uncomfortable. His trousers were still deuced snug. He strode toward her anyway.

"Lady Grenfell." Brandon bowed formally when he reached her, taking her hand in his and bringing it to his lips for a lingering kiss on the knuckles.

He had dispensed with his gloves, but she still wore hers, and the impediment was nettlesome. The pleasant scent of roses, tinged with a hint of violets, reached him. She must have dabbed some scent on her inner wrist during her *toilette* that evening.

"Your Grace."

He suddenly wished to tug her glove away and know the softness of her bare skin. But that could come later. For now, he couldn't afford to luxuriate in seduction. And damn it if that wasn't a rarity for him.

He straightened but didn't relinquish his hold on her hand. "Call me Brandon. Surely there is no need for formality between us."

She inclined her head, still holding his gaze in that brazen way of hers he found so deliciously enticing. "As you wish. You may call me Lottie if it pleases you."

Lottie. The name suited her. Bright and lovely, rather like a butterfly.

"Lottie," he repeated, trying the name on his tongue and finding he liked the feel of it as well. "Come and have a seat, won't you?"

Her brow furrowed, as if she found his request puzzling. "Of course."

She believed he had invited her to the emerald salon for a

tryst. Her befuddlement was understandable, and God knew he wished he had brought her here for that purpose instead. He offered her his arm, escorting her to the seating arranged before the hearth, a generously sized *Louis Quinze* settee and a pair of wingback chairs.

A sudden sense of indecision struck him.

He had never proposed marriage to a woman before. Brandon had made innumerable indecent and wicked proposals over the years. But never a *proper* one. Good God, what did one do? He ought to have prepared some manner of speech whilst he had been awaiting her. What should he say? Something flowery? Something pragmatic? A false declaration of love? An ode to her breasts?

Well, Christ. What a conundrum.

Brandon guided her to the settee and then settled himself at her side, her cream-and-crimson silk skirts brushing his trousers. It was bold of her, pairing her vibrant red hair with such a daring gown. But the effect was undeniable. At this proximity, she was even more exquisite. Her eyes were pale blue with a ring of gray circling the irises—quite unusual. He didn't think he'd ever seen such a shade before.

Long, coppery lashes swept over the eyes he'd been admiring. "This room is…quite…green."

Her polite, if somewhat grim, observation jolted him from his thoughts.

Brandon gave her a wry grin. "Hence the reason it is known as the emerald salon. Do you find fault with it? I must confess, I've never had an eye for such matters. The wall coverings, furniture, and even the pictures hanging are relics from Dukes and Duchesses of Brandon past."

"I don't find fault with it," she assured him, a small smile flirting with the corners of her sultry lips as she discreetly tugged off her gloves and laid them in her lap. "I was merely surprised at the prodigious amount of the color. A Duke or

Duchess of Brandon past must have been inordinately fond of the shade."

"My paternal grandmother, I believe."

"Oh dear." She bit her lip, and that had his unruly cock awakened once more. "I do believe I've just insulted your grandmother. Quite unintentionally, of course. Forgive me."

He shifted in an effort to lessen the effect her mouth and nearness were having on him. "I scarcely use this room. Think nothing of it."

They stared at each other, the ormolu clock on the mantel —another relic from past dukes and duchesses—ticking into the silence, the muted strains of music and voices in the distance as its sole accompaniment. How the devil was he to proceed?

He knew everything about seduction.

But he knew absolutely nothing about proposals of marriage.

"Is this—" she began.

"Perhaps I—" he started in unison.

They both stopped. This was proceeding wretchedly. He was going to have to revert to what he knew best. On any other occasion, he would have already had her skirts around her waist. She would have been moaning his name by now.

Maybe that was the answer he was seeking. He could combine a seduction with a proposal.

Brandon reached for her, cupping her cheek, the smooth warmth of her skin sending searing awareness careening through him. Her gaze fastened on his. He stroked the lip she had been abusing with the pad of his thumb, and then he angled his head toward hers, hesitating for a moment, curiously entranced by the golden flecks dancing along the bridge of her nose.

A potent awareness blossomed between them. She was the first to break the moment, moving toward him swiftly, their mouths meeting. Lottie kissed him with unabashed ardor, her lips as silken as the rest of her, hot and damned drugging. They were soft, laced faintly with champagne. He thought he'd never tasted anything better.

He caught her waist with his one hand, pulling her more snugly against him as he slid the other to her nape, his fingers slipping into her cool, sleek chignon. He knew how to kiss without affecting a lady's coiffure, but there was some elemental need within him, urging him to pluck pins away, to unravel her long, flaming hair so that he could revel in its glory as it cascaded down her back. Her lips parted, and he took advantage, delving inside with his tongue.

One pin slid free, and then another. A small sound of need came from low in her throat. The desire that roared through him took him by surprise. They had been dancing about each other—literally and figuratively—for weeks now. But she was close to his friend's most recent inamorata, and he had known he needed to tread lightly where Lottie was concerned. However, all that had changed because, now, he was desperate.

It wasn't desperation he was feeling at present, though, nor was it desperation that threatened to consume him. It was something far more potent. Because nothing could have prepared him for the way her lips felt on his, her tongue gliding boldly into his mouth.

Or for her hand on the fall of his trousers, lightly skating over his rigid cock in a tease that set his jaw on edge.

He jerked his head back as she gave him another slow, more thorough caress that made his ballocks tighten, holding his stare all the while. Her boldness pleased him so much that a rush of lust knifed through him with enough violence that he hissed in a breath, as if wounded.

Here was a woman who knew what she desired and wasn't afraid to take it. To take *him*. And sweet Christ, if that wasn't the most potent aphrodisiac he had ever known, he hadn't an inkling what was. His breathing was ragged, his heart galloping. Everything in him screamed to tear open the buttons on his falls and let her do what she would with him. But no, he hadn't invited her to the emerald salon for a frantic fuck. He had brought her here for another reason entirely.

Summoning all the control he possessed, Brandon snatched her hand away from his raging cockstand and brought it swiftly to his lips for a reverent kiss instead. "Lottie."

"Mmm." Her eyes were slumberous, lids low, eyes darkened with desire, twin pools of wintry, storm-ravished seas, and her glorious hair had begun to come undone, curls spilling over her shoulders.

He had to swallow hard against a new rush of need and remind himself that, for the first time in his misbegotten life, his responsibilities outweighed his own selfish wants. He couldn't allow Lottie to unbutton his trousers, take out his cock, and ride him until they both came.

No, he had to ask her the last question in the world he had ever wished to ask of a woman.

One deep breath, and he blurted it.

"Will you marry me?"

CHAPTER 3

Lottie disentangled herself from Brandon, recoiling to the other end of the settee.

For the second time in the span of one evening, she was convincing herself she had misheard him. And yet, this time, there wasn't the cacophony of a ball to blame. Nor did she think she had misunderstood his question.

No, indeed, he had enunciated it quite clearly.

And he was staring at her now, unfairly handsome, a wavy lock of hair fallen over his brow in a rakish manner. The expectation on his face was sincere, having replaced the look of sullen desire he had been wearing when her hand had been upon the thick ridge of his cock.

He had asked her to *marry* him.

Good God, was he mad?

"Are you jesting?" she demanded, struggling to form her thoughts after the turbulent desire that had roared through her at his kisses.

He was unsmiling. "I can assure you that I would never joke about so serious a matter."

"But-but you are London's greatest lover," she sputtered.

He inclined his head. "I am aware of the somewhat dubious title. But I'm afraid I've no source of comparison. I cannot lay claim to the veracity of it. My pride, however, would certainly delight in doing so."

The carved wood of the settee's arm pressed into her back through her corset. "Are you soused?"

One corner of his lips curved in a mocking half smile. "Unfortunately not."

Her mind whirled. "Then why…? That is to say, I don't understand. I thought this was to be an assignation."

"That is apparent, and as much as I adored your hand on my cock, I'm not in search of that sort of diversion this evening."

Your hand on my cock.

Her cheeks went hot, and she knew she was flushing like a blasted tomato. "You needn't be so vulgar, Your Grace."

Your Grace. How strange and formal the honorific felt on her lips so soon after his tongue had stroked against hers and her hand had covered the indecent bulge that was still present in his trousers. At least his desire hadn't been feigned, even if his ruse in inviting her here to this room had been.

He lifted one shoulder in an elegant shrug, his eyes—even more vibrant here in the emerald salon, surrounded by shades of green—burning into hers. "I was being honest. There was nothing I would have liked more than to let you have your wicked way with me. There are simply other concerns awaiting me that can't be ignored. I need a wife, and with great haste."

Let you have your wicked way with me.

Her ears were burning now. Burning with shame. Which was a most unusual response. Since rebelliously embracing her widowhood and seeking her own pleasure, she had never been ashamed. She had held her head high. There was nothing wrong with desire. She could experience it—and want it, for that matter—just as well as any man could. Moreover, unlike Grenfell, she was *not* being faithless. Her loyalty was to no one, save herself.

Lottie tipped her chin up with defiance. "Perhaps I am the one who must beg forgiveness, Your Grace. I was under the mistaken impression, based upon our past interactions and your reputation, that you were amenable to a tryst."

A new, small smile curved the duke's beautiful lips. "Do you think you could have been satisfied at just one tryst with me, darling? If so, I daresay my reputation is in dire need of repair."

He was making light of this wretched circumstance, but Lottie found no levity in it Quite the opposite. She was horrified, but her pride refused to allow him to see that.

It required every bit of sangfroid she possessed to hold his stare and raise an indolent shoulder of her own. "Perhaps I wanted to see if you were a worthy enough lover for a second such arrangement."

"How prettily you speak of fucking, dancing around the subject, neglecting to call it what it is."

His voice was low, deceptively smooth, and it poured over her like warm honey. Nary a hint of censure or bite, and yet his words held the distinct note of challenge.

Unflinchingly, Lottie met it, smiling back at him, summoning all her bravado. "But we didn't fuck, Your Grace. If we had, I would well understand the reason for your proposal. Men have a habit of begging me to marry them after they've been in my bed you see."

That wasn't entirely true. But neither was it a lie. Her first lover after Grenfell's death had been a kindhearted widower as nervous as she. But when he had professed his love and asked her to marry him she had felt vaguely ill at the notion and thrown him over shortly thereafter, having learned her lesson.

Or so she had believed.

Brandon's grin deepened. "No doubt the poor bastards do."

She considered him, trying not to be distracted by his smoldering air and aristocratic good looks.

And failing miserably.

He was easily the most handsome man she had ever seen in her life. Far more so than Grenfell, but it had been Grenfell's charm that had won her over, not his massive, burly frame. Unfortunately, she hadn't been alone in finding him dashing.

"You said you need to marry in haste," she pressed, curious now in spite of herself about why the Duke of Brandon, whose rakehell ways were as infamous as they were legendary, would wish to take a wife. "Why?"

"Tut-tut, darling." His grin faded, his expression going somber. "If you don't accept my proposal, there's no need to discuss the matter further, is there?"

How soundly he parried her every thrust. She wanted to know now more than ever. "You must admit that it's quite unexpected. You *are* the Duke of Brandon, after all."

"And I can assure you that I pride myself in never doing what's expected of me." He winked. "Unless you wish to accept my offer, that is?"

"No." Her answer was swift, torn from her marrow. "I doubt that God himself could persuade me to marry again."

"Ah, a pity. Even I must accept I'm a mere mortal. Thank you for your time, dear lady."

He rose from the settee, flouting convention by standing in her presence. Lottie sat there, flummoxed, the heat of his lips still burning on hers, her body newly awakened, nipples hard beneath her corset, aching in her core.

"Where are you going?" she asked.

His grin returned, the corners of his eyes crinkling, those eyes of his sparkling to rival the color of the damask walls. "To redouble my efforts, of course. I still find myself in need of a bride. Are you certain I cannot persuade you?"

"N-no," she stammered, standing, feeling quite as if she had drunk too much champagne.

And perhaps she had.

Brandon bowed. "Then I bid you good evening, lovely Lottie, and good luck on your own particular quest."

And then he was gone, leaving Lottie standing in the midst of the emerald salon, wondering what in heaven's name had just happened.

CHAPTER 4

"*D*-duke?"

Brandon awoke, as he had each day since his daughter's arrival at his town house, to a tremulous, girlish voice calling him from the foot of his bed.

He sat up, already wearing a silk dressing gown for this very reason, blinking the sleep from his eyes. "Yes, Pandy?"

"The wolf m-man was comin' to get m-me again."

Bloody hell. Yet another nightmare. His poor, sweet girl—her sleep was riddled with them after her mother had abandoned her. He didn't count himself particularly paternal, but even a dissolute rakehell like him could see quite plainly that the child needed protection and comfort.

He held out his arms to her, forcing a reassuring smile. "Come here, my darling girl."

His sentence was scarcely finished before she launched herself at him, a tiny bundle of arms and legs and a fat braid that slapped him in the cheek as she landed in his embrace. He cradled her against his chest, patting her back gently as she pressed her wet face to the crook of his neck and sniffled loudly.

Good God, he didn't know if that was tears she was smearing on his neck, snot, or both. Likely a combination of the two. He really needed to begin keeping a handkerchief by the bed.

"The wolf man cannot get you," he promised her, laying his cheek atop her head and reveling in the miracle that was this tiny body, somehow a part of him. "I won't let anyone hurt you, I promise."

She sniffed loudly, confirming his suspicion that snot was involved. "I tried w-wakin' Nurse, but she t-telled me good little girls must go b-back to sleep after n-nightmares."

"The devil she did," he muttered, thinking he would have a talk with Miss Partridge tomorrow. Or was the woman's name Wren? Pheasant? Something avian, he was sure of it.

"Y-you mustn't s-speak of the d-devil," Pandora warned him. "M-mama said so."

"She's not wrong, Pandy," he conceded. "I ought to watch my tongue."

Having a child running about his home was still new. He had yet to curb all his base impulses, cursing being one of them.

"B-but she was wrong a-about some things," she said, clinging to his neck with the tenacity of a hangman's noose.

He continued patting her soothingly. "What things, my clever girl?"

"That I w-wouldn't miss her," his daughter said, her chest rising and falling with uncontrollable dry sobs. "I m-misses her lots."

That heartless witch. First, she had kept his daughter a secret from him for four years, and then she had abandoned Pandora without a backward glance to sail off with her lover.

"Of course you do, sweeting." His voice was thick with his own barely suppressed emotion.

"And I m-miss Papa," she said.

Brandon kissed the top of her head, a pang going through his heart at the way she referred to Helena's former husband, Mr. Booth, as Papa. He didn't blame the child, of course. Booth, who had apparently taken ill and died just before Helena had found her new lover, had been the only father Pandora had known. Until she had been unceremoniously dumped at his grandmother's town house like an outmoded hat, that was.

"I've no doubt you do, Pandy," he said, still patting her small back.

He had never paid much attention to children. Had never supposed he would have a child of his own. Brandon was not the dutiful sort who was happy to carry on the family line. Quite the opposite. He'd been pleased at the notion of it ending with him, just to spite the bastard who had sired him. But there was something undeniably wondrous about the small form clinging so tightly to him. The moment her green eyes had met his, he had seen himself in her, and the accompanying surge of protective instincts had proven unstoppable.

And now? He would burn down the world just to make her heart hurt less.

"I dreamded the wolf man h-hurt Papa," Pandy said, her frame shuddering with a new onslaught of tears. "He m-made Papa die."

Sniffle, sniffle.

Something was dripping down Brandon's neck, but he ignored the sensation and the troublesome question of what that something was. He was too preoccupied with comforting his daughter. He hated the fear in her voice. Hated the way she trembled and sobbed in his arms, the uncertainty and fear.

He swallowed his resentment down, however, knowing

he needed to remain stoic for her sake. "It was only a nightmare, Pandy girl. You're safe with me always."

"Thank y-you, Duke." Another sniffle.

He wished she might call him Papa one day. But he was willing to wait and not press the matter. Pandora had been through enough in her short, young life. He had no wish to add to the upset.

"You needn't thank me. I'm meant to protect you." He gently shifted her so that she was no longer sliming his neck with snot and tears, looking down at her through the shadows. "I was intending to venture to the kitchens and see if Mrs. Willoughby has left any sweets about to eat, but you wouldn't want to do that, would you?"

"Of course I w-would!" she exclaimed.

Although she was still overset, the enthusiasm in her voice made him smile. Distraction was in order, and he wasn't afraid to employ his cook's decadent confections for that purpose, even if it was the midst of the night.

She was already scrambling from his lap in a flurry of bounding curls and ruffled nightgown and girlish enthusiasm. Brandon threw back the bedclothes and rose as well, making certain to discreetly obtain a handkerchief and mop up his neck before tucking it into a pocket on his dressing gown. Taking up a candle to aid them on their journey, he lit it, light flaring to life in the room.

The flickering flame illuminated Pandora's tearstained cheeks. He forced a smile for her benefit and took up a fresh handkerchief to dry her face as well.

"I do believe we may find some of Mrs. Willoughby's famed cabinet pudding," he told Pandora with a conspiratorial air.

He had begun asking his cook to leave some of Pandora's favorites aside in the evenings for just such occasions. He already knew the Savoy cake laden with candied angelica and ginger and sultanas awaited them.

His daughter clapped excitedly. "Oh, I hopes we will, Duke."

"Come," he said gently, offering her his hand.

She slipped her small fingers trustingly into his, and he led Pandora to the kitchens.

∽

"Have you heard the latest *on-dit*?" Rosamund asked Lottie over tea that afternoon, bearing the air of someone who couldn't wait to relay the scandalous gossip she'd recently learned.

"*On-dit, on-dit,*" squawked Megs from Rosamund's shoulder.

Her somewhat eccentric friend had brought her African grey parrot along for her call.

Megs was a brilliant bird, but Lottie couldn't help but to be perpetually disconcerted by the parrot's presence. She felt quite as if they were being eavesdropped upon.

"I don't believe that I have," she said mildly, taking a sip of her tea.

"I should think you would find it most intriguing as it pertains to a certain duke."

"A certain duke, a certain duke," Megs added.

"Hush, darling," Rosamund chided the parrot, offering her a bite of sliced apple that Lottie had requested from the kitchen for just such a purpose. "The Duke of Brandon, to be precise."

Lottie's stomach performed a little flip at the mentioning of Brandon. Although several days had passed since their ignominious meeting at his most recent ball, she had been haunted by the memory of his mouth on hers.

But she schooled her features into the blandest expression she could muster, not wanting a hint of her conflicting emotions to show. "I'm sure I don't have any interest in gossip concerning His Grace—or anything else regarding him, for that matter."

Megs blinked at her, chewing on her apple from Rosamund's shoulder. Lottie swore the parrot knew she was lying. She narrowly resisted making a face at the bird, who was far too wise and knowing for a creature so small.

Rosamund pursed her lips. "With the way the two of you were speaking together at the ball, I thought that perhaps you had an...*understanding*."

As a single woman, Rosamund was not meant to know such things.

"Your mother would be horrified to hear you speak thus," Lottie reminded her, feeling that as the older, if not wiser, of the two of them, and certainly as the more experienced, she bore a responsibility.

Rosamund grinned, unrepentant. "I have no doubt that Mama would, which is why I never mention such subjects in her presence."

"Never mention to Mama," Megs said. "Do keep it a secret, Megs. Do keep it a secret."

A slight flush gilded Rosamund's cheekbones at the parrot's telling musings. "Never mind you," she scolded Megs quietly, offering up another bit of apple before turning her attention back to Lottie. "Don't you wish to know? I couldn't very well tell my mother about it since she disapproves of gossip. But I've been seething with the need to confide in someone."

How ironic. Lottie found herself feeling quite the opposite. She could see, however, that her friend would tell her whether she wished to hear the *on-dit* or not.

She sighed, settling her teacup in its saucer with a small

rattle. "What is the gossip you have heard concerning Brandon?"

Lottie could only presume that what her friend had heard had been positively scandalous.

Rosamund leaned forward in her chair, lowering her voice as if they were in a crowded room and anyone might hear. "I have it on good authority that he has an illegitimate daughter who is *living* with him now. She is a young child, no more than five years of age, and she was recently abandoned at his poor *grandmother's* town house."

Lottie bobbled her tea and sent it raining down her silk skirts to pool on the Axminster underfoot. "Oh drat."

"Spilled tea, spilled tea," Megs chirped. "Hell's bells, hell's bells."

"Good heavens, Megs," Rosamund scolded. "I told you that you were to be on your best behavior today, and you agreed that you would."

"What a good little bird," Megs chirped. "Good little bird."

Lottie might have found mirth at the ridiculousness of the scene—she covered in tea, Rosamund attempting to admonish her wayward feathered companion, and the gray parrot seeming to be laughing at them both. But all she could think about was Brandon offering her marriage. Brandon dismissing her offer of a night in her bed.

And everything began to make perfect, horrid sense.

Little wonder he hadn't seduced her further in the emerald salon. He likely hadn't wanted her at all. Rather, he had been seeking out a mother for his bastard daughter. The utter nerve of the scoundrel! She had spent the last few days turning his behavior over in her mind, utterly perplexed, wondering what was wrong with her. And here was her answer.

Nothing was wrong with Lottie.

The Duke of bloody Brandon was the problem.

"Lottie? Shall I ring for a maid to sop up the mess?"

Rosamund's concerned voice broke through Lottie's whirling thoughts. She blinked, disconcerted by the way the parrot on her friend's shoulder continued to eye her frankly, as if the bird could see into her soul.

"I shall do it, of course," she said, recalling that she was the hostess. "You mustn't trouble yourself for a moment."

Rising, she strode to the bellpull with determined steps, yanking on it with more force than was necessary. She wasn't angry with the domestics or the corded bellpull or even herself for spilling her tea. No, indeed. She was furious with the Duke of Brandon. What a liar he was, flirting with her, leading her on a merry dance, and all the while, he had been searching for a wife to mother the child who had been born on the wrong side of the blanket.

"I don't suppose he would take responsibility for such a child," she said. "Not in truth. No, he must be seeking a wife upon whom he can foist the girl so that he can carry on with his cavorting."

"Carry on with cavorting," Megs said. "Fucking, fucking."

Lottie's eyes went wide.

Rosamund bit her lip. "Pray excuse her. She knows not what she is saying."

"You know me, my dear. Candid speech is always preferable to subterfuge," she reassured her friend, not offended by the parrot's language in the least, merely surprised.

Although it was not the first occasion on which her friend had brought Megs to pay a call, Lottie had never heard the parrot swear before. How amusing to think Megs might blurt such coarse language before a stern matron. Little wonder Rosamund preferred to keep to the periphery of polite society.

"You mustn't say naughty words, Megs," Rosamund cautioned the parrot sternly.

"Naughty words, naughty words. Fuck, fuck." Megs blinked, looking distinctly unapologetic.

"Perhaps we ought to ignore her," Rosamund suggested. "She seems to be having one of her moods. Have you heard from Hyacinth recently? I expected to see her at Brandon's ball."

Ah, so Lottie wasn't the only one concerned about their friend's recent absence from gatherings.

"She wrote to me that she is indisposed." Lottie sighed. "But it's been far too many days now. I believe I'll pay her a call to be certain nothing is amiss."

Rosamund nodded. "Capital idea. Please do let me know how she is faring. I've missed her."

A maid gave a discreet knock at the door then, indicating her arrival. Lottie bid her enter and directed her to the tea spill, hoping Megs would at least behave herself before the servant. As if sharing Lottie's concern, Rosamund distracted the parrot by feeding her another slice of apple. The maid hastily completed her task and left the room.

Lottie waited for the door to close before recalling her conversation with Rosamund at Brandon's ball. "Speaking of the Duke of Brandon's fête, did you ever speak with Camden?"

She had been dreadfully curious since that night, she couldn't lie. But Lottie also wanted to distract herself from all thoughts of a certain handsome, green-eyed duke.

"I did," Rosamund said enigmatically.

"And?" Lottie pressed. "What have you decided?"

A secretive smile curved her friend's lips. "I've decided that I need more time to consider His Grace's offer."

Lottie understood Rosamund's desire for revenge. However, she didn't understand how or why the Duke of Camden would facilitate it. She had a suspicion her friend wasn't ready to tell her just yet either.

"I reckon you will tell me more when it suits you," she drawled, pouring herself a second cup of tea.

"Of course." Rosamund fed Megs another bite of apple.

"With all this marriage nonsense in the air, one might think it catching. Fortunately, I am well armed against it. My past experience with that terrible institution is my suit of armor and shield."

Rosamund's brow furrowed. "Was it truly so horrid?"

Lottie thought of the heartache she had experienced when she had first discovered the man she loved was bedding another woman. He had left her after consummating their marriage, only to return in the early hours of the morning, smelling of another woman's scent, his hair ruffled, a bruise on his throat from someone else's mouth. When she had confronted him, he had acknowledged his infidelity.

"This sort of arrangement is done all the time, my dear," he had said, without a hint of compunction. "It is good for a marriage."

And then he had kissed her lightly on the cheek and told her he was weary, that she ought to return to her own bed, quite as if he hadn't just destroyed her entire perception of him. To say nothing of her heart.

With a grim jolt, she realized that she had been woolgathering, and she had added far too much sugar to her tea. She took a sip of the sickeningly sweet brew anyway.

"It was the second biggest mistake of my life," she told Rosamund frankly.

The first had been falling in love with the Earl of Grenfell to begin with. But she had learned her lesson all too well. She would never allow herself to be so weak and vulnerable again.

CHAPTER 5

*L*ottie may not have excelled at being a wife; her marriage had been a miserable failure, though the fault had not been hers alone. She may not have had her own children—to her everlasting regret, her miserable union with Grenfell had not even produced a single pregnancy. But she was quite excellent at being a good friend.

And that was why she was presently sitting opposite her dear bosom bow Hyacinth in her salon. When one's friend suddenly became a hermit, one needed to pay her a call and discover the reason. Hyacinth must have fallen in love with Viscount Sidmouth, with whom she had been having a torrid affair that had recently come to an end. And Lottie strongly suspected it was a broken heart that kept her friend confined to her home.

Oh, Hyacinth had continued to plead illness, of course, sending notes round to Lottie at regular intervals. But Lottie had decided that she'd had enough of Hyacinth's avoidance. The time had come to discover what was truly afoot.

Lottie waited until they were comfortably settled in Hyacinth's salon, the servants dismissed for privacy's sake.

"How much longer do you intend to hide from Sidmouth?" she asked her friend without preamble as soon as the door had closed.

Hyacinth frowned at her, looking lovely in a green afternoon gown, if a trifle pale, her golden hair plaited in a Grecian braid. "I am not hiding from Sidmouth. Nor am I *hiding* at all, in fact."

Ha! Did she truly think Lottie would believe such a lie?

Lottie raised a brow. "You have not left your home in a fortnight. You cried off for the opera, Lady Siddon's ball, Lord and Lady Maplethorpe's masque. You told me you were too ill to go shopping, for heaven's sake, which we both know is blasphemy."

To say nothing of her lack of appearance at Brandon's latest ball. Lottie knew Hyacinth had been invited, for invitations had gone out before Hyacinth and Sidmouth had ended their understanding. Sidmouth and Brandon were thick as thieves, and Hyacinth had no doubt skipped the ball to avoid her former lover.

"I *have* been ill," Hyacinth claimed.

Lottie studied her friend more closely, thinking she'd never seen her looking so wan, plum bruises denoting her lack of sleep beneath her blue eyes. Now that Lottie looked more closely, there was a gauntness to Hyacinth's form too.

"You *do* look pale," she acknowledged. "Have you been eating properly?"

"I have scarcely been able to keep anything down, save tea and toast."

That was rather worrying indeed. Perhaps Hyacinth had been unwell after all.

"You mean to say you are truly ill? Hyacinth, why did you not say so?"

"I *did* say so," her friend pointed out wryly. "Several times over the last fortnight. And again just now."

Lottie made a dismissive gesture. "Yes, but I thought you were lying."

"The illness should subside in a few weeks' time, according to Dr. Hayes," Hyacinth told her. "But I shall have another problem forthwith. My gowns will all need to be altered."

"You shall have to have them taken in, do you mean? You do look terribly thin, dearest. I did not want to say so, but there you have it. Honesty is best, or at least that is what my mother always said. Has your physician given you anything to ease this illness of yours?"

Her friend shook her head. "I am afraid there is no cure, save time."

"Time?" Lottie repeated, mind whirling with possibilities, heart lurching at the thought of some mysterious, prolonged ailment.

What in heaven's name could be wrong with her friend?

"Most ladies in a delicate condition are only ill initially," Hyacinth said.

"Ladies in a delicate condition," Lottie repeated, the words taking on a new meaning. "Hyacinth, what are you saying?"

"I am with child, Lottie."

The bald announcement, without fanfare or preface, left Lottie stunned.

But only for a moment. In the next instant, she shrieked and rose from her chair. "*Enceinte*? Hyacinth! You cannot be. I cannot believe it. How? My God. Whose? Is it Sidmouth's?"

Her friend winced. "Do cease shrieking, Lottie. And have a seat. You are making me seasick with all your carrying on. Of course it is Sidmouth's. He is the only lover I have taken."

Astounded by the revelation—and not just a bit jealous, if she were perfectly honest with herself—Lottie collapsed into her chair with a distinct lack of grace. "Have you told him?"

"No, nor shall I," Hyacinth answered quickly and firmly. "Our *affaire* is over. He has not attempted to contact me once in the last fortnight, and I expect he has already quite moved on and is charming the next lady."

That hardly made sense. Viscount Sidmouth was not a cunning rake. He had followed the Marchioness of Needham about like a lovelorn puppy for some time before that lady's husband had returned from abroad and won back her favor. The viscount had been notoriously faithful to Lady Needham, despite her marriage.

"I do not know, Hyacinth. Do you truly believe him that inconstant? He doesn't seem the sort."

Tears sparkled in her friend's eyes. "I scarcely know him. But I feel certain he would not have simply ignored me for the last fortnight if he cared."

"You have ignored him as well," Lottie pointed out, thinking of the way Hyacinth had withdrawn from society. "And you are the one who disappeared, are you not?"

Hyacinth's shoulders stiffened. "I hardly disappeared."

"That isn't what you said," she countered, thinking of the story Hyacinth had previously relayed to her.

Hyacinth had left Sidmouth in the midst of the night, sneaking away like a housebreaker.

Her friend glared at Lottie. "Whose side are you on? You are *my* friend, are you not?"

And it was the job of every good friend to harness common sense where it was lacking. To be the voice of reason.

"Of course I am on your side, and I *am* your friend. One of your best friends, I hope," Lottie said gently. "Which is why I feel compelled to counsel you in your best interest. You have broken not one but two cardinal rules of taking a lover. You fell in love with him, and now you are carrying his child."

The tears that had been welling in Hyacinth's eyes rolled down her cheeks. "I hardly set out to do either of those things. I thought I was barren. I had believed there was no possible means for such an event to occur. And I certainly never meant to fall in love with him…"

A sob racked her friend, and Lottie felt it as surely as if it had been a blade. Because she knew those feelings, those feminine fears and beliefs, the disappointments and the hope, all too well. And because her friend was hurting and the knowledge broke Lottie's heart.

"Oh, my dearest." She rose once more and crossed the room, this time sinking to the settee at Hyacinth's side and gathering a comforting arm around her shoulders. "Do not cry, if you please. I didn't mean to cause you distress, and surely it is not good for your condition."

"I don't know why I am weeping." Hyacinth hiccupped.

"You are weeping because you are pregnant, my dear," Lottie said. "My elder sister Caro wept for a full month straight when she was carrying my nephew. And my cousin Elizabeth could not stop eating chocolate cake and pickled herrings."

"I hate him."

"Of course you do, darling." She nodded and rubbed her friend's back in soothing motions.

"But I also love him," Hyacinth admitted on another sniff.

Just as Lottie had suspected. And she had seen the way the viscount looked at her friend, quite as if she were the only woman who had ever graced *terra firma*. She would wager Sidmouth was in love with Hyacinth as well. Now, there was a baby to consider too.

"You must tell Lord Sidmouth about the baby, dearest," she said gently. "He is the child's father. He has a right to know. Even if you have no wish to marry, he deserves to be told."

"No." Hyacinth shook her head vehemently.

"Hyacinth, I love you like a sister, but you must see reason," Lottie pressed.

"Do not take me to task, I beg of you." Hyacinth pressed a hand to her stomach, her pallor heightened, looking as if she were about to retch. "I have seen reason, Lottie. I am not meant to be the merry widow. I tried, but it is not in me. And now that I am carrying a child, I have been thinking about what I must do for the babe. Not just for myself. I am going to go away, to the countryside where no one knows me."

Lottie was aghast at the notion. "You cannot mean it, Hyacinth. What of Town? You have scarcely been here but two months' time. I refuse to believe you will leave me so suddenly. I *need* you."

Hyacinth's smile was wistful. "You are being silly, Lottie. You do not need me."

"Of course I do." Lottie bumped her elbow into her friend's in a teasing fashion, attempting to lighten the mood. "Who shall accompany me on all my shopping excursions? And how shall I woo the Duke of Brandon without you?"

Never mind that she no longer intended to woo the man. Hyacinth didn't need to know that just now.

"Most importantly," Lottie continued, "who will have tea with me whenever the notion strikes me? Who shall tell me when I am wearing something garish? You know I favor bold colors, and no one else will tell me the truth, save you."

"You may visit me in the country if you like," Hyacinth said quietly.

Lottie shuddered, for the last place she wanted to go was the country—nothing but dreadful memories dwelled there. "More blasphemy."

They were silent, seated together, nothing but the steady thrumming of a mantel clock to interrupt the quiet.

"It is what has to be, Lottie," Hyacinth said at last. "It is for the best. You shall see."

And Lottie's heart sank to the soles of her handsome new silk-and-satin embroidered boots.

Blast.

She despised meddling of all forms. But one thing was painfully clear to her after her chat with Hyacinth. She was going to have to seek out Sidmouth on her friend's behalf, before it was too late for Hyacinth to find the happiness she deserved.

∽

"You look like a drowned puppy," Brandon observed grimly as he took in the sight of his old chum, Viscount Sidmouth, dripping and bedraggled, in his entry hall.

"I went for a walk," Sidmouth explained with a drunken half smile. "And it began to rain."

Bloody hell. It was a damned good thing Brandon had left Pandy in the care of her nurse. He hadn't expected a caller at all, let alone a soused one. And although his daughter had no doubt witnessed all manner of scenes she ought not to have in her young life, he had no wish to expose her to more.

"Towels, if you please," he called to his servants, all of whom were remaining discreetly out of sight.

The quiet scurrying of footfalls told him they hastened to do his bidding. Thank Christ. Sidmouth was making puddles all over the polished marble. Apparently, the viscount had ventured on his walk without an umbrella or top hat to blunt the sting of the rains.

"Towels would be welcome," his friend said, listing to the right. "And mayhap some whisky."

Brandon sniffed the air, which was redolent with the scent of spirits, and raised a brow. "*More* whisky, old chum?"

Sidmouth's inebriated state was somewhat troubling. He had always been one of the most staid, dependable chaps Brandon had known, and he was certainly not given to excess, whether it be food, drink, or the pleasures of the flesh. Indeed, he had never joined in any of the festivities at Wingfield Hall.

"Shut up," Sidmouth slurred, swaying to the left now.

He attempted to avoid falling and slipped on the marble.

"Bloody hell, man." Brandon caught his friend in a staying grasp before he toppled to his arse or, worse, to his head. "Are you well?"

"Yes," Sidmouth said brightly.

That was a lie if Brandon had ever heard one. A maid scurried forward bearing towels, one of which a footman threw over Tom's dripping shoulders.

He thanked the domestics before dismissing them, sensing his friend required privacy for the conversation that was about to ensue.

Sidmouth dried his sodden hair with the towel as footsteps faded away once again. "I owe you a debt of gratitude for giving me shelter from the storm."

"And I owe you a sound trouncing for gadding about Town in the midst of a thunderstorm with nary an umbrella," Brandon countered. "What the devil are you thinking, Sidmouth? And if you prattle on about that taking-a-walk nonsense, I will smite you."

Sidmouth swayed again, unsteady on his feet. "I *was* going for a tidy little walk. It merely turned into a longer walk than I had supposed it would be. One involving lightning and profuse amounts of thunderclouds."

Brandon shook his head. "To the study with you, sir. I despair. I cannot whip your arse in billiards when you are in such a state. Is this because of the lovely widow? Lady Southwick?"

Sidmouth and the widow had been lovers, but Brandon rather suspected his gentle giant of a friend—who had been brokenhearted after being thrown over by Lady Needham—was about to see that tender organ dashed once more to bits. Poor Sidmouth didn't stand a chance, particularly since Lady Southwick ran in a fast set with Lady Grenfell. He firmly tamped down all thoughts of the flame-haired beauty—those luscious kisses they had shared, in particular.

Sidmouth was clenching his jaw, looking desperately forlorn. "Of course not. I found myself in need of diversion. That is all."

Ah, Christ. Sidmouth had it worse than he'd realized.

"*Sid*," Brandon said, using the voice he reserved for Pandy. The fatherly one.

The one that was equal parts fond and firm.

Sidmouth finished drying his hair and glanced at the marble, which had been spread with now-dampened towels all about him, quite as if he were viewing his surroundings for the first time. "Am I that much of a ruin, old chum?"

How to answer that? Brandon didn't know. Fortunately, the timely sound of footsteps yet again approaching in the cavernous marble entry hall saved him from having to respond. It was Shilling, his august butler, his countenance expressionless.

"Another carriage has arrived, Your Grace," the butler announced.

More visitors? Damn it, he hoped it wasn't Grandmother. All he needed was for her to pay him a call when he had a drunken, heartbroken friend dripping all over the marble. She'd take one sniff of the air and know Sidmouth had been imbibing.

"In this deluge?" He frowned, wondering at who would unceremoniously visit on such a day. "Is the carriage marked?"

"A footman ventured out," Shilling intoned, "and it would appear Lady Grenfell is within. She wished to be assured of her welcome before she braved the storm. Her ladyship desired to impart that her visit is of the utmost importance."

Lady Grenfell.

Damnation. He had hoped their paths might never cross again after the debacle of his proposal. It would seem he had been wrong. What would she be doing here, paying him a call? Surely it wasn't that she had changed her mind, was it?

No. More than likely, her presence at his town house had something to do with the sodden Goliath before him.

He scowled. "Curse you, Sid. This has your mark upon it."

"Do I know Lady Grenfell?" Sidmouth asked, sounding genuinely puzzled.

Brandon bit back a groan. Just how drunk was the viscount?

"Your Grace?" his butler prompted. "Shall I send the carriage on its way?"

"No." Brandon heaved an irritated sigh—he couldn't well refuse Lady Grenfell, even if that was precisely what he wanted to do. "See her inside, Shilling. The emerald salon, I suppose. To the devil with my study. And see that tea is brought round, if you please. This afternoon is turning into quite the unexpected social gathering."

Sidmouth cleared his throat. "Have you another engagement this afternoon, Brandon? I admit, I was not thinking when I arrived at your door, other than that my boots were quite soggy and there was the slight possibility I would be struck by lightning."

"Good God," Brandon muttered. "Imagine this. The Duke of Goddamn Brandon, the soul of reason. The entire world is going to the dogs."

"That is what my *grandmère* assures me," Sidmouth offered.

He toweled off his shoulders next, wringing the excess water in the cotton onto the towels at his feet.

"Christ, Sid." Brandon sighed, feeling responsible. Becoming a father had changed him irrevocably. "You are still soaked to the bone. You will catch your death."

"Also something *Grandmère* would say." Sidmouth grinned. "Why, Brandon. Your grandmotherly affection for me is quite comforting."

Just how sotted was his friend?

Brandon scowled. "I am nothing like your dragon of a grandmother, you arse. I want what is best for you, and she wants what is best for herself."

Which was entirely true—the Duchess of Arrington wanted her grandson to marry a woman of her choosing.

"I cannot argue the point,' Sidmouth said, his tone resigned.

"Come and get settled in the salon. We cannot very well greet Lady Grenfell in the entry hall," he invited with great reluctance, thinking of the last time he had met the countess in his emerald salon and the ignominy with which it had ended. "Of course, I suppose we could. But it would be dreadfully *de trop*."

But Sidmouth stood there like a dolt, still dripping into the towels, staring at him instead of moving.

"Why are you looking at me as if I have just announced you must take up embroidery?" Brandon glowered at his friend. "To the salon with you, old chap."

Thankfully, Sidmouth obeyed. They had scarcely ensconced themselves in the room when more footfalls intruded.

Shilling had returned, bringing with him the woman who had all but laughed in his face at his proposal of marriage. *Lovely.* The day, begun before dawn when Pandy had awakened him, was only continuing to improve, he thought, darkly amused.

"Lady Grenfell, Your Grace, Lord Sidmouth," Shilling intoned with icy formality

The butler took his duties quite seriously, which was ironic because Brandon—and his household—was far from serious.

"Thank you, Shilling," he said mildly. "Just the tea, if you please."

The butler bowed his way out of the room, forcing Brandon to acknowledge the countess whose kisses had kept him awake at night. All these years of debauchery, and it would seem that rejection was his preferred aphrodisiac. Perhaps because it was so rare that he experienced it.

He smiled as politely as he might to a maiden aunt. "Please be seated, my lady."

Her light-blue eyes lingered on him, and for a moment, he swore he saw reflected in her gaze the heated memory of those passionate kisses before his proposal had shattered an otherwise perfect interlude. The air between them hung heavy with all that was unspoken. But then she swept past him with the regal air of a lady who knew her true worth and seated herself.

He took note that it was not on the same settee as the last time.

He and Sidmouth followed suit. Silence descended.

"To what do I owe the honor of your call, Lady Grenfell?" he asked.

A slight flush crept over her cheeks. And damn, but he couldn't help but to admire the way that rosy hue painted her ivory, copper-flecked skin. She was astoundingly lovely, but it was her innate sensuality that drew him more than her appearance. Her unapologetic attitude toward pleasure was refreshing; he had only encountered the like in the demimonde.

Her gaze remained steadfastly upon Sidmouth, however, her countenance stern. "I was searching for Lord Sidmouth. He was not at home when I called."

"You were looking for me?" Sidmouth sounded perplexed before alarm had him straightening in his chair, some of the whisky fog apparently having been lifted. "Is it Hy—Lady Southwick? What is the matter?"

"It is indeed about Lady Southwick." The countess cast a calculating glance in Brandon's direction. "It is, however, a matter of a more personal nature. I must speak with you alone, Lord Sidmouth."

The daring minx. If she thought she was going to toss him out of his own bloody salon, she was decidedly wrong.

He pinned her with a narrow-eyed stare. "Alone? Whatever news you have to impart may be spoken before me. We are like brothers, are we not, Sid?"

"Yes," Sidmouth agreed, sounding far less inebriated now that he had something to fret over. "Tell us, my lady."

Lady Grenfell fidgeted with her skirts, wearing a sudden air of uncertainty that was unlike her. "Very well, my lord. You are going to be a father."

Brandon nearly swallowed his tongue. Perhaps fatherhood was catching.

Sidmouth blinked, looking as if the countess had just spoken a language he couldn't comprehend. "I beg your pardon, my lady?"

But Lady Grenfell's chin tipped upward. "Lady Southwick is carrying your child."

A light rap at the door denoted the arrival of their tea. The news Lady Grenfell had imparted had rendered Sidmouth incapable of speech for the moment. The tea service was left on a table, and the capable Lady Grenfell began to pour.

"None for me," Sidmouth said suddenly, his voice hoarse with emotion.

The countess glanced up, surprise etched on her countenance. "I thought a bracing cup might be the thing."

But the viscount shook his head. "No. I need to rectify this matter at once."

Lady Grenfell frowned. "How will you do so?"

"By marrying her, of course."

"Why do you wish to marry Hyacinth, my lord?" the countess pressed. "She was trapped in an unhappy marriage once, and as someone who suffered the same fate, I can assure you that the last thing I would want is for her to find herself similarly constrained again."

Lady Grenfell hadn't been contented in her marriage, then. It was news to Brandon, who had never particularly troubled himself with society gossip. Perhaps that explained her reticence. *I doubt that God himself could persuade me to marry again*, she had said, and not without corresponding bitterness.

"I love her." Sidmouth announced. "No tea. I must go."

His friend rose quite as if a fire had been lit under his arse.

"It's still raining," Brandon pointed out dryly, wondering if the viscount had forgotten he'd walked through the driving rain on his way here. He was still waterlogged. "My carriage is at your disposal. Take it, if you please, and avoid a lung infection. I'll not have you meeting an untimely end when you're about to become a father."

Sidmouth nodded, lost in his thoughts. "Thank you, Brandon. I'm indebted. You'll come to the wedding, of course?"

"Rather putting the cart before the horse, are you not, Sid?" he teased.

Another nod. "Of course. Yes. I'll have to ask her first. She'll have to say yes. God." He shook his head. "Thank you for telling me the news, Lady Grenfell."

The countess inclined her head regally, her expression solemn. "I hope I've done what is right."

"You have, my lady." A bow, and then Sidmouth all but raced from the room.

Brandon watched the door snap closed behind his friend, bemused by this unexpected turn of events. And by Lady Grenfell's presence in his emerald salon once again. More silence ensued, punctuated only by Sidmouth's diminishing footfalls and the sound of rain lashing the windowpane.

Lady Grenfell's gaze slipped to her tea, avoiding him, he thought, the notion vexing. He intended to say something clever. To offer a quip that shook her from her lack of engagement, but then the door to the salon opened and a small creature raced across the Axminster, followed closely by a flurry of ringlets and colorful skirts.

The furred thing ran directly toward Lady Grenfell.

"Pandy," he warned, rising from his chair as he realized what was about to unfold.

Lady Grenfell screamed. Tea flew everywhere. And the creature raced beneath the hem of her gown.

Bloody hell.

CHAPTER 6

Something furry flew beneath Lottie's skirts.

She screamed, upending her teacup, and jolted to her feet. Grasping fists of silk and petticoats, she lifted her hem to her knees in an instinctive reaction, trying to make certain that it—whatever it was—was disabused of the notion it might make a home beneath her gown.

"Cat!" cried a girlish voice.

Belatedly, Lottie became aware of the presence of a small child. Her cheeks were rosy, her green eyes were dancing, and she had a head full of dark ringlets. Her small face gave no doubt who she was—Brandon's illegitimate daughter.

"Pandy, what manner of scrape have you found yourself in now?" he demanded of the girl, his voice stern.

"I'm playing chase-chase with Cat," the girl explained.

Lottie glanced frantically about her ankles just in time to watch a streak of brown-and-white fur disappear under the settee. She could have sworn the creature had appeared a bit large to be a feline.

"Who is Cat?" Brandon asked patiently, "and what, my darling girl, is chase-chase?"

Her heart still pounding over the sudden interruption and ensuing fright, Lottie glanced in the duke's direction. Which proved a dreadful mistake. Because he was on his haunches, at eye level with the child, putting his handsome profile and muscled thighs on display. And he was speaking with such tenderness that something inside her that had previously been all hard, jagged edges smoothed and softened, despite her every inclination to remain as impenetrable as granite where the Duke of Brandon was concerned.

"Chase-chase is when I tries t'catch Cat," the girl said with the excited guilelessness only the truly young can muster. "Cat's my dog friend. It be great fun, Duke. Wanna play?"

"You've a dog named Cat?" Brandon's brow furrowed. "Since when, Pandy?"

"Since yesterday. I finded her in the garden whilst Nurse were napping. I gived her a stewed pig trotter, and we've been friends ever since."

Brandon winced. "What the devil were you doing with a pig trotter?"

"You mustn't say *devil*," the girl chided, her eyes wide, whispering the last word. "Someone might hear."

Lottie rolled her lips inward to keep from laughing. She couldn't help herself. The scene before her was, quite possibly, the most ludicrous she had ever encountered. To be sure, it was positively scandalous. Most aristocrats kept their bastard children discreetly housed out of sight, cared for financially, if in no other manner. Their miscellany certainly weren't running about their town houses. And they absolutely weren't luring stray dogs with pig trotters and naming them Cat.

"Forgive me," he offered with a sigh.

"You'd best 'pologize to the lady too," the girl said.

Grimly, Brandon turned to Lottie, his vibrant eyes

causing a frisson of unwanted awareness as they connected with hers. "I beg your pardon as well, Lady Grenfell."

What was it about the sight of this gorgeous man with his daughter that moved her? It wasn't merely that he was handsome. She had seen any number of handsome rogues in her day. And it wasn't the lingering, persistent memory of his mouth on hers either. Rather, it was something far more complex. Something she refused to examine too closely, for fear of what she would discover about herself.

No, best to place those dangerous feelings where they belonged—buried deep and forgotten.

"Your apology is accepted, Your Grace," she said, striving for a suitably serious tone. "Er, perhaps we should attempt to rescue...Cat."

It truly was an unusual name for a dog. And the creature had darted beneath the furniture faster than a streak of lightning across the sky. He was decidedly not accustomed to so much commotion, which perhaps explained the game of chase-chase that the child was engaging in. The girl chased, and poor, startled "Cat" hid.

"You gots to be quiet." the girl told Lottie solemnly, pressing a finger to her lips. "Shh."

For a wild, foolish moment, Lottie was struck by the realization that this cozy little gathering of father and daughter could have been something she would have been a part of. Had she accepted the duke's proposal of marriage, she would have been his wife. The mothering of the child—who had presumably been left to the care of the duke—might have fallen upon Lottie's shoulders. And oh, how she would have enjoyed it, regardless of the scandalous nature of the girl's birth.

Once upon a time, she had wished for children of her own. But now she understood that being a mother was a dream she must forget. Not just because she remained uncertain whether she was barren—which was a distinct possibility, for neither her marriage nor her liaisons had produced issue, though she had taken great care with her lovers to prevent such an outcome. But also because she couldn't bear to ever be so vulnerable by marrying again. Having endured the misery of unrequited love once, she knew she couldn't survive it a second time.

No indeed, children and a husband were not for her. Fortunately, Grenfell had left Lottie a more than generous widow's portion and a town house unencumbered by the entail. She was a woman of means and independence, and that—she reminded herself sternly—was how she preferred it to be.

"Come, Cat," the girl was saying, peering beneath the settee, her ringlets dancing about her small head. "Come out, sweetheart. I ain't gonna let the wolf man get you. I'll save you from that rotter always and forever and ever and ever."

The wolf man?

Lottie turned a questioning look upon Brandon. He sighed again, rising to his full, impressive height and running his fingers through his dark, wavy locks, leaving it tousled in a rakish manner that only served to heighten his appeal.

"She has been having nightmares about the wolf man ever since she arrived," he confided in Lottie, keeping his tone quiet.

"I dreamded 'bout him," the girl insisted, giving Lottie a wide, green-eyed look. "Ever since Mama goed away. She's gone on a grand adventure, 'n young girls can't go on adventures. Did you know that, missus? They might fall off the ship and get drowneded."

Lottie bit her lip, her heart squeezing with a pang of sympathy. She knew she ought to be scandalized, for it simply was not done to parade one's natural child before company. However, the child was innocent and sweet, and

Lottie couldn't help but to be charmed. And saddened to have her suspicions confirmed. The girl's mother had indeed abandoned her to Brandon.

She cleared her throat against a rush of emotion. "I hadn't realized that, my dear. You ought to call me Lottie if we shall be friends. And what shall I call you?"

"My name's Pandora,' the girl said, straightening with almost comical speed, throwing her thin shoulders back. "Duke calls me Pandy. You can call me either, but I reckon Pandy suits me better 'cause it sounds far more lovelier, don't it?"

Lottie's heart gave a pang. "It does indeed sound lovely. It's settled, then. I shall call you Pandy, and you shall call me Lottie. Now, then. Shall we rescue Cat from her hiding place?"

The girl shook her head, her expression adorably serious. "Can't say as I've ever managed to get her out of a hiding place unless I offer her food. Her likes tarts, cheese, roast chicken, and all manner of puddings. But thus far, it's pig trotters what's her favorite. Have you got any of those?"

"I always keep a spare pig's trotter in my reticule," she teased.

The girl's eyebrows rose. "You do?"

Oh dear. She hadn't recalled the penchant of the very young to take every utterance literally.

"Goodness no, I was jesting, my dear girl. I would shudder to think of what my reticule would smell like should I keep a spare pig's trotter in it,' she explained, smiling gently at the child. She truly was a sweet girl, and her resemblance to her father was undeniable. "But I have a feeling we might lure Cat from beneath the settee just the same. Would you care to hear my plan? Before you listen, I must warn you, Pandy, that we have to keep it strictly secret in order that it shall work. Can you do that?"

Pandy glanced in her papa's direction, looking uncertain. "May I keep a secret with Lottie, Duke?"

"We can tell Duke as well," Lottie said, winking at Pandy. "It shall be a secret just between the three of us. One mustn't keep secrets from an adult, after all. How does that sound?"

"Capital," the girl declared, grinning as if Lottie had just announced her intention to give her a basket of sweets, the sole caveat being that she must eat them all at once.

"Duke?" Lottie asked politely, glancing at the unsmiling Brandon. "Have you any objections?"

"None," he said grimly in a tone that suggested the opposite.

It occurred to Lottie—quite belatedly—that she was overstepping her bounds. But it was too late for such concerns now. Pandy was eyeing her expectantly, Cat was still cowering beneath the furniture, and Lottie had offered her plan as a solution.

She decided to ignore Brandon's brooding intensity and settled her attention upon the girl instead, using a loud whisper. "Now then, you've said that the only way you've been able to lure Cat is with food, yes?"

Pandy nodded solemnly. "But I don't got no food now."

"*But I don't have any food now.* That is the proper way to say it, my dear," she corrected gently. "However, Cat doesn't know we haven't any food, so what we shall do is use our imaginations."

"Magination?" Pandy's eyebrows rose. "What's a magination?"

"Im-a-gin-a-tion," she said, enunciating the word with slow, deliberate care. "It's simple. We will pretend we have food in our hand, and Cat will think we have something for her to nibble on, and she'll come out of her hiding place. When she does, Duke will scoop her into his arms."

"Here now. I've not offered myself for such a service. The

shabby little sack of fleas can go back to where she belongs, which decidedly isn't under the settee in my emerald salon. Pandy, what were you thinking, bringing a mongrel into the house without my permission? Where have you been keeping the creature?"

Pandy sniffed, batting her long lashes against gleaming tears, her small countenance clearly on the verge of shattering. "But Duke, Cat ain't a mongrel."

"Of course she isn't," Lottie hastened to reassure the child, casting a disapproving frown in Brandon's direction. "And every young girl must have a dog. Why, did you know that I had a faithful hound myself when I was about your age, my dear?"

"You did?"

Fond memories of her beloved pup Fancy brought a smile to Lottie's lips. "I did indeed. And a cat as well."

Pandy grinned, her tears forgotten. "Then you know all about how to rescue dogs 'n make them come without pig trotters, doesn't you?"

"Of course I do," she said with far more confidence than she truly possessed, for there was no telling how tame the dog was. "First, we must get down on our knees so that Cat can see we aren't a tall threat looming over her." Grasping silk, Lottie lowered herself to her stockinged knees on the Axminster. "Like so."

With far less ladylike aplomb, Pandy dropped to her knees as well.

"And now, we must pretend as if we are eating something. The most delicious something we have ever eaten," Lottie explained, holding her palm open and then using her other hand to pluck an imaginary delicacy out of it before holding it to her lips and pretending to eat.

To her amusement, Pandy mimicked her motions, pretending to stuff a bite of imaginary food into her mouth. "Oh, missus, this is the best something what I ever did eat."

"Lady Grenfell, Pandy," Brandon said, presiding over their imaginary feast with a forbidding air. "You must refer to the lady properly."

"This is the best something what I ever did eat, Missus Lady Grenspell," the child parroted brightly.

With a long-suffering sigh, Brandon raked his fingers through his hair, leaving it in disarray that Lottie was bemused to discover she longed to smooth into place. That simply wouldn't do. The Duke of Brandon had already made himself clear. He wanted a wife. Lottie wanted a lover. No complications, no vows, no rules, no nonsense. Nothing but pleasure, her autonomy, her life to live as she saw fit.

With that reminder, she turned her attention back to the settee, where a wet black nose had made an appearance, followed by the swipe of a long pink tongue.

"It is working, Pandy," she said quietly. "We must keep eating."

They continued consuming their imaginary sweets, and Cat became a bit bolder, her stomach apparently getting the better of her instinct for self-preservation.

"Cup your hands together now, my dear," she instructed softly. "Pretend as if you are guarding something delicious there, and hold your hands just out of Cat's reach. When she comes nearer, slide slowly away until she has emerged enough that I can scoop her up."

The girl did an excellent job of heeding Lottie's advice, making a show of "eating" her imaginary food and offering it to Cat, whose nose poked farther out of the shadows beneath the settee. A few more moments of luring, and Cat emerged sufficiently that Lottie was able to swoop, gathering the surprisingly strong bundle of wriggling fur in her arms.

"Hush," she told the dog, trying to calm her when she attempted to escape. A decided odor rose up from the spaniel's long, matted fur. "I do believe Cat is in need of a bath."

Brandon muttered something beneath his breath that sounded suspiciously like an oath. But he wasn't the one holding the squirming, smelly dog and befouling his fine silk bodice, was he?

"Perhaps Duke will give her a bath," she suggested slyly.

"Oh yes, will you, Duke?" Pandy asked, unaware of Brandon's displeasure.

Brandon's eyes narrowed on Lottie. "One of the footmen shall have the honor, I believe. Thank you for your assistance, Lady Grenfell. I'm sure you must be ready to go on with whatever amusements you've planned for this afternoon."

The rotter

He was essentially telling her to leave.

Well, two could play at this game.

Smiling sweetly, she rose to her feet and unceremoniously offered the stinky, writhing beast to Brandon. "Here you are, Your Grace."

"Thank you," he gritted, taking the dog in a reluctant hold.

Cat twisted about and licked his chin, then his mouth before settling upon his earlobe, the flash of sharp little teeth the only warning the dog was about to bite before Brandon emitted a startled yelp. Lottie couldn't suppress a chortle, which only made him glare at her more.

"Good day to you both," she said cheerily. "It was ever so lovely to meet you and Cat, Miss Pandy."

"And you, Missus Lady Grenspell," the girl said, attempting a curtsy and nearly tripping over her own feet. "I do hope I'll see you again."

That same, troubling shift happened in the vicinity of Lottie's heart.

She swallowed against an unwanted rush of tenderness for the girl. "Perhaps we will one day, my dear."

But as Lottie took her leave, she knew that, more than likely, she'd never see the charming little spitfire or her odiferous rescued dog "Cat" again. She wouldn't allow herself to feel sad over it, however. She was perfectly happy with her life just as it was.

~

BRANDON WAS SOAKED and irritated when he stalked into his library, shoes sloshing, hair plastered to his forehead, shirt and coat and trousers thoroughly sodden, and found his irreverent friend King awaiting him, glass of wine in hand.

King flicked an indolent glance over him and raised a brow. "Is this a new sort of excess of which I'm blissfully unaware? Bathing with one's clothes on and then…carrying on with one's day?"

"Ha bloody ha," he growled. "Give me some wine, will you?"

As it had turned out, washing the furred demon his daughter had discovered in the gardens had required not just the determined ministrations of two of his burliest footmen, but his intervention as well. He'd only realized as much when the drenched beast had gone tearing up the staircase at breakneck speed, however, forcing Brandon to engage in a rather humiliating game of "chase-chase" which had led to him falling on his arse, knocking a picture off the wall, and ultimately resorting to having Pandy fetch a pig trotter from Mrs. Willoughby to lure the little devil from her hiding place under his *own* damned bed.

From there, he had decided that the monster was going to have a thorough cleaning by his own hand.

King obligingly poured him a glass of *Chateau Margaux* and offered it to him. "Here you are, old chap. You look as if you need it."

"I do." He took the glass and poured half its contents down his throat in one long gulp, heedless of the wine's excellent notes.

King grinned, gesturing toward his dripping person. "Care to explain?"

"It's a long and tiresome story." He glowered over his wine. "Suffice it to say that it involves a mongrel and the maddening Lady Grenfell."

"Ah, dear Lottie," King said with barely disguised amusement and a note of self-assured familiarity that suddenly had Brandon's shoulders tensing.

"The countess is a friend of yours?" he asked, striving to keep his tone mild as he took another bracing sip of wine, trying to ignore the drip-drip-drip from his trouser leg onto the carpet.

"We've been known to travel in the same set," King said in a smooth tone, cleverly avoiding the question.

Brandon scowled. "That isn't what I asked, and you know it."

King raised his glass in mock salute. "A gentleman need not tell everything he knows."

"Damn it, King," he bit out, vexed beyond reason at the thought of his good friend enjoying an intimate friendship with Lady Grenfell.

Touching her.

Kissing her.

Bedding her.

It shouldn't matter to Brandon. She had already refused him. He needed a wife to soothe his grandmother's ruffled feathers. He most certainly didn't need a red-haired Siren who distracted him with her lush mouth and her generous breasts and the stunning fit of her walking gown and…

Stop it, damn it, he ordered his recalcitrant mind. *Cease this vein of thoughts at once.*

King tapped at the dimple in his chin. "It seems to me as if you are asking something more than whether dear Lottie is my friend."

He couldn't say why, but the phrase *dear Lottie* boiled his blood.

He drained the remnants of his glass. "Did you fuck her?"

King chuckled, clearly enjoying himself, the perverse bastard. "My, how crude of you. The answer is *not yet*. But that isn't to say that I don't have designs upon her virtue."

"She's a widow," Brandon snarled. "Virtue is for virgins and debutantes."

"Yes, but it sounds so much better than saying I plan to shag her silly, doesn't it?" King drawled.

Brandon found himself seriously considering his choice in friends. "Stay away from her."

The words fled him, ill-advised and thoroughly witless.

Both of King's eyebrows rose this time. "You plan to bed her yourself?"

"No," he bit out the denial hastily. "I need a wife, not a mistress."

And the lady had made it more than clear she only wanted to occupy the latter role rather than the former.

King choked on his wine. "A wife?"

It occurred to him that he had yet to share his unfortunate news with the other members of the Society. Pandora's arrival had been a whirlwind, and suddenly, she had become the center of his universe.

He sighed. "Yes."

"*You?*"

King's tone was incredulous. Brandon couldn't particularly blame his friend for his reaction.

"Me," he confirmed with a dramatic shudder. "Perish the thought, I know. However, circumstances have recently changed."

King stalked to the sideboard and poured the rest of the *Chateau Margaux* into his empty glass. "Is this somehow related to your sudden proclivity for bathing whilst fully clothed?"

He winced. "Indirectly, yes. It's not terribly sporting of you to drink all my wine and not save even a drop for me."

"You have the largest wine cellar of anyone I know," King pointed out.

Brandon shrugged. "Yes, well. I don't suppose you brought any of your particular potions along with you?"

Wishful thinking, he knew. Given the afternoon's unexpected twists and turns, he would love nothing more than to erase his worries with one of King's mysterious elixirs.

"I'm afraid it's only the *Chateau Margaux*. Shall I ring for another bottle?"

Brandon crossed the chamber to the bellpull, his shoes making a squelching sound with each step. "I'll ring for it."

He yanked the cord, nettled with himself. Nettled with his friend. Nettled with his grandmother and with Lady Grenfell and with that blasted mutt who had invaded his town house.

King gave the air a pointed sniff. "Something smells like a wet dog in here, Brandon. Perhaps you ought to have your domestics give the rugs a thorough cleaning."

Brandon lowered his head and tested the air, confirming his suspicion. "I'm afraid it's me."

"You?" King's dark brows snapped together. "Never say you were bathing with a canine, old chap."

"I was." He paused, shaking his head as he realized how

that sounded. "Rather, I was helping the footmen to bathe a runaway dog named Cat who smelled like a Whitechapel alley and who had hidden himself beneath my bed."

Hell. He passed a hand along his jaw, realizing that sounded even madder aloud than it had in his head.

"I think you had best start at the beginning of this tale," King said.

A servant arrived just then, and Brandon requested another bottle of *Chateau Margaux* from his impressive London stores. Once it had arrived, he wasted no time in pouring another glass and beginning to unburden himself.

They were two bottles in when he finished. "So, you see? I've no choice but to do my grandmother's bidding if I wish to keep Wingfield Hall. The stubborn woman has promised me she will forfeit it to a distant country booby cousin if I don't find a wife and soon."

"I'm still having the devil's own time believing you're a father," King said, shaking his head in disbelief.

"I'm yet growing accustomed to the notion myself," he said wryly. "Pandy is an intrepid girl. I haven't an inkling of what to do with a child her age. She terrifies me."

His friend chuckled. "You must admit the irony—you, the man among us all who has been most vocal in disparaging marriage and children, now have a child and must also secure himself a wife."

Grimacing, Brandon took a long sip of his wine. "I wish I could find the levity in the circumstances."

"Is it absolutely necessary that you marry to secure Wingfield Hall?" King asked.

"Grandmother assures me that it is. And you know what we've built there with the Society. We cannot simply start anew somewhere else. The improvements we have made to the estate, the servants, the grotto…it's all too perfect."

"Can you not reason with your grandmother?"

DUKE WITH A REPUTATION

"Reason and my grandmother do not belong in the same sentence," he grumbled. "She is the most stubborn woman I know."

Well, perhaps there was another woman he knew who was equally obstinate, but he wasn't about to allow the Countess of Grenfell back into his thoughts yet again. He firmly banished her.

"So you truly believe that if you don't marry, she'll leave Wingfield Hall to this country cousin of yours," King said, his tone contemplative.

"I have no doubt. You don't know her as I do. The woman is as formidable as an army."

"Blast." King took another draught of his wine. "Quite the quandary you unexpectedly find yourself in, old chap."

"I am aware."

"You really ought to have changed into dry clothes," King pointed out. "You're still dripping onto the Axminster."

He glanced down at his sodden trousers. "A bit late now, isn't it?"

"There is also the matter of the unfortunate scent," King said unkindly.

"Go to the devil," he said without heat.

"You never did explain what Lottie has to do with all this, however," his friend said.

Lottie. There it was again, the reminder that King was on far too friendly terms with her. And there *she* was again, invading his thoughts, taunting him when she was nowhere near and he shouldn't be thinking about the way she kissed or how deliciously all her soft curves had melted against him.

"She paid a call earlier, looking for Sidmouth. After he had gone, Pandy and Cat the dog swept into the room and mayhem ensued."

King chortled some more.

Brandon glared at his friend.

"Cat the dog," King explained. "Surely you can admit that's quite amusing."

At least one of them was finding the humor in the sad state of his life. "Not as amusing as the thought of upending a bottle of my finest wine over your head."

"I know you'd never waste it. To do so would be sacrilege, particularly with the phylloxera in France." King was smug.

And correct.

Brandon sighed. "Lady Grenfell helpfully suggested that the dog needed to be bathed before she took her leave and handed her off to me. Of course, the little beggar *did* need a sound washing. She also bit my ear and licked my mouth. It took two of my most strapping footmen to wrestle her into a bath in the kitchens, but the mongrel is diabolical. She escaped and went on a tour of my town house that ended with spiriting herself beneath my bed and refusing to emerge until I offered her a pig trotter. I decided to take matters into my own hands and oversee the bath so that it could be completed without further escapes. When I emerged, I was wetter than the blasted dog, and Shilling informed me that I had a visitor. You, as it happens. Hence my present state."

"Perhaps we should call for another bottle," King observed.

"Not a terrible idea," he admitted, returning to the bellpull and giving it a tug.

The glasses of wine had lessened the discomfort of sporting cold, sodden clothing. And with everything that had happened over the past few weeks, losing himself for a few moments with his old friend felt like an excellent way to spend the time until dinner.

"Now, then," King said when additional bottles of *Chateau Margaux* had been requested, "tell me why your sainted grandmother has chosen now, of all times, to issue an ultimatum concerning your marriage."

Brandon drained his glass. "Perhaps it had something to do with the fact that my illegitimate daughter was abandoned at her town house so that my former mistress could run away to America with her lover of the hour. Or the fact that when she arrived to give me a thorough tongue-lashing, an opera singer burst into the drawing room wearing nothing but my dressing gown."

"Christ," King muttered. "Discussions concerning the next meeting of the Wicked Dukes Society can wait. You're fortunate indeed that I paid you a call, old chap."

Brandon didn't feel particularly fortunate as he settled in for another glass of Bordeaux in his now-damp clothes. But diverting his mind from tempting thoughts of Lady Grenfell was just the thing. He had no doubt that, as with so much of his misbegotten life, he'd regret it later.

CHAPTER 7

Her friend's wedding day had arrived. Hyacinth and Lord Sidmouth had chosen to wed in haste in the interest of avoiding scandal and protecting their baby. But they were both blissfully happy. Indeed, Lottie had never seen her friend so content.

Lottie spent the ceremony trying not to weep at how beautiful a bride dear Hyacinth made. Nor to fear that her friend was making a dreadful mistake in marrying. Sidmouth was a good man. He loved Hyacinth. And he would be a loyal husband. Of that, Lottie had no doubt.

Not every man was cast from the same mold as Grenfell, after all.

Sometimes, she simply needed to remind herself of that fact. Repeatedly and with firm, unwavering determination. Her marriage had been dreadful. But that did not mean that all marriages would be.

By the time the wedding breakfast was at an end, she was beside herself with the need to take her friend aside for a moment of reassurance, however. For Lottie knew she was the catalyst who had catapulted Hyacinth and Sidmouth back together. If she hadn't revealed Hyacinth was carrying his child, no doubt the viscount and her friend both would have continued to be stubborn. She wanted to know without a doubt that her friend wasn't upset with her for her interference.

The bride and groom were preparing to say their farewells before she managed to take Hyacinth aside. "Are you sure you forgive me for telling Sidmouth?" she whispered.

Hyacinth embraced her warmly, dispelling any lingering doubts. "How could I be angry with you for making certain everything worked out the way it should have?"

Lottie returned her embrace, relief washing over her. "Oh, thank heavens, dearest. You have no idea how much I struggled over the decision. But I feared you were making a grievous mistake."

"And naturally, you thought you would intervene."

The cutting, masculine voice that intruded upon their private tête-à-tête was familiar. Too familiar. And although his tone was biting, the Duke of Brandon's baritone still slid over her like a caress. He had joined them where they stood on the periphery of the immense gathering. His green stare was cold and assessing as it landed on her. Perhaps he was still nettled over her intervention with Pandy's dog.

More than once during the course of the wedding breakfast, she had found her gaze wandering to the handsome, elegant figure he cut. And more than once, his eyes had ensnared hers, telling her that she hadn't been alone in stealing looks. Still, nothing could come of her irritating attraction to him. The Duke of Brandon simply wasn't the lover for her.

"My intervention was timely," she informed him coolly.

"Lord and Lady Sidmouth love each other and are destined to be together. Anyone can see that. I merely did what was in their best interest."

"Hmm. Best interest as you deemed it," Brandon drawled.

Hyacinth frowned, looking from Lottie to the duke and back again. The last thing Lottie wanted was for her friend to deduce there was something between herself and the Duke of Brandon. For there most certainly wasn't.

Lottie gave a disdainful sniff. "At least they are not living a lie, Your Grace."

It was bold of her, she knew, referencing their ill-advised assignation in his emerald salon. But Hyacinth couldn't possibly know what she was speaking of, and the need to put the arrogant duke in his place was strong.

His jaw tightened, the only sign that her words had hit their mark. "Perhaps we have different definitions of what is a lie and what is the truth, my lady."

Sidmouth appeared suddenly at Hyacinth's side, tall, golden-haired, and handsome. The two truly did make a delightful couple. Lottie wished them all the happiness, for they deserved it.

"The carriage is ready, darling," the viscount told Hyacinth. "Shall we go, Lady Sidmouth?"

Hyacinth beamed at her new husband, any worry that had been marring her furrowed brow instantly smoothed by the sight of him. "Yes, Lord Sidmouth. I do believe we shall."

Feeling an unwanted pang of envy at the undeniable love between the couple, Lottie watched her friend being escorted away to her honeymoon by the viscount. To her irritation, the Duke of Brandon didn't stray from her side.

"How dare you speak ill of my daughter?" he demanded, voice low and angry, all the easy charm of moments earlier having fled.

Startled, Lottie cast a glance in his direction, momentarily distracted by his stinging ire. "What in heaven's name are you speaking about, Brandon? I've not said a word about that sweet child."

"Of course you did. Just now, accusing me of living a lie."

"I was referring to your reputation as a rake," she countered quietly, "which is quite at odds with a man who declines an assignation in favor of a proposal of marriage."

He gave her a brooding stare, likely pondering whether he believed her. His daughter was unmistakably a sensitive subject for him, and she could understand that all too well. Pandy would have a difficult life as an illegitimate daughter. Some lords raised their bastard children along with their own, whilst others hid them away, out of sight and forgotten. Either way, the boundary was there, and polite society was nothing if not unforgiving.

Even if the scandal was no fault of the child's.

"Forgive me," he said grudgingly then. "I stand corrected."

His concession surprised her, and despite herself, Lottie felt a surge of admiration for his protective instincts where Pandy was concerned. "Thank you." She pursed her lips, not wanting to know and yet feeling the need to be polite as she continued, "Tell me, how is the hunt for a bride coming?"

"As well as can be expected." He gave her a considering look. "And how is the search for a lover?"

The word *lover*, uttered in his deep, decadent voice made an unwanted frisson go down her spine. Try as she might, she hadn't forgotten those stolen kisses they'd shared.

Nettled with herself for her weakness where he was concerned, she slanted him a disapproving look. "Who said I was looking for one?"

"You did, in my emerald salon. Or have you forgotten what happened there?"

Dreadful man. They were surrounded by well-wishers seeing off their friends, gossips and scandalmongers amongst their swelling ranks, and this was what he chose as polite conversation?

She gave him a quelling frown. "I said no such thing. All I recall is a smelly dog and an adorable child."

His glittering green eyes narrowed, and she wished she didn't find them nearly as mesmerizing as she did. "You and I both know it is a different occasion of which I speak."

"I've quite forgotten that unfortunate little incident already," she told him with a bright smile.

A lie, of course.

She'd thought of little else.

"How well do you know Kingham?" he asked her suddenly.

His abrupt shift in subject startled her. "The Duke of Kingham and I have traveled in some of the same circles over the last few years. Why should it concern you?"

"No reason," he said.

Which she knew was also a prevarication, unless she missed her guess. The Duke of Brandon wasn't a man who asked questions without purpose. What a pair they made, liars, the both of them.

They stared at each other, surrounded by the chattering of their fellow guests and the jangling of tack and plodding of horses on the street beyond. Hyacinth and her viscount were ensconced in their carriage now. Lottie really ought to take her leave, for there was nothing left to see, the wedding breakfast quite at an end.

But she found herself reluctant to leave the duke's side. To put an end to their verbal sparring.

You truly ought to go, Lottie, she cautioned herself inwardly. *Be practical for once. Forget all about the Duke of Brandon and his masterful kisses and that impressively thick ridge you had the fortune to feel swelling beneath his trousers.*

But that was the thing about Lottie. She never did listen to her own good sense. And the wickedest part of her was remembering exactly how his cockstand had felt beneath her questing hand. That part of her wanted more. Wanted to return to those stolen moments in the emerald salon.

This simply wouldn't do.

"Never say you are jealous, Your Grace," she taunted with a smile, careful to keep her voice low.

A muscle in his jaw tensed. "Jealous? Hardly, my dear. Warm his bed all you like."

"Perhaps I have."

"Lovely for the both of you, I'm sure."

"You *did* deny yourself the opportunity."

"I do believe it's called responsibility, my dear Lady Grenfell. Some of us have to bear it more than others, however."

"You know nothing of what I've had to bear," she told him frostily, thinking of Grenfell and the countless lovers he had flaunted before her and hidden in secret.

Each time she had discovered another infidelity, a new woman to whom he had given that most sacred part of himself that should have been reserved for her, Lottie's heart had withered and died a little more.

"I could say the same, madam."

They glared at each other some more, in a contest of wills.

Finally, she tore her gaze away in time to see the carriage bearing Hyacinth and Lord Sidmouth rumbling into motion. At last, it was done, their fates sealed. Her friend had been undeniably happy today, radiating a joy Lottie had never seen before. She hoped it lasted.

"And away they go," she murmured. "I suppose that is that, then."

As the carriage moved farther into the distance, the finality of the moment settled over her—the beginning for Hyacinth and her viscount, the end for Lottie and Brandon. If indeed there had ever truly been a beginning.

"I wish them happy," Brandon said. "Sidmouth is a good man."

"And Lady Sidmouth is a wonderful woman," she pointed out loyally.

He looked over her shoulder then, a ferocious frown overtaking his features. "By God, where is he going with my bloody carriage?"

Lottie turned to follow the duke's stare, finding a lacquered carriage bearing his ducal crest pulling past them into the street and moving away.

"Someone has thieved your carriage?"

"Not someone," he muttered, passing a hand over his jaw. "Camden. He accompanied me here, and now it would seem he has decided to carry on without me."

Lottie couldn't quite stifle her laughter.

He slanted a wry look in her direction. "Amused, are you?"

"You must admit that it is rather humorous, the Duke of Brandon's carriage being commandeered by his friend, leaving him stranded on the street. Will you take a hack home? Perhaps an omnibus." She chortled again.

"I could walk. The day is a fine one."

As he made the statement, a fine mist began to fall.

Lottie compressed her lips, trying and failing to keep from grinning. "You may accompany me, and I'll see you home. I'd hate to be responsible for you catching an ague."

He was silent for a moment, and she thought he might argue. But then he inclined his head. "With both my friend and the skies conspiring against me, it would seem I've no choice but to accept."

His grim response further entertained her.

At least it would be an interesting carriage ride home.

~

BRANDON SAT opposite the Countess of Grenfell in her gently swaying carriage, trying to look anywhere but at her. It was a task he was failing at quite miserably. Because it was impossible to avoid noticing her. Everything about her was mesmerizing, from the vibrant cinnamon-gold of her hair peeping from beneath her jaunty hat to the cream-and-pink silk gown she wore, which emphasized her lush curves to mouthwatering perfection.

Even her stubborn chin, the slight dimple in it, the curve of her eyebrows, and, sweet God, her mouth. When those seductive lips of hers were smiling at him with haughty amusement, he wanted to do nothing more than take them with his and kiss her breathless. This was proof—all of it— that he was going mad.

He was going to damned well box Camden's ears for running off with his carriage and leaving him to suffer the temptation of enduring a ride to his town house in a confined space with a tempting vixen he couldn't afford to want. He didn't need the distraction of a woman at the moment, particularly not one he wanted in his bed. He needed a wife, and as his grandmother had paid him a call the day before to remind him, he was running out of time to find one.

No amount of attempting to dissuade Grandmother had rendered her any more amenable to abandoning her threat of willing Wingfield Hall to horrible Cousin Horace. He sighed, drumming his fingers on his thigh, ready to escape this carriage. Grandmother had also managed to inveigle a dinner invitation out of him for this evening, and he needed to prepare himself.

"Deuced crush of carriages," he muttered. "And at this time of the day."

"The Duchess of Arrington invited half of polite society to Hyacinth and Sidmouth's wedding," Lady Grenfell said, her disposition as sunny as her voice. "What did you expect?"

The duchess was Sidmouth's grandmother. Impossible to believe that the curmudgeonly woman had deigned to accept Sidmouth's sudden nuptials. But somehow, she had. If only his own grandmother were so easily won.

Lady Grenfell—Lottie, though he told himself he must not think of her in such familiar terms—was staring at him, a small smile curving her full, pink lips that made him think about how soft and warm they had been beneath his.

She was enjoying his irritation.

Of course she was.

"At this rate of speed, it will take us half a year just to get off this street."

"You could always walk," she suggested kindly.

A grim look out the window confirmed that the earlier mist had descended into a sodden, miserable downpour.

"I reckon I can wait," he told her through gritted teeth.

"So eager to return to the business of courting unsuspecting debutantes?" she mocked.

Scandalously, she had tugged off her gloves, and they were lying in a tidy pile on her lap. But then, she had done far more scandalous things than removing kidskin. He had a sudden, intrusive mental image of one of those dainty, freckled hands wrapped around his aching cock.

He jerked his gaze away from her folded hands and the coppery flecks so deliciously decorating her creamy skin. Up to her eyes, which were watching him intently, those brilliant, light-blue orbs assessing. Seeing far too much.

"Eager to be free of this carriage," he grumbled, sliding a finger beneath his necktie and tugging. "I've been trussed like a Michaelmas goose all bloody day, and the Duke of Camden made off with my carriage and coachman. My grandmother insisted upon inviting herself to dinner, a dog named Cat chewed up my favorite pair of shoes last night, and I inadvertently stepped in a cold puddle of dog piss this morning. If I am lacking in cheer, pray forgive me."

To say nothing of the fact that Grandmother was demanding that he marry and that, quite unbeknownst to him, Pandy had been eavesdropping upon every word. After his grandmother had taken her leave, Pandy had popped up from behind a settee and blithely suggested he marry *Missus Lady Grenspeil* if he needed a wife.

No, best to keep that particular reason for his sour mood to himself.

"What do you suppose Camden is doing with your carriage?" she asked, sounding curious.

And not at all sympathetic to Brandon's own plight.

"I'd prefer not to contemplate it."

"He seems determined to marry Miss Rosamund Payne," she said, continuing the same bland, imperturbable mannerism that she'd managed for the duration of the carriage ride thus far, as if her sangfroid were unassailable.

As if she didn't feel the same potent spell of attraction that was driving him to distraction.

"Who seems determined to marry Miss Payne?"

"The Duke of Camden."

He blinked. "Cam wants to marry? This is news to me."

He wasn't sure he liked the notion.

"It would seem that a number of rakish dukes are eager to make matches suddenly," she added. "It's almost as if marriage is catching."

"Like a lung infection," he grumbled.

None of the members of the Wicked Dukes Society had married. They had all vowed to avoid carrying on their rotten family lines.

She chuckled. "Don't sound so enthused."

"I'm glad my misery is cause for such amusement."

"Why should you be miserable? No one is forcing your hand and making you marry."

He felt heat creep up his throat, his ears going hot. He tugged at his necktie again, glaring out the window at the lashing rains.

"Oh," she said, so much in that lone word. "I begin to think I understand."

"Leave it," he snapped, not wanting to be poked and prodded for her diversion any longer.

"Are you funds to let?" she asked softly.

"No, madam."

"Your grandmother, Mrs. Carrington-Smythe, then," she guessed correctly. "Is she pressing you to marry?"

He plucked off his hat and raked his fingers through his hair, feeling unaccountably weary. "That's something of the way of it."

"I must admit, I admire her daring."

"How lovely for her," he drawled, and not without a hint of bitterness.

"Have you settled upon a lady yet?" she asked, tilting her head curiously.

He resisted the urge to point out that he had already done so and she had soundly turned him down. "Not yet."

"I could help you."

If he'd just taken a sip of something, he would have spat it everywhere, so great was his shock at her offer.

"You?"

He didn't bother to hide his incredulity.

"Me." She smiled brightly. "I have a tremendously large

circle of friends and acquaintances, you know. Why, I've just played matchmaker for Hyacinth and Sidmouth, haven't I? Only think of how well I would do for you."

"That is rather a different beast. Sidmouth and his new wife are hideously in love."

"They are, aren't they?" Her smile turned wistful. "I am glad for her. Hyacinth deserves nothing but happiness. But you aren't looking to fall in love with your prospective bride, are you?"

"Christ no." He shuddered. "I don't even want a bride. Her role will be to appease my grandmother."

"As I thought." She tapped her chin, her quick mind clearly at work. "What of Pandy? Will your future bride be expected to take a role in her life, or are you intending to send her away to avoid scandal?"

The very notion of sending his daughter away had something seizing within his chest.

"She will remain with me. The woman I marry will need to accept her presence in the household."

"Do you have a preference in appearance?"

He blinked. "You aren't playing matchmaker for me."

"Why not?"

Because he wanted to bed her. He wanted to tear away her demure silk and find all the places where those coppery flecks adorned her skin. Because he wanted to sink his hand into her cinnamon hair and wrap it around his fist and...

Damn it, no. He couldn't keep thinking this way.

Brandon shifted on the Moroccan leather squabs, his cock stirring, and cleared his throat. "Because I don't want you to."

"Why, Brandon? Surely you agree that I did an excellent job of bringing Sidmouth and Hyacinth together, do you not?"

"I'm not certain I would call it excellent."

"Well, what would you call it, then?"

He thought for a moment, recalling poor Sidmouth dripping all over his floor, learning the news that he was to be a father before an audience and not from the woman he loved. "Untidy."

Lady Grenfell gasped. "*Untidy?*"

She was beginning to give him a headache. The woman was a whirlwind, packed inside a thunderstorm, hidden within a maelstrom. *Trouble.* She was nothing but tempting, ludicrous, wayward, beautiful, utterly maddening trouble.

"Do lower your voice," he said. "I'd rather not have your coachman think we're having a lover's quarrel."

"Ha! You would have to be my lover for us to have a lover's quarrel."

Oh, how his pride stung at the way she scoffed at the notion.

"Yes, but your coachman doesn't know that, does he?" he ground out.

"John Coachman knows all my secrets. Who else am I to trust, if not him?" she asked defiantly.

Good God, was she saying that her coachman knew whose bed she was warming at any given moment? And why did he hate the thought of her in anyone's bed but his? Most specifically, in King's? Swiftly, he banished all such questions from his mind.

"The coachman of your paramour," he suggested. "Is that not how these matters are usually conducted? With proper discretion?"

"John Coachman *is* discreet. You can't have believed I would allow myself to be at the whim of a lover's coachman and carriage. I see to myself, as I've always done. I trust myself, you see. I trust my judgment, and I trust my loyal retainers. They would go to their graves keeping all my secrets for me."

There was a note of pride in her voice, and yet he couldn't help but to hear what she was truly saying—that no man had ever taken care of her. He didn't know if she was referring to what happened in the bedroom, beyond it, or both. But he wouldn't—couldn't—allow himself to care. This magnificent woman and her frank sensuality and bold personality and her freckles and gorgeous hair were not a part of his future.

"No doubt they would go early were they forced to endure a carriage ride with you," he said uncharitably.

"I ought to box your ears for saying something so wretched."

Yes, she ought to. However, she was forgetting something.

"I happen to be twice your size, madam. To do so would be inadvisable."

She raised a brow, unmoved. "It wouldn't be the first thing I've done that was inadvisable. After such rudeness, it would serve you right if I were to rescind my offer. However, because I am good-natured, I won't."

Her offer.

For a wild moment, he thought she was speaking about her blatant invitation in the emerald salon, her hand on his cock, knowing, stroking.

Then he realized she was talking about bloody matchmaking, and he regained his senses. "I am fully capable of finding a wife on my own, thank you."

She raised a brow. "And yet, have you found one?"

Blast the woman.

"I haven't had time to do much reconnoitering, as it happens," he defended himself. "If you'll recall, I've been chasing after a spirited child, a stray dog with a penchant for eating things she ought not, wayward friends, and attending weddings."

"Do you have any preferences?" she asked.

What the devil was she talking about now?

"Preferences?" he sputtered.

"Hair color, eye color, figure?" she enumerated in a methodical tone. "Do you prefer ladies who are clever or dull, quiet or outspoken? Must she be a virgin, or can she be a widow?"

Good, sweet Lord, she was going to drive him to madness.

"Has anyone ever told you that you are infuriating, madam?"

"Never." She grinned unrepentantly, her eyes sparkling. "And I wouldn't recommend that you do so either, because this is my carriage we are in, and you would hate to walk the rest of the way to your town house in this deluge, wouldn't you?"

The minx. She had him there.

He couldn't say why, nor did he know what devil prompted him to do it, but he leaned forward across the carriage, forearms resting on his thighs. "Cinnamon-gold, blue, and lush. Clever and maddening. I prefer a woman of experience. One who knows what to do with my cock."

He was talking about her, of course. Because when she had listed off her questions concerning his requirements in a woman, all that had come to mind was the sultry woman whose kisses had been haunting him since their ill-advised assignation in the emerald salon.

Her eyes widened, her pink lips parting in surprise, and for once, he had rendered her speechless. Victory was his, and just in time too. The carriage had finally lumbered onto his street.

"Nothing to say, my dear?" he asked with feigned innocence.

Her chin went up, the fight returning to her. There was nothing more glorious than the Countess of Grenfell when she'd been challenged.

"I'll send a list of prospective brides around to you."

The carriage rocked to a halt. "I'll await it with bated breath. Good day, Lady Grenfell. I thank you for the ride."

He slid from the squabs and threw open the carriage door, leaping into the rain in the hopes that it might cool some of the fiery lust burning through him.

Damn her, he should have known she wouldn't allow him to win.

CHAPTER 8

"Is there any correspondence for me?" Lottie asked her lady's maid nonchalantly that afternoon as she drank her tea before a crackling fire, a novel in her lap.

Rising late on cool days, luxuriating before a fire in her dressing gown well past luncheon, reading as long as she liked—these were private pleasures she afforded herself now that she was no longer at the mercy of Grenfell's daily demands of her. Pleasures which, unfortunately, were not proving sufficient distraction at the moment.

"Nothing so far," Jenkinson announced cheerily. "Are you expecting something, my lady?"

Yes, she was.

She was expecting a response from the Duke of Brandon. After hours of careful deliberation the day before, she had produced a list of several ladies and sent them to him. Naturally, she hadn't been able to satisfy all his requirements—those had been made to discomfit her, she knew. And it had worked, the rotten man.

But after all the effort she had gone to on his behalf—taking him home from the wedding breakfast, composing a thoughtful list of potential brides—the arrogant wretch hadn't even deigned to respond.

Presciently, Lottie didn't confide any of that in her lady's maid. She did trust Jenkinson implicitly, of course. But there were some things one necessarily kept to one's self.

She forced an unconcerned smile. "Not anything in particular, Jenkinson."

"I've selected the pink silk for you this morning, Lady Grenfell," her lady's maid told her. "It complements your lovely hair so well."

Lottie could privately concede that her hair was one of her vanities. Grenfell had once told her it was brazen; he'd preferred icy blondes. When he'd confided that to her in one of his crueler moments, she had vowed to make her hair her crowning attribute. Jenkinson was a dab-hand with all manner of hairdressing. No braid had been too elaborate, loose tendrils artfully curled to frame her face, accented with twinkling diamonds or fresh flowers. Her admirers often remarked upon her hair, which she refused to cut—it curled long past her waist, down over her bottom when fully unbound.

But no one had ever described her hair as cinnamon-gold before.

"An excellent choice," she praised her lady's maid absently, trying to dismiss all thoughts of yesterday's carriage ride and the Duke of Brandon from her mind.

And failing.

It had been torture. Pure, sensual torment. He had been so handsome in his elegant blacks, a shadow of whiskers on his strong jaw. His scent had filled the carriage—musky, citrusy, decadent. How impossible it had been not to admire him. The Duke of Brandon was the picture of masculine beauty. Almost too pretty, with a strong, muscled form that perfectly accented the striking perfection of his face. His mouth was made for kissing. His hands, large and long-fingered and elegant, had been made for pleasing, touching, caressing. She had wanted them on her body, the entirety of the ride passing in torpid torment, her nipples so hard she'd imagined they might poke through her corset, the ache between her legs impossible to ignore. She'd distracted herself with conversation and her perhaps ill-advised crusade to find him a match.

After leaving him at his town house, she had returned home to a long, hot bath during which she had pleasured herself twice to thoughts of him. And she wanted him still. He was a poison in her blood. The time had come for her to take a new lover. That was what she needed—diversion. Pleasure. She'd been suffering from the dreaded empty bed for far too long.

Yes, that was all. This inconvenient longing had nothing to do with the Duke of Brandon.

"Are you ready for your *toilette*, Lady Grenfell?" Jenkinson asked, pulling her from the web of her thoughts.

"I am," she decided. "But take out a promenade gown instead, if you please. I do believe a walk in Hyde Park will be just the thing."

An excellent way to settle upon someone else, she decided. Someone who *wasn't* a dashing, marriage-minded duke. Someone who wanted to bed her and never wed her.

"Of course, my lady."

They set to work on her *toilette*. By the fashionable hour, Lottie was wearing a favorite navy silk gown with overskirts accented by plaid ribbons and blonde lace at her throat. Her hair had been plaited into an intricate braid and coiled low beneath her smart matching hat, curls framing her face. She was dressed impeccably, newly determined to forget all about the Duke of Brandon as the gravel crunched beneath her booted soles while she took the air.

She heard the commotion before she saw it.

Loud barking, a young girl's shouts.

And then she rounded the bend and discovered that everything she had been attempting to forget had found her right here in Hyde Park—well almost everything, anyway. The brown-and-white-furred blur racing toward her was followed by a dark-haired girl whose skirts were flapping wildly about her knees as she ran.

"Cat! Cat! Come back here, Cat!"

Cat didn't appear inclined to slow down or halt. She was galloping toward Lottie, an abandoned leash dangling down her back.

"Cat!"

It was the desperation in Pandy's voice that prompted Lottie into action.

She bent her knees and spread her arms wide, attempting to block the runaway dog's escape route. "Come here, you little scamp."

Seeing her chance to flee blocked, Cat darted to the right. Lottie followed, lunging toward the dog. And in that same moment, the toe of her embroidered walking boot hooked in the hems of her petticoats and tiered promenade gown. She scrambled to correct herself, but it all happened too quickly.

Lottie landed in the gravel, her outstretched hands catching the brunt of her fall and keeping her face from connecting with the earth. Cat collided with her in the next instant, and she instinctively grabbed the wriggling dog to her breast, holding her there as Lottie struggled to regain her breath.

"Cat! Missus Lady Grenspell!"

Small feet trampled toward her, and then Pandy was there, hovering over her, grasping Cat's abandoned leash. "Are you hurt?"

Worry creased the child's countenance as she peered down at Lottie.

She might have laughed had she been capable of it. But her palms stung, her pride hurt worse, and she had just gasped in a breath that her blasted corset was attempting to deny her.

"Pandy," she croaked.

"You saveded Cat from running away," Pandy said excitedly. "A mean lad throwed a stone at her, and it frightened her, and I losed her leash." Tears glistened on the girl's cheeks. "I thought Cat was gone forever."

"There now," she tried to comfort Pandy, whilst heaving herself into a sitting position. "Cat is here, and you haven't lost her."

"Oh, thank you, Missus Lady Grenspell," Pandy exclaimed, launching herself at Lottie.

She caught the child with a startled grunt, her body still smarting from her impact with the ground. But what a precious bundle, small arms wrapped tightly around her, gleaming mahogany curls tickling her face. Such childish exuberance. It touched Lottie's heart and, strangely, made her own eyes sting.

"You are quite welcome, child," she said. "But tell me, what are you doing racing through Hyde Park alone?"

"Nurse is here somewheres," Pandy told her. "She didn't wanna chase Cat, so I runned here without her. Let the mongrel go, she said. Good riddance to it."

Lottie patted the girl's back reassuringly, thinking that there were now two people she'd like to give a sound verbal drubbing to—the awful boy who had thrown a stone at poor Cat and Pandy's nurse as well. How dare the woman be so unfeeling? Couldn't she see how much the dog meant to the girl?

Cat had calmed down sufficiently from her race now—

her tongue was lolling, and she was panting, sitting calmly on the gravel and watching Lottie with big brown eyes.

"That wasn't very nice of Nurse at all," Lottie said grimly. "I am glad that I was walking today."

"I am too, Missus Lady." Pandy released her and leapt to her feet, patting the top of Cat's head with a chubby, gloved hand. "There's a good lass, Cat. You need to apol-gize to Missus Lady Grenspell for knockin' her to the ground."

Just as Lottie was wondering how the dog might *apol-gize*, an older woman dressed in a plain dove-gray walking gown rounded the bend.

"Miss Pandora," the woman scolded. "What manner of trouble have you found yourself in now?"

"Missus Lady Grenspell saved Cat," Pandy told the nursemaid excitedly.

"Forgive me, my lady," the nursemaid said. "The child is dreadfully ill-mannered. Her upbringing is coarse, I'm afraid. The mother was a common trollop who abandoned her."

Lottie was appalled that the nursemaid would speak so ill of Pandy and her mother before her. "Madam, it does not behoove you to speak so plainly of such matters," she informed her icily, wondering if the duke knew that his nursemaid was carrying tales to anyone who listened.

But the nursemaid had already turned her attention to Pandy, wagging a scolding finger at the girl as she scowled. "You are going to be punished for this, you rotten little imp. Nothing good comes of children born into sin. It's what my mother always told me, and you're proof of it."

"Please not the rod," Pandy pleaded.

Heaving herself to her feet, Lottie brushed off her gloves, finding them shredded, her hands bleeding and raw from the impact on the sharp gravel. But that scarcely mattered. What did matter was that the nursemaid before her, to whom the Duke of Brandon had entrusted his daughter's care, had nearly lost her in Hyde Park and then had insulted her repeatedly. Worse, it would seem she had struck the poor child in the past and intended to do so again.

"You've earned it, miss," the nursemaid snapped. "Running about the park like a wild creature, insisting upon bringing that flea-bitten mongrel…"

"Cat's my dog, not no mongrel," Pandy declared, tears glistening anew in her eyes. "I love her, and she loves me."

By now, they had created quite a scene, and Lottie had heard and seen more than enough. "Of course she is your dog, my dear," she told the girl, before pinning the nursemaid with a pointed glare. "I'm a friend of the duke's, madam, and I do not think he will care to hear the report of what has happened here today."

The nursemaid paled. "The girl will be punished for what she's done, my lady. I assure you. There's no need to speak with His Grace."

"Judging from what I've heard, there is every need," she said coolly. "Indeed, I think it best if Miss Pandora and Cat accompany me back to the duke's town house in my carriage."

"I can't leave her in another's charge," the nursemaid protested.

"Yes, because you have taken such excellent care of her yourself," she said, unable to keep the acid from her voice.

Not only had the woman been unkind and cruel to Pandy, but she had also clearly been striking the poor girl. If the Duke of Brandon didn't sack his daughter's nursemaid after learning of what had happened and what she'd said to Pandy, Lottie would personally box his ears.

Twice over.

Pandy threw her arms about Lottie's skirts, clinging to her as best she could, given the voluminous nature of her promenade gown. Cat barked and then resumed panting, apparently still worn out from her adventures.

Lottie drew a protective arm around the child. "Pandy, would you and Cat like to come in my carriage with me?"

"Oh yes, Missus Lady Grenspell," the girl declared. "Me and Cat wants t'go with you."

Lottie glared at the nursemaid, daring her to defy her.

"As you wish, my lady," the nursemaid relented, twin patches of color on her cheeks.

"Very good." She took Pandy's hand in hers, wincing when the child gripped her cut palm with excited pressure. "Come along, my dear. I'll see you and Cat home."

∽

"Duke!"

Brandon was in the midst of reviewing the correspondence from the servants he had permanently installed at Wingfield Hall when his daughter's cry echoed beyond his study, punctuated by three barks and a series of racing feet slapping the marble.

Where was her blasted nursemaid? He had warned the woman not to allow Pandy to race across the marble. She would slip and fall and crack open her head. Christ knew how many times he had done so as a lad when no one had been watching him. To say nothing of the many times he had slid down the railing of the grand staircase when he'd been alone. Once, he'd nearly broken his leg for his troubles. On another occasion, his neck. Fortunately, Pandy hadn't discovered that dangerous source of entertainment just yet. Though, if she took after him at all, she would soon enough.

"Miss Pandora, do please walk," cautioned a well-modulated lady's voice that decidedly did *not* belong to Miss Partridge, the nursemaid.

No, this was a voice he recognized all too well, and not just because it made his stupid prick twitch to attention.

Lady Grenfell. What the devil was she doing here at his town house, and with Pandy?

He rose from his chair, frowning, gratified that his daughter's footfalls had slowed. The dog barked again.

"And you must be a lady as well, Cat," she cautioned the dog quite as if she were speaking to a human.

"Yes, Missus Lady Grenspell."

"I told you that since we are friends, you are to call me Lottie, my dear."

The voice was kind and warm, and it wrapped around his heart like a vise. Curse it, why was he eavesdropping in his own home, at his own study door? And mooning over the countess's voice at that? He shuddered, disgusted with himself.

There was a small knock at his door that he recognized as well.

"Enter," he called, trying to summon his composure.

The door burst open to admit Pandy, Cat, and an unsmiling Lady Grenfell presiding over them. She was predictably lovely in navy silk and...dust. Her cinnamon-gold hair had come partially free from her elaborate coiffure, and her hands were red and scraped.

He strode forward. "Lady Grenfell, what has happened?"

"Lottie saved Cat," Pandy told him, adoration evident in her voice and eyes as she gazed up at the countess and continued with a breathless explanation of events. "A mean boy throwed a rock at Cat in the park, and Cat runned away. I loseded her leash. Miss Partridge telled me to let Cat go, that she has fleas. But I runned after her, and Missus Lady—Lottie—catched her and then she falled over 'n hurted herself on the stone path and Miss Partridge catched up to us and said she'd use the rod on me again. Don't let her use the rod on me again, Duke. *Please?*"

The rod.

The nursemaid was *striking* his child? Why did he not know this?

"That was rather a lot of information, Pandy girl," he said gently, taking in the tear-streaked nature of her small, cherubic cheeks.

She'd been crying.

He wanted to tear the paper hangings from the damned walls until his fingers bled.

"Your Grace, I hope you'll forgive me for overstepping my bounds and bringing your daughter and Cat here myself," Lady Grenfell interjected. "However, after I ran across Pandy in Hyde Park, it was plain to see that my intervention was necessary."

Dear God. He had never felt more like a failure in his life than he did in that moment.

"You are injured, madam," he observed grimly.

"I am perfectly fine. A few mere scrapes. But I would like a word with you before I go, if you please." She sent a telling glance in his daughter's direction.

"Of course." He moved to the bellpull, and when Shilling dutifully appeared, he asked the butler to have one of the chambermaids escort Pandy and Cat to the kitchen to see if Mrs. Willoughby had any treats to offer them. He also requested a wash basin, soap, and cloths.

The maid arrived posthaste, depositing the basin, soap, and cloths on his desk as he instructed, and whisking away Pandy and Cat. Pandy, pleased at the notion she might soon have her hands on one of Mrs. Willoughby's sweet confections, waved gaily at Lottie as she took her leave.

"Thank you for saving Cat, Lottie!"

"Any time, my dear child," Lottie told her with a fond

smile and a wave of her own that served to remind Brandon of the injuries she'd sustained on his daughter's behalf.

Or perhaps on behalf of his daughter's dog named Cat.

Either way, the fault was his.

The door closed, leaving him alone with her.

"Come and have a seat, Lady Grenfell, whilst I tend to your hands."

"I will see to them myself when I get home," she countered, predictably stubborn.

"Nonsense. You were injured by helping my daughter. The least I can do is offer my aid."

"I would like to speak with you about the nursemaid," she insisted, frowning.

Deciding to take matters into his own hands, he caught her elbow in a gentle grasp and guided her toward his desk and the waiting basin and soap. "Speak as I work, then."

Although she held herself stiffly, she allowed him to move her to the desk. "You must sack the woman, Brandon."

He took up a cloth and wetted it in the basin. "Your hands, if you please."

To his surprise, she didn't argue, offering them palms up. "The nursemaid had allowed Pandy to run off after Cat on her own. Anything might have happened to her. What if she had found her way into the Rotten Row thoroughfare and been hit by a carriage?"

The very notion was incomprehensible. It made his gut clench and his heart tighten painfully. "I'm grateful you were there."

Nascent guilt mingled with fear. He had selected the nursemaid. He had placed Pandy in her care. If anything had happened to his daughter today, the fault would have been his. Jesus, he was just as bloody terrible at being a father as his own sire had been. But there wasn't time to dwell on his vast insufficiencies, for he had a countess to tend to.

Brandon settled on her right hand first, which had suffered more damage than the left. Angry red gashes marred her palm, and though the bleeding had stopped, the fall had clearly been a serious one.

"As am I. She said all manner of awful things by the time she caught up with us," Lady Grenfell continued, hissing when he gently applied the damp cloth to her cuts and scrapes. "She told Pandy that she had been born from sin and that no good would come of her, and I do believe she has been striking the poor girl with a rod."

Clenching his jaw, he scrubbed the cloth over the brick of Winters soap before bringing it back to Lady Grenfell's waiting palm. Lightly, he dabbed, trying to cleanse the grit from her injuries as the floral scents of the soap rose. "I'll be sacking her forthwith."

"I'm relieved to hear it." She made another sharp inhalation as he continued his ministrations.

"Forgive me," he murmured. "I'm trying to be as gentle as I can."

"It stings a bit. I am perfectly capable of seeing to the scrapes myself."

"Yes, but you championed my daughter today," he countered, trying not to allow their proximity to affect him, nor the way her hand felt in his, dainty and warm and soft and right, so blasted right. "You stopped Cat from running off, and you brought them both safely home to me. Furthermore, you informed me about the nursemaid, and I'm grateful to you. Cleaning the wounds you received because of all that is the least I can do."

"It is wholly unnecessary," she protested, but she allowed him to continue.

He finished with her right hand, wringing out the cloth in the bowl to rinse it before gently patting it dry. "I insist." Brandon took up her left hand and cleansed it as well.

A heavy, almost companionable silence fell between them as he finished his task, blotting her left hand dry. Still holding her hand in his, he made the mistake of meeting her gaze. There was a small, plum-colored bruise on her cheek, he realized.

Without thought, he cupped her cheek, gently touching the bruise with his thumb. "You've a mark here."

"Oh." She winced as he brushed over the purple skin again. "I suppose I did strike the ground with my face after all. It was a most ignominious fall. Quite murderous on the pride."

She was attempting to make a jest, but there was nothing funny or lighthearted about what had happened today, nor about the way he was feeling just now.

"Lottie," he said roughly, her name torn from him.

He wanted nothing more than to kiss her. He couldn't kiss her. He shouldn't kiss her. He needed a wife and not the complication of a mistress. She didn't want to marry. And yet the tenderness she had shown Pandy, the concern for her welfare...and the way she was looking at him now.

Ah, hell.

He was going to kiss her.

How could he not?

"I'm sorry you were hurt," he said softly, his thumb stilling over the purpled flesh. "Your hands, your cheek, your pride."

"All shall heal." Her sky-blue gaze dipped to his mouth.

The desire that had never been far from the surface brazened forth, roaring like an uncontrollable fire. *Do not kiss her*, he admonished himself sternly. *Do not dally with this woman. You need a bride.*

And the widowed Countess of Grenfell had made it more than clear she wasn't it. But he didn't want a wife, and that was the trouble. In this moment, he wanted nothing so much as he wanted *her*. Her with her wild red hair, her audacious ways, her staunch defending of his daughter, her mesmerizing blue eyes, the freckles that gilded her nose, calling for his lips...

"If you don't move away from me, I'm going to kiss you," he warned Lottie.

She didn't go anywhere. Just stayed there, still and tempting, her eyes like twin pools of endless sky, burning into him.

"Lottie," he said again. "Last chance."

Suddenly, she did move. But it wasn't to leap away from him. Instead, she grasped a handful of his necktie and pulled him into her, her mouth hard and hot and open on his. With a growl, he hauled her into him, kissing her back with all the yearning he'd been attempting to control.

Her name was an absolution, singing through his mind, his blood.

Lottie.

Lottie.

Lottie.

She tasted sweeter than he remembered, her lips lush and full beneath his, her tongue invading his mouth just as she had stormed into his town house. As if she belonged there. And God, it felt like she did, her sweet perfume surrounding him in a haze of sensual delight, her breasts crushing into his chest, her fingers sifting through his hair. She kissed him as if she wanted to devour him, and he kissed her in kind, spinning them about so that her bustle pressed into his desk and she was trapped between his body and the immovable carved mahogany at her back.

He ravished her mouth, starved for her, this magnificent woman he couldn't stop wanting, no matter how hard he tried. But kisses were woefully insufficient. He needed more. Needed her completely undone for him, crying out his name in helpless abandon as she came. He gave her his tongue, and she sucked on it, making a low sound of need that went straight to his ballocks.

The hand that had been holding his neckcloth in a fervent grasp moved, gliding down his chest, over his abdomen, perilously near to the waistband of his trousers. His cock arrowed upward, straining against his falls, needing her hand on him, just *needing*.

As if she'd read his mind, those nimble fingers found the buttons on his waistband, plucking them from their moorings one by one until his trousers opened. She slid her hand inside the slit in his drawers, wrapping her fingers around his cock and giving him a decadent stroke from root to tip.

He groaned into her mouth, their tongues dueling, their breathing ragged. It hadn't been his intention to ravish her in his study in exchange for protecting his daughter today, but here he was. And there was no denying that she wanted him every bit as much as he desired her. She tipped her head back, breaking the fusion of their mouths, her lips kiss-swollen and dark red, moving her hand up and down his shaft in a tantalizing rhythm that had his hips jerking as if he were a green youth enjoying his first frantic frigging. He wasn't, of course. But he didn't remember the last time he'd been so desperate to be inside a woman.

Maybe never.

She swirled her thumb over his crown, and he forgot what day it was. Forgot everything that wasn't her.

"I want you," she murmured, her voice throaty and low. "Now, here."

Sweet God, no. He couldn't. Could he?

Her grasp on his cock tightened.

Yes, he decided. He most certainly could.

Brandon planted his hands on her waist and lifted her to his desk. He'd forgotten about the wash basin. Her tournure knocked into it, sending water raining to the Axminster.

He'd deal with that later. For now, he caught a fistful of silk and petticoats and lifted it, his hand finding the silken recess behind her knee, higher to the curve of her thigh, tantalizing him through her fine drawers.

"You're sure?" he asked hoarsely, some dim part of his brain still functioning sufficiently to recall that he ought to be a gentleman and give her the opportunity to change her mind.

That a frantic fuck on a desk was likely not what she had intended this afternoon any more than it was what he had planned.

With the hand that wasn't tormenting his cock, she reached for his, bringing it between her parted thighs. "I'm certain."

Wetness kissed his fingertips as she pressed his hand to her hot, silken quim. He took her mouth again, finding the tender nub of her pearl and teasing her. She was so slick, so ready for him. He sank a finger deep, her inner muscles clenching hungrily on him, and both of them moaned as one. Her thumb slicked the mettle seeping from him over his cock head, and she nipped at his lower lip, the stinging pain mingling with pleasure.

Damn. If she didn't stop, he was going to spend in her hand.

He jerked his mouth from hers and withdrew his finger from the hot clutch of her velvety cunny.

"Hold up your hems," he ordered her, his voice hoarse.

She released her hold on his cock and did as he asked, grasping her voluminous navy skirts to her waist. He was treated to the decadent sight of her deliciously curved calves encased in silk stockings above her embroidered boots, a lacy, almost transparent pair of drawers clinging to her luscious thighs above, trimmed in ribbons. But what he wanted to see most remained hidden by the spurious fabric.

"Wider," he said. "I want to see you."

Wordlessly, she obeyed, her legs parting more fully, the split in her drawers gaping to reveal the glistening pink heart of her. Her scent, musky and feminine, blended with roses and violets, thoroughly intoxicating. He wanted to bury his face between her legs and lick her until she came. But he also wanted to sink his cock inside her and fuck her until they both came.

A dilemma.

His head was filled with fire and few thoughts. Words, reasoning, ration…beyond him, all of it. There was only action. Seizing. Claiming. If he only had her once, he wanted to know what she tasted like.

Brandon dropped to his knees, hands framing her hips, and took her clitoris in his mouth, sucking hard.

The sound of her breath fleeing her lungs gratified him, but not as much as the needy tip of her hips as she thrust herself more firmly into his face. Yes, this was what he needed. Although, in a different time and space, he'd have preferred her to sit on his face so that he could recline and fully enjoy devouring her. This, however, would have to suffice.

He laved her with his tongue, licking up and down her seam, then found her entrance and delved deep into the honeyed recesses he was about to fill with his aching cock. She writhed and said his name, and he rewarded her by returning to her swollen bud, licking and sucking with renewed abandon until she stiffened and cried out, shuddering against his mouth as she reached her pinnacle. Damn, he loved the way she tasted. He could lose himself in nothing more than pleasuring her with his mouth.

But his rampaging cock had other ideas.

Swiftly he rose to his feet, licking his wet lips to savor her as he grasped his cock, rubbing himself up and down her folds until he was coated in her dew. He took a moment to drink in the sight of Lottie on his desk, sated and lost in her passion, her customary thorns momentarily stripped. Her head was back, her eyes heavy-lidded and glazed with passion, her cheeks flushed.

"Inside me," she demanded.

And she didn't have to tell him twice. Brandon aligned himself with her center. She released her hems to grasp his shoulders, but it didn't matter. His body was holding them in place now. He cupped her nape and took her mouth in a fiery kiss, feeding her the taste of herself on his tongue as he sank inside her body with one swift thrust.

And sweet Lord, it was glorious.

She was snug, wrapped around him in pulsing heat, her legs locked about his waist. For a moment, he could do nothing more than remain as he was, consumed by the sheer bliss of being planted deep within her. He wished he had a mirror properly positioned so that he could have the pleasure of watching as he fucked her, their bodies moving rhythmically together.

But there was no mirror, only the two of them, their bodies one, her breasts surging into his chest, their mouths fused. Needing to move, he withdrew almost entirely, still kissing her, their lips never parting, before sliding deep. Slowly, he began a rhythm that was agonizing and yet incredible, savoring the warm glide of his cock in and out of her grasping sheath.

Slowly enough to torture them both.

Lottie apparently grew impatient.

She tore her lips from his as he pumped into her with agonizing care. "Faster, Brandon," she demanded, breathless.

But the more she wanted him to hasten his pace, the more he, perversely, wanted to take his time. To pleasure her slowly, until they were both delirious with wanting. He buried his face in her throat, inhaling deeply of her scent, finding her racing pulse with his tongue.

"Damn you," she ground out, her nails biting into his shoulders. "More."

He chuckled and kissed his way to her ear. "Patience, sweet Lottie."

Then he slid his hand to the place where they were joined, his fingers finding her pearl and teasing her until she bucked and gasped, shuddering around him as she climaxed again. But he wasn't finished. Not until he wrung every drop of pleasure from her that he possibly could. He licked the hollow behind her ear, plunging deeper now, faster, her cunny so slippery that the wet sounds of their lovemaking echoed around them. Somehow, her head slipped to his shoulder, and he felt the mark of her teeth through his coat and shirtsleeves.

He bit her earlobe and pinched her clitoris at the same time, and she gave a little scream, shaking against him as she tightened on his cock with so much force, she almost pushed him from her body. He continued keeping her pearl in his hold, feeling it throb between his forefinger and thumb for just another moment until he released her finally. Surging in and out, he pressed his face to her temple, fucking her hard and deep and then, at the last moment, forcing himself to withdraw, shooting creamy ropes of spend all over her silk drawers.

Blood rushing in his ears, his vision speckled with black stars from the force of his release, Brandon collapsed against Lottie and the desk, breathing harsh, heart pounding. Belatedly, he realized that his shoes were soaked through and there was a puddle on his carpet. But he didn't give a damn.

Because for the moment, he had her pliant and warm in his arms, and everything in his tumultuous world felt inexplicably—if fleetingly—*right*.

CHAPTER 9

*L*ottie had bedded the Duke of Brandon.

No, that wasn't true. Not precisely. Rather, she had rutted with him on his study desk like a common doxy. After which, she finally had gathered her wits and slid from the waterlogged correspondence-strewn surface, shaking her skirts back into order. They had fallen around her, perfectly in place, yet hopelessly wrinkled from their frantic coupling.

"Thank you for tending to my hands, Your Grace," she had managed. "Good day."

"Lottie," he had called after her, tucking his spent cock back into his trousers.

She had ignored him and fled, of course. Because when he had been holding her in the aftermath, she'd known a moment of tenderness for him. A moment of contentedness that did not belong between two lovers with no future together. And it had terrified her.

That had been mere hours ago, but it may as well have been a lifetime. Now, Lottie stood on the periphery of the ballroom floor, watching Brandon dancing with a young debutante who was perfect for him in every way—eighteen, golden-haired, beautiful, and innocent. Everything Lottie was not.

"Are you attending me, Lottie?"

Her friend's voice jolted her from her disquieting reveries. She turned away from the ballroom crush and the sight of Brandon smiling down at the lovely Lady Lavinia Westermere and tamped down all hints of jealousy she had no right to feel.

"Of course I am, Rosamund, darling," she chirped with feigned brightness.

But her dear friend was not so easily convinced.

"What did I say?" Rosamund asked, pinning Lottie with a shrewd look.

Lottie bit her lip, trying to recall any hints of conversation flitting about in her mind. But all she could think about was the moment she'd spied Brandon across the ballroom with Lady Lavinia in her pale-pink silk gown. Watching the two of them spin together had caused a physical ache deep within her.

"Was it something about Megs?" she guessed weakly.

Rosamund arched a winged brow. "No."

"The Duke of Camden?"

"Not in this instance."

Blast.

"The ballroom being a crush?" she tried next.

"What I said was that you certainly do seem preoccupied with the Duke of Brandon and his dance partners this evening," Rosamund said pointedly.

She'd been caught. Heat crept up her throat.

"Is he in attendance? I hadn't noticed." She shrugged one shoulder, feigning indifference.

"You needn't try to fool me, you know," her friend said

conspiratorially. "Something is going on between the two of you."

"Whatever it was, it's passed," she muttered, trying to keep her gaze from seeking him out again and failing miserably.

He was one of the tallest gentlemen in attendance, which made him easy to spy. Curse the man. What a dashing figure he cut, far more handsome than any man had a right to be. Her heart pounded as she thought about him on the floor before her, on his knees, his tongue and mouth doing wicked, delicious things. His reputation as London's greatest lover hadn't been wrong. She simply hadn't expected to receive that confirmation on his study desk when she was dusty and disheveled from a fall in Hyde Park.

"Then why are you staring at him?" Rosamund asked.

Lottie's ears went hot, and she forced her eyes back to her friend, who looked resplendent herself in a becoming purple silk evening gown. "I wasn't staring at him. I was…taking note of how poorly he dances."

Another lie, but she didn't want to confess the raw truth to Rosamund here in the midst of the ballroom, that she had been as intimate as a man and woman could be with the Duke of Brandon earlier that afternoon, and that they were now in attendance at the same fête, avoiding each other as if they were strangers.

Which was how it ought to be. How she wanted it to be, she reminded herself sternly.

Brandon glided expertly through another turn as Lottie and Rosamund watched.

Rosamund sent her a wry smile. "It looks as if he dances quite well to me."

"To you and Lady Lavinia both," she grumbled before she could help it.

"Are you jealous?"

Lottie flapped her fan wildly, making the fringe of curls artfully arranged on her forehead flutter. "Don't be ridiculous, Rosamund. Why should I be jealous of Lady Lavinia Westermere? She's a mere babe. Only look at her, fresh from the schoolroom. I've no doubt she scarcely knows anything at all."

As the bitter words left her, Lottie realized just how very envious she sounded. Petty, as well. She heaved a sigh, disappointed in herself. She didn't compete for a gentleman's affections. Grenfell had been the last man she had shared, and she had vowed never to do so again.

"I do believe she is newly eighteen," Rosamund agreed mildly. "If the Duke of Brandon is looking for a biddable young wife, Lady Lavinia would be an excellent choice."

Yes, she would. Admittedly, Lottie had placed Lady Lavinia on her list of prospective brides for Brandon. But that had been before, when she had been secure in her belief that she would never be intimate with him herself. The notion of crossing out the debutante's name was undeniably appealing now.

"Indeed."

Oh, how the concession cost her pride. Lottie was not so very old, but compared to a young chit like Lavinia, she felt positively ancient. To say nothing of the trials her marriage had put her through.

"They do make a well-matched pair," Rosamund continued thoughtfully. "His dark to her light, his height to her shorter stature."

"You make them sound like horseflesh, my dear."

"Finding a husband or a wife is scarcely any different," her friend said. "Bloodlines are considered. Teeth must be examined, et cetera."

Lottie laughed. "What a sight it would be, the Duke of

Brandon inspecting Lady Lavinia's teeth on the ballroom floor."

It certainly would have improved her mood to see such a scene. It would have made her feel less...*raw*. She didn't know why she should be affected so. She'd taken lovers before. But then, none of her past lovers had been interested in marriage. Their needs had been as clear and plain as hers. Pleasure, nothing more. Nothing permanent. No emotions involved—purely the physical.

Not that she had developed anything so foolish as feelings for the Duke of Brandon. Because she most assuredly hadn't. It was merely that watching him with another woman who might become his wife and the mother of his children...well, it left her at sixes and sevens.

"We couldn't be fortunate enough to have that much entertainment," Rosamund said. "Balls are dreadfully dull affairs, are they not?"

"Quite tiresome," she agreed, taking note of the way Brandon leaned nearer to his dancing partner, murmuring something in her ear.

Lady Lavinia laughed. She looked even comelier in the throes of her amusement. Lottie was sure the sound was as clear as tinkling church bells.

"Perhaps a glass of champagne would help," Rosamund observed kindly. "You seem in need of distraction."

Her friend caught the eye of a liveried servant passing with a tray of champagne glasses. The servant hastened in their direction. Lottie quickly snapped her fan closed and hung it from her wrist before snatching up some champagne. Rosamund accepted a glass as well, and the two of them drank in companionable silence for a few moments.

"I think I'm going to marry him, you know," her friend said at last.

Lottie slanted a surprised look in her direction. "The

Duke of Brandon? I do believe the champagne has gone right to your head, darling."

Rosamund chuckled. "Not Brandon, you goose. Camden."

Relief and shock warred with each other within her. "You're going to marry the Duke of Camden? Truly?"

As the heiress to unimaginably vast sums, Rosamund would be best served—in Lottie's opinion—to never marry and to keep her funds wholly under her own control, along with the rest of her life, regardless of how great her yearning for vengeance was.

"I do believe that I am, yes," Rosamund acknowledged quietly.

Almost wistfully.

"What has so persuaded you?" Lottie wanted to know. "You are currently firmly in possession of the reins, my dear, in control of your fortune and all that comes with it. Why would you wish for your circumstances to change? And marrying a cad like the Duke of Camden? I don't think the man has it in him to make a good husband."

"That wouldn't matter," Rosamund said. "Not truly. It isn't a husband I want, of course, and you know that. It's revenge."

She knew about the retribution her friend sought, and she well understood the reason for it. Women with broken hearts were forces to be reckoned with, and no one deserved to be meted his punishment more than Lord Wesley.

Lottie took another sip of her champagne. "Revenge at the expense of your freedom, however? Do you truly think it would be worth it, Rosamund? Would you chain yourself to Camden just to spite his brother?"

"He destroyed me, Lottie," her friend said, her voice low but laden with emotion. "And I understand Lord Wesley all too well. It will eat him alive to know that his brother has married the fortune he once coveted for himself."

Lottie noted that Rosamund spoke of her inheritance and not herself.

"You are worth far more than your money," she told her friend staunchly. "Surely you know that."

"I don't know that. For the entirety of my life, I've been the Payne heiress. Men look at me and see a fat golden cow to milk. That is how it has always been, and that is how it shall always be. Camden is no different, but at least he was honest about what he wanted."

The sadness in Rosamund's voice made her heart clench. "You are beautiful, clever, witty, and amusing. To the devil with any man who cannot see that."

"I am plain, of moderate intelligence, and eccentric. Even I know my faults, though I do thank you for your loyalty."

"I love you dearly, Rosamund, which is why I must tell you that you are wrong."

"We shall agree to disagree," her friend said, raising her brows. "We're about to have company."

"Company?" Frowning, she followed Rosamund's gaze, startled to realize that the dance had finally come to an end, the Duke of Brandon having separated from Lady Lavinia.

And he was striding in their direction. Her foolish body's reaction to his powerful form was instant and nettlesome.

"Why is he coming over here?" she muttered to Rosamund.

"He looks as if he's quite intent upon you," Rosamund said *sotto voce*, no help at all.

"Is it too late to hide?"

"I'm afraid so," her friend said as Brandon reached them.

"Lady Grenfell, Miss Payne." He bowed, and somehow even the ordinary, polite act was rendered indecently sensual. But then he held her gaze with his emerald-green one and spoke, shocking her even further than his presence before her already had.

"I believe this is my dance, Lady Grenfell."

~

CHECKMATE, Brandon thought smugly as he watched realization dawn in Lottie's brilliant blue eyes.

It wasn't his dance, of course. He hadn't asked her. But he'd pinned her neatly in a difficult situation. She could either call him a liar before her friend or quietly accompany him.

"So it is," she said at last with a marked lack of enthusiasm, offering him her hand.

He took it, bringing it to his lips for a lingering kiss, inhaling deeply, searching for hints of her scent. And there it was, violets and roses and Lottie, making his randy prick go instantly hard in the midst of a crush of people. It seemed an eternity had passed since those forbidden moments of passion this afternoon, and he remained as desperate for more of her as he'd ever been. He tucked her hand into the crook of his elbow, guiding her toward the sea of dancers who were assembling for the next song.

"You need not look so enthused at the prospect of waltzing with me," he told her wryly as they took up their positions opposite each other, making certain to hold her body closer to his than propriety called for.

"Why are you dancing with me?" she asked, unsmiling. "Surely there is another debutante eagerly waiting her turn with you. Lady Lavinia is an excellent choice for a bride, but there are others who are every bit as lovely."

Hmm, so she *had* been watching him dance with Lady Lavinia, then. He didn't miss the bitterness in her voice now, and he couldn't say why, but it pleased him.

"Why would I not dance with you?" he countered, lacing their hands together as the waltz began.

What did she expect after what had happened today in his study? That he would simply never speak to her again? Clearly, she hadn't thought he would approach her this evening. But how was he to stay away? He'd been able to think of nothing but her every second since he'd watched her flee his study in a swirl of dusty navy skirts.

"Because I am not a prospective bride," she said through gritted teeth as she smiled at him. "And you are in dire need of one."

"But I like you," he countered smoothly, turning them with effortless precision.

An understatement. He more than liked the woman. It was reasonably possible that he worshiped her. His inconvenient preoccupation with shagging her was already growing tiresome.

She scoffed. "Not a sufficient reason."

He leaned nearer, his lips close to her ear. "Perhaps I've been thinking of being inside you again ever since you left my study, and dancing with you is the closest I can find myself at the moment."

Her swift inhalation was his reward. He'd hit his mark. She stumbled, nearly tripping on her hems. Brandon saved her, turning her about once more, unable to keep from grinning.

"Are you always this scandalous when you dance, Brandon?" she asked sharply, distinctly unamused.

"Only with you," he told her easily, bewitched by the smattering of freckles on her nose.

"I cannot think Lady Lavinia would approve," she said, holding herself stiffly, her gaze trained on a point over his shoulder.

"Since she is neither my wife nor my betrothed, her opinion doesn't signify at the moment."

Lady Lavinia, he had already decided, was not for him.

She was pleasant enough. Pretty enough. Hailed from a fine enough family. She was even an excellent dance partner and witty conversationalist.

But he didn't want to fuck her on a desk. He wasn't obsessed with the color of her hair or the tilt of her lips or the sounds she made when she came.

Most of all, she hadn't championed his daughter. Hadn't caught a runaway mongrel to her own detriment. Hadn't taken a cruel nursemaid to task.

She wasn't Lottie.

"Truly, Brandon," Lottie said, still frowning at the place beyond his shoulder. "It looked as if the two of you were thick as thieves. You needn't prevaricate on my behalf. I know that what passed between us today was an aberration. You're hardly my first lover, nor shall you be the last."

He wasn't sure if she meant that as a challenge, but he took it as one. He looked at her, stunning in the glow of the chandeliers, her fiery hair glinting with hints of spun gold, and was possessed by the sudden, fierce notion that he *would* be her last lover. To make it so. The emotion accompanying this tremendous realization confounded him. This time, Brandon nearly tripped, only catching himself at the last second before the two of them landed in an unceremonious heap.

But he would show none of this to her, for he knew instinctively that a woman as clever as the Countess of Grenfell must never be permitted the upper hand. She would be ruthless with it.

"An aberration," he repeated. "Yes, of course. It shan't happen again."

"It cannot," she insisted crisply.

"I was simply caught up in the passion of the moment."

"It was a mistake."

"A dreadful one."

By this point, he had maneuvered them so that they were positioned near one of the doors leading to the hall. Without hesitation, he danced her over the threshold. He was familiar with the Earl of Abernathy's town house, and he knew there was a convenient salon adjacent to the ballroom.

"Brandon, what are you doing?" Lottie asked him in hushed tones. "You've moved us into the hall."

"Oh dear, have I? Allow me to rectify that."

He spun them into the salon, closing the door behind them, and whirled again, so that her back was to the portal. She was flushed, her lips parted, eyes glistening.

"This isn't the ballroom," she said, breathless.

"Do you want to return?" He held his own breath, awaiting her answer.

So much hinged upon it.

The very world, it seemed.

"No," Lottie told him, softly, quietly.

Lust arced through him, intense and potent. It didn't matter that he'd had her this afternoon on his desk. If he didn't slide inside her again within the next five minutes, he would combust like dry kindling.

He allowed himself the pleasure of drinking her in—the gown she was wearing was a marvel, fitted to the architecture of her body like a sleek glove. The silk was neither purple nor blue, but some mystifying shade in between that rendered her eyes a stunning iolite hue. Her creamy breasts were mounded high above the bodice, a cluster of silk flowers and fine tulle adorning them. It occurred to him that he had yet to see her breasts, and this seemed an egregious lapse on his part.

He needed to be alone with her, with the luxury of time and without the fear of interruption.

But that was a worry for later. For now, his aim was simple and single-minded. He passed the backs of his fingers slowly, lightly, over the soft swells of her breasts, reveling in the hiss of her breath as she inhaled. How satiny her skin was, gilded with coppery flecks. Deliberately, he ran his caress along the ridge of her collarbone, pausing in the dip at the base of her throat to feel her pulse throbbing in time to his.

He could explore her all day. Every inch of her was a revelation, but desire had cast its heady spell over him, and he couldn't resist lowering his mouth to hers. He kissed her with all the longing that had been burning within him, devouring her lips, giving her his tongue and tasting the sweetness that was Lottie mingling with champagne.

She made a low, throaty sound of need, clutching at his coat with one hand whilst the other found the fall of his trousers. His cock was already rising toward her, and the brush of her palm over his erection was enough to make him groan in turn. Was she as mad with wanting him as he was for her? He had to know.

Grasping her voluminous skirt and petticoats in one hand, he lifted them high, his hand unerringly seeking her cunny. She was wet and ready for him, his questing fingertips finding her swollen clitoris and strumming over her. Her hips chased his hand, her tongue greedily invading his mouth.

He toyed with her, rubbing, stroking, lightly at first and then with greater pressure, wanting to prolong her pleasure and torment both. She found the buttons on his falls and flicked them open, his cock springing free into her waiting hand. As if she had been waiting all evening, she stroked his rigid length firmly from base to tip, her tight grasp and hum of appreciation making him harder.

Brandon traced her seam to her entrance, sinking a lone finger deep. The velvet grip of her cunny was almost enough to make him spend in her hand. All the while, he fed her kisses, long and slow and demanding, their tongues tangling, their ragged breaths and sounds of frustrated need blending to become one. His thumb fluttered over her pearl as he worked in and out of her. He needed to make her lose control, to make her come here pinned against this door while just beyond, a ballroom laden with people danced and laughed and made merry.

And he wanted, with sudden, possessive need, to know that his seed was inside her. For her to return to the ballroom filled with his spend. He didn't know where this urge was coming from, only that it was. Foolish. A risk he couldn't take. He didn't need another bastard child in the world, particularly when he was trying to find a wife.

But he couldn't excise the thought from his mind, from his blood, and when she reached her pinnacle, her cunny tightening on his finger as she moaned into his kiss, he knew he couldn't resist. He had to be inside her, to claim her. To make this woman his.

She was still pulsing around him when he withdrew and shifted their positioning, hooking her leg around his hip so that he could have her as he wanted. She was open to him, ready and waiting, soaked. No words were exchanged. There was nothing left to say, their lips and bodies communicating for them.

Lottie guided his cock to her center, slicking him up and down the wet petals of her sex before bringing him to her entrance. He gave them what they both needed, sliding into her in one deep thrust, the door at her back making a small creak of protest at the sudden motion. Sensation flooded him. He was intensely, almost violently aware of the place they were joined, his cock clenched in the silken hold of her cunny. Aside from this, they were fully clothed, adding to the erotic, forbidden nature of the moment.

Despite his rakish reputation, he could honestly say that

he had never, in all his years, fucked a woman against a door in a secluded little salon at a ball. Taking Lottie like this was perilous—she had not been wrong in her earlier assessment that he needed a wife. Impressing debutantes was not achieved by clandestinely shagging one's lover.

But nothing else mattered. He was inside her, where he belonged, and every single second that had passed between them had led them here, to this inevitable moment of utter sensual abandon.

Lottie was impatient as he held himself still, buried within her, reveling in the feeling of her wrapped snugly around him. Her hips swiveled against him, her head falling back against the door with a soft thud as she broke the kiss.

"More," she demanded.

And he gave it to her, losing all restraint. He took her mouth as he withdrew and then plunged into her again and again. He scarcely had the presence of mind to reach between them and stroke her clitoris until she was crying out into his kiss, her body trembling from the force of her release, the clamp of her cunny on his cock nothing short of exquisite.

He pumped in and out of her, riding the ripples of her orgasm. The *thump, thump, thump* of him driving her into the door rose to rival their ragged breaths and the faint din of the orchestra from the ballroom. If anyone were to pass on the other side, there would be no doubt of what was happening within. Somehow, that only made him harder, more frenzied. He wanted all of London to know this woman was his, to carry her out of this room and take her away with him. To strip her naked and tie her to his bed and fuck her a hundred different ways.

For now, he had to settle for this one way. Part of him knew he ought to exercise caution. To withdraw from her. But the other part of him, the primal part of him, didn't want to stop. One more thrust, the angle of her hips nothing short of exquisite, and white-hot bliss rolled up his spine, pouring out of him. Brandon surrendered himself to the beautiful oblivion of release, filling her with his cock, with his seed, with everything he had, giving her some intangible part of himself he hadn't known existed.

Filling her until he collapsed against Lottie and the door, his heart racing hers.

CHAPTER 10

"You have callers, my lady."

Her butler's report startled Lottie from the book she'd been halfheartedly reading. It was a dreary, rainy day, and she had overslept this morning, having spent most of the night at the Abernathy ball, much of which had passed in a champagne-soaked blur following her mad coupling with Brandon in the salon.

She wasn't expecting visitors.

"Did you tell them I'm not at home?" she asked patiently, closing the volume and setting it aside.

For she had made it clear this morning—or perhaps, rather, this afternoon—when she had risen, that she was in no mood for callers. Everything yet felt far too raw and jagged within her, after her second encounter with Brandon. Twice in one day. And once in public, no less. Her body ached in strange places thanks to the creative nature of their couplings.

How had she managed to find herself in such a delicious, foolish predicament?

"Er, yes, madam," said her butler with politic parsimony of phrase. "I did indeed say that you are not at home."

A muffled bark drew her attention then, sounding from somewhere in the hall beyond.

Cat?

It couldn't be. Could it?

Another bark, and she had to believe that it could.

Lottie frowned. "Does the caller have a young girl with him and a spaniel, by any chance?"

"He does."

Brandon was here. With his daughter and her willful little dog. Her heart leapt, and she couldn't say why.

"See them in, if you please."

"Of course, madam." With a bow, the butler disappeared.

The energetic hound entered first, bowling into the room in a flash of brown-and-white fur. Pandora came next, trotting in a girlish skip that was hardly well-mannered. Brandon, elegant and wickedly handsome, was last to cross the threshold.

Cat launched herself into Lottie's lap and instantly began licking her face with unrestrained exuberance.

"Oh Cat, you mustn't. Missus Lady Grenspell don't want no face lickings," Pandora announced as Lottie attempted to placate the spaniel with some ear scratches.

"Blast it, Pandy. I told you the damned dog should stay at home," Brandon growled, stalking across the room to pluck Cat from Lottie's lap.

But not before she had received a sound tongue bath from the pup. Idly, she wondered if dog saliva was dripping from her chin.

"Duke, you ought not to say no-no words," Pandy informed him, eyes wide.

He muttered something that sounded suspiciously like another oath. Lottie tried not to be amused by the vignette before her and failed. There was something undeniably adorable about watching father and daughter. Pandy was the perfect, rambunctious foil for the devastatingly handsome rakehell duke. But she would not allow herself to soften toward the man any more than she would allow herself to make love with him again.

Twice had been enough. She'd had her pleasure, and now she'd happily find it somewhere else.

Liar, said a voice within that she promptly ignored.

"Brandon," she greeted with a cool aplomb that belied the fluttering in her stomach. "To what do I owe the dubious honor of your call?"

"Dubious? I'm affronted." Holding the wriggling pup against his broad chest, he seated himself on a nearby settee. "I have a favor to ask of you, if you must know."

Interesting. Also, not what she had expected.

She watched him struggling to contain Cat with undisguised amusement. "A favor? Of me? I'm positively agog."

"Pandy, no playing with the *bric-à-brac* on Lady Grenfell's tables," he sternly advised the girl, who was unabashedly exploring the room with her hands rather than her eyes.

At that moment, she was holding a framed picture of Grenfell in her hands. Lottie didn't know why she kept it about—perhaps as a reminder of how dreadful a mistake she'd made in marrying him. As it was, she didn't think she'd mind if the girl dropped it and the glass shattered to bits.

"It's only Grenfell," she said. "She may as well pitch it into the fire."

"Hardly the tender sentiment of a contented wife," Brandon observed shrewdly.

Cat finally succeeded in extricating herself from his hold and leapt to the carpet, trotting after Pandy.

Lottie had no wish to discuss her unhappy marriage with him. Or anyone.

So she raised a brow. "What is the favor you need, Brandon?"

He winced. "No time for small talk?"

"*Brandon.*"

"What's this, Missus Lady Grenspell?" Pandora asked loudly from across the room.

Lottie glanced in the girl's direction and realized she was now holding a sketch that Lottie herself had drawn what felt like a lifetime ago.

"You must call me Lottie, dearest," she reminded Pandy. "And what do you think it is?"

"A cat?" Lottie guessed, wrinkling her brow as she studied the framed sketch in her chubby-fingered hand.

"Pandy, my girl, look with your eyes alone," he said, with another long-suffering sigh.

"It is indeed a cat," Lottie answered. "But you may hold the sketch if you like, dear."

"Missus Lady—Lottie," Pandy corrected herself belatedly, regarding Brandon with triumph, "has said I may hold it."

"It's only a sketch I made in my youth," she explained to Brandon. "My favorite cat, Mr. Whiskers."

"Where's Mr. Whiskers now?" Pandy asked with the naïve innocence of a child who has no notion of mortality.

"He was quite old, and he grew sick several winters ago," she explained gently, her throat going thick with sadness at the reminder of her beloved cat, even after the passage of so much time.

"Oh," the girl said with feeling.

"Do put the frame back where it belongs, Pandy," Brandon commanded. "Before Cat eats it."

Lottie eyed the dog, who was sniffing at Pandora's skirts. "Has Cat been eating things she shouldn't?"

"She appears to have a fondness for table legs and the gowns of nursemaids," he drawled.

"Oh dear." Lottie cast a speculative glance in the direction of her own tables.

"Fortunately, you're not a nursemaid," he said.

"But I *do* have tables, Brandon."

"Pandy will make certain Cat doesn't cause mischief whilst she's visiting."

Her eyes narrowed, and she swiveled her head back to the handsome duke currently inhabiting her settee. "What do you mean, *whilst she's visiting?*"

"Ah." He gave her a rueful look, running a hand along his sharp, whisker-shadowed jaw. "That is the, er, favor I must beg you."

She sighed. "Go on."

"I had to sack the last nursemaid after what you told me," he said quietly. "And the maid I cozened into taking up the situation had a fit of the vapors last evening when I was at the ball and Cat tore away half her skirts."

"Oh dear."

"Quite." His smile was pained.

Lottie couldn't say why she was taking an absurd enjoyment from his plight. Only that she was.

"Cat has discovered she possesses an affinity for eating skirts," she mused. "What makes you think she won't attempt to make mine her dinner?"

"Yours are silk."

Quick with an answer, every time. The man's tongue was despicably talented, and Lottie could attest to that personally, in more ways than one.

"I fail to see why that should matter," she countered, clinging to her patience.

"Cat doesn't prefer to eat silk, as far as I can tell."

She stared at him, searching for a hint of laughter. A tiny twitch in his jaw. The wink of an eye. Anything to suggest he was jesting.

Nothing.

"Have you offered her silk as a dining option?" she asked suspiciously.

"Er, no. Pig trotters, cheese, and black French twill appear to be favorites, however."

"Perhaps Cat is a dog who is also part goat," she reasoned with a grin.

Brandon winced. "Either way, I must attend to a meeting where I cannot, for reasons you likely can discern, have Pandy as an accompaniment. You have been her champion. I was hoping you might be amenable to keeping her here with you for several hours."

A meeting where the child wouldn't be welcome. Her mind instantly flew to his need of a bride. Was he depositing his daughter with her so that he could court another woman? And after what had happened between the two of them yesterday?

She stiffened her spine, her levity dying, for she disliked the notion immensely. "As you said, Brandon, I'm not a nursemaid."

"Must I beg?"

A vase containing freshly cut flowers teetered as Pandy picked up another frame to examine it, and Cat stood on her hind legs, her front paws on the girl's skirts.

"Do try not to knock over the flowers, dear," she called. "I'm afraid Cat would try to eat them and get dreadfully sick."

"I'm sorry, Lottie. I didn't mean to," the child said, her voice contrite.

"Lottie," Brandon said urgently, his voice low. "I'm desperate. It's only for a few hours."

"Off to court Lady Lavinia?" she asked, turning her attention back to him.

"Jealous, my dear?"

It scarcely behooved him to taunt her. She might have

pointed that out to the conceited oaf seated in her drawing room requesting a favor of her. But she didn't want him to see just how affected she was by the thought of him gallivanting with another woman.

"Why should I be?" she asked coolly, fussing with the gathering of her overskirt. "Our association is at an end."

"Is it?" His eyes flicked over her body with frank sensual intent.

And damn the man, but that green-eyed glance alone was enough to make her nipples hard.

"Of course it is. As we discussed, it was nothing more than a temporary aberration. A brief surrender to madness."

"Not the table leg, Cat!" Pandy declared.

Lottie diverted her attention to her *Louis Quinze* table, which was being gnawed on by the spaniel.

"No, Cat," Brandon commanded. "Bad Cat."

"Do you think her name ever confuses her?" Lottie wondered idly.

Looking guilty, the dog backed away from the table, leaving it relatively unscathed.

"It was hardly an aberration, and I believe you know that," Brandon added to her in a low aside. "Nor was it madness."

Heat blossomed in her belly. The very air in the room suddenly felt heated and sparking with electricity. But she wouldn't think of that now. Wouldn't focus on the sensations he evoked. The yearning starting to burn deep within her. She'd had what she wanted from him. At least, that was what she was telling herself.

"Whatever it was, it shan't be repeated," she told him sharply.

"Have you any sweets?" Pandy wanted to know, apparently having grown weary of inspecting the framed pictures and sketches Lottie kept on the low table and moving on to the window, where she peered into the street below, her face so near to the pane that it left a smudge when she backed away.

"I'm certain my cook has some in the kitchens," Lottie told her, a rush of fondness for the child going through her.

It was impossible not to like the girl. Pandy was filled with energy, boundless spirit, sweet charm, and a hint of naughtiness. She ran circles around her father, and that also pleased Lottie. If anyone needed to be brought to his knees by a tiny human, it was the Duke of Brandon. His love for his daughter, however, was undeniable. And remarkable. Many men in his position would have sent her away and never thought of Pandy again.

"Does that mean you will grant me this favor?" Brandon asked.

She wished she didn't find him every bit as charming as his daughter, albeit in a different sense. But she did. When he smiled at her, it was difficult to deny him anything he wanted. Including herself.

But she was wise enough to know that she could use the circumstances to her advantage.

"I will," she decided, "in exchange for a favor of my own."

He grinned. "I ought to have known. What is the favor?"

"When I decide upon it, I'll let you know," she told him.

His eyes narrowed. "What if I don't like the favor in question?"

She beamed at him. "I'm afraid you don't have a choice."

He glowered at her for a moment before relenting. "Very well. You'll have your favor in return for mine."

"Excellent." It required all the self-discipline she possessed to keep from rubbing her hands together in diabolical glee.

Now to think about what favor she would request. And to keep Cat from eating her tables. She rose from her chair and shook out her gown, casting a wily eye in the direction of the spaniel, lest she hatch any ideas about the ribbon trimming and gauzy overskirt.

"Come along, Pandy. Let us see what treats we can find for you and Cat." She held out her hand to the girl.

Pandy happily skipped toward her, the dog racing her until the child nearly tripped. Lottie had a feeling it was going to be an interesting several hours. And strangely, she was looking forward to it.

~

THE WICKED DUKES SOCIETY—or, to be more specific, its founders—convened in the drawing room at the Duke of Camden's Grosvenor Square town house. There was brandy and cheroots. Bawdy jokes and an overuse of curses. It was decidedly not an appropriate setting for one's still relatively newfound four-year-old imp and her table-and-nursemaid-eating dog.

"There's been some news from Wingfield Hall," Brandon announced grimly to the assemblage when a lull in discussion had occurred.

"News?" Riverdale repeated. "I don't think I like the sound of that or the accompanying expression on your face."

Brandon took a fortifying sip of brandy. "And well you shouldn't. It's my grandmother, I'm afraid. After all these years of abandoning the estate to my care, she has apparently made an unexpected visit."

"Bloody hell," Camden swore.

"Have you received word from her?" King asked, drinking something that decidedly didn't resemble brandy.

Another of his potions, presumably.

"From the servants," Brandon clarified.

"And?" Richford wanted to know, raising a brow. "What have they said?"

"Grandmother is suspicious," he said, repeating verbatim what his butler had relayed. "There are certain…rooms that are likely a concern. To say nothing of our next house party, which is set for a month from now. If she chooses to remain in residence…"

"We'll have to cancel the house party," Whitby finished for him.

"But the invitations have already been accepted, as have the payments," Riverdale pointed out.

And they all knew the payments were an immense sum, divided six ways still enough to be considered a small fortune for each of them. The lucrative nature of the Society was one of the reasons they continued hosting their lavish fêtes at Wingfield Hall. Earning their own funds rather than accepting the familial coffers that had been left them—in varying states of empty and full—had given each man a sense of purpose that had been previously lacking.

But for Brandon, it was more than that. He had been diverting the sums to the orphanage that had been his mother's favored charity. A small, secret way to pay her honor, but one that was important to him.

He sighed now, raking his fingers through his hair. "I'm well aware of all the problems facing us if my grandmother insists upon staying at Wingfield Hall, and I greatly regret offering it as the location for our Society gatherings, given what she's been doing."

Forcing him to marry. Threatening to give Wingfield Hall to Cousin Horace. Now intruding upon the estate she hadn't visited in years, a month before they were to host a gathering with carefully selected members of the Society. His head was beginning to ache just thinking about it all.

He took another hearty drink of brandy, hoping to dull some of the pain.

"Wingfield Hall is perfectly situated near to London,"

King said. "We all agreed upon it for its convenience and the grotto. The fault isn't yours, old chap."

Not entirely, perhaps. But he would be the one to pay the price with his own sacrifice. Which brought him to another topic of concern he needed to raise with the rest of his friends.

"As King knows, my grandmother has recently taken a notion into her head that I must marry or she'll give Wingfield Hall to a distant cousin," he blurted. "It's her estate, inherited from her family, and she has the right to do it. I simply…never thought I'd see the day when she would take my birthright and give it away to someone else."

"You have to get *married?*" Whitby choked out, looking not just astonished but horrified by the idea.

Indeed, with the inflection he put on the word, Whitby might have said *you have to take a leap from the nearest pier whilst wearing leaden weights about your ankles* instead. The revulsion was the same.

"I do," he admitted grimly, thinking of Lottie again.

She had looked nothing short of luscious this afternoon. He'd wanted to devour her. To gather her up in his arms and carry her to the nearest room containing a bed, where he could happily enact all the lurid fantasies that had been haunting his thoughts last night when he'd been alone in the darkness of the night.

"My sincere condolences." Whitby shuddered, then raised his glass in a mock salute. "To the memory of the Duke of Brandon. May he rest in peace."

"I'm marrying, not dying, you arse."

"Is there a difference?" King asked wryly.

Damn it. Not much of one, as far as Brandon was concerned. Even if the thought of wedding one woman in particular didn't terrify him nearly as much as it ought to. Indeed, the notion of marrying Lottie somehow held unexpected appeal. Waking to her every morning, shagging her silly each night...

But no, he mustn't think of that now. There were five pairs of eyes trained upon him, awaiting his answer.

"Perhaps not. But rest assured, I'll do whatever it takes to secure Wingfield Hall for the Society's sake," he vowed.

"Even so, *marriage*, Brandon?" Whitby shook his head. "You needn't go that far. Surely there's another way. One that isn't so drastic. So completely bloody terrible."

"Have you made the acquaintance of my grandmother? She has the tenacity of an ox, a dog, and a mule combined. I am persuaded she could put any general on a battlefield to shame."

"I *have* met her," Whitby conceded with a wince. "Excellent point, old chap. The old harridan is rather terrifying."

"Sounds as if the both of us will be married men soon," Camden announced grimly.

"You?" Brandon turned to his friend, still surprised though Lottie had warned him as much on their carriage ride from Sidmouth's wedding breakfast.

"Me," Cam confirmed. "Although the lady has only just consented to be my wife—and with a list of stipulations five times longer than the bloody Magna Carta."

"Stipulations?" Now this was interesting to Brandon, the very thought of his iron-willed friend bending to a prospective bride's demands. "Never tell us you've fallen in love."

"Christ no," his friend reassured him. "You know I haven't a heart. Nothing but a husk where it ought to have been."

Brandon would have said the same for himself not long ago. But that had changed when Pandy had stormed into his life with her outrageousness, her utter lack of proper manners, and her dog perversely named Cat. Now, by contrast, he felt too much. It was as if his heart had grown large and tender and new again, softened by his daughter's innocence in a way he otherwise would never have known.

He didn't like it, but that didn't make it any less true.

"Who is the fortunate lady in question?" King intoned, raising his glass. "Perhaps a toast is in order."

"Miss Rosamund Payne," Cam said.

"The chit with the pet squirrel who rides on her shoulder?" Riverdale inquired, sounding aghast.

"It's not a squirrel, Riverdale," Cam corrected. "It's an African grey parrot, and yes, she does occasionally squire the thing about on her shoulder. Her name is Megs, and she delights in calling me all manner of names. The latest is 'gormless shite,' I believe."

"I thought the chit's name was Rosamund, not Megs," King said, frowning into his glass. "And that's a hell of a thing to be calling one's future husband."

"The parrot, you dolt," Cam elaborated. "Her parrot is called Megs, and the bird in question is the one who has been heaping insults upon me. Miss Payne is quite obviously called Miss Payne."

"Miss Payne. How very formal. I reckon you don't have to marry her because you've bedded her, then?" Whitby inquired.

"Has anyone recently told you that you're a rude prick?" Cam asked him conversationally.

"Always." Whitby took a deep inhalation of his cheroot and blew a perfect cloud of smoke into the air above him, unrepentant.

"Stop nattering, the two of you," Riverdale admonished. "You're worse than a pair of squabbling biddies. We need to come to a decision about Wingfield Hall and the Society house party. If we want to cancel it, then we should act now."

"I can't afford to cancel it," Cam admitted, his cheeks going ruddy.

"Can't afford it?" King frowned. "What the devil do you mean?"

"I mean…I need my share of the funds," Cam said. "I'm pockets to let, and I've already spent the blunt. It's also why I need to wed Miss Payne."

"And her squirrel," King reminded him.

"Damn your hide, it's a parrot, not a squirrel," Cam gritted. "A parrot I strongly dislike, mind you."

"Pockets to let," Brandon repeated. "This is bloody news, Cam. Why did you not say something sooner? I'd be more than happy to lend you some funds."

"This isn't the sort of debt that can be erased with a mere loan," Cam said, "though I do thank you for the generous offer."

"I'll gift it to you, then," Brandon suggested. "Your problem is easily enough solved without resorting to nuptials."

But Cam shook his head, his expression turning mulish. "I don't want a gift. A man does have his pride, even if it's all that he has left."

"Still," King argued, "you should have told one of us."

"For what purpose? I'll not accept alms from any of you. The funds from the Society were sufficient to keep me afloat for a time…until they weren't. I'm afraid when my father decided to apply himself to the family tradition of being a dissolute wastrel, he excelled. In fact, it was probably the only thing he was good at, aside from bedding light-skirts and making my mother miserable. But even his profligacy pales in comparison to my brother's."

Like Brandon and the rest of their inner circle, Cam had no loyalty to his dead sire. They were united in their cause—pursuit of pleasure and the destruction of their fathers' bitter legacies of unhappiness and destruction. For Brandon, that cause had taken on a new shape. He hadn't ever supposed he would marry, but now that Grandmother demanded it, he hadn't a choice.

He wondered idly if he ever had.

Likely not, and it had been the height of foolishness to imagine he'd had the liberty to rule his own life as he saw fit. He'd been born to be the next Duke of Brandon, and nothing had altered him from that course. He could almost hear his bastard of a father laughing from the grave.

"You're certain you want to marry the squirrel chit?" Whitby asked Cam, retrieving Brandon from his wool-gathering.

"Damn you, it's not a squirrel but a parrot, and I don't want to marry her, but it seems the preferable option at the moment."

"Preferable to?" Brandon prodded.

"Selling my soul to the devil," Cam offered, and not without bittersweet irony.

"I do hate to tell you, old chap," King drawled, "but you've just given the very definition of the parson's mousetrap."

"Better the devil you know, et cetera," Cam said, raising his brandy in salute, his features set in grim acceptance of his fate.

And in that moment, something occurred to Brandon. The devil one knew was decidedly better than the devil one didn't. He knew Lottie—intimately, if not the depths of her soul. He liked Lottie. Pandy liked Lottie. This was the devil he knew.

She was also the devil he intended to marry. He just had to convince her. He had offered for her once and she'd refused him, but that didn't mean he couldn't ask her a second time. He didn't want to marry a debutante. He wanted her.

"To what must be done," he said, raising his own glass, "like it or not."

"To what must be done," his friends echoed in unison, clinking their goblets together.

"And to *who* must be done," Whitby added slyly to ensuing laughter.

King raised his glass again. "Also, to squirrels."

"Bloody hell, King, it's a goddamned parrot," Cam grumbled.

CHAPTER 11

Lottie woke the next day when her lady's maid brought in a massive vase of fresh flowers.

"For you, my lady."

She could understand Jenkinson's excitement—the woman was practically floating above the Axminster as she glided into the room with an arrangement that was almost the size of a small country.

Lottie blinked blearily at the blossoms, wondering what time it was as she sat up, the bedclothes pooling around her waist. "Thank you, Jenkinson. However, I didn't ring for you just yet."

It was a gentle reminder that her slumber had been interrupted.

She'd spent the previous day racing after the giggling, wayward blur that was the Duke of Brandon's daughter. And her impetuous dog too, of course. By the end of the quite massive favor she'd given Brandon, Lottie had abetted in the thieving of biscuits from the kitchen, in the charcoal sketching of admittedly unrecognizable self-portraits—Lottie's skill at drawing had waned in recent years without practice—and she had played a game of hide-and-seek that Pandy had inevitably won, thanks to her smaller stature and lack of bustle.

"Oh, I know you didn't ring for me, my lady, and I must beg your pardon. But the young man who brought the flowers insisted upon waiting until you offered a response to the note that accompanied them. He's been waiting in the kitchens for nigh on three hours now, and Cook has grown tired of him eating all her sweets." Jenkinson settled the vase on a table and straightened, beaming. "I feared incurring her wrath, Lady Grenfell."

Cook's wrath was indeed quite legendary. She was temperamental, yet undeniably talented. It was her culinary marvels that made keeping her on—and keeping her happy— a necessity.

"Three hours," Lottie repeated, frowning. "What time is it, Jenkinson?"

"Half past one, my lady."

She had slept through luncheon.

"Goodness, having a miniature caller about must have exhausted me."

Pandy's boundless energy certainly had been taxing. Enjoyable, but taxing nonetheless.

"Children oft tend to be wearying," Jenkinson agreed, offering her the missive. "The note, my lady."

"Thank you." Lottie took the sheet from her lady's maid and unfolded it, reading the slanted, undeniably masculine scrawl.

Lottie,
Kindly consider these flowers my insufficient means of expressing gratitude for the favor you

paid me yesterday. I eagerly await the favor you shall, in turn, request of me.

Pandy tells me that you are quite clever at hide-and-seek and that you were infinitely patient with Cat, who only managed to eat a small bite of one table leg on account of her being provided with a soup bone from your cook.

I am forever indebted to you. Do enlighten me as to the favor.

Suspense renders me bilious.

Yours,

Brandon

As she finished the letter, Lottie realized she was smiling. Oh, this wouldn't do. She tamped down her levity. He wanted to know her favor already? She hadn't even considered what she would ask of him yet. The reason he had instructed his servant to await her response was clear, however.

She folded the epistle again, holding it as she slipped from the comforting warmth of her bed. "I suppose I must provide an answer, then, so that the young man belowstairs can cease disturbing Cook."

"It would be most beneficial if you did, my lady," Jenkinson offered as she fussed busily over some of Lottie's garments across the room.

Lottie padded to her writing desk and sat, taking up pen and paper.

Your Grace,

Thank you for the flowers. The gesture was unnecessary, though appreciated. I fear I haven't had sufficient time to ponder the favor in question. I do hate the notion of being responsible for your biliousness. Perhaps a cup of tea would ameliorate your condition.

Yours,
Lady Grenfell

THERE. It was a subtle reminder that there must be a return to formality between them. He was going to marry soon, and she had to accustom herself to that reality. She folded the missive and gave it to her lady's maid, who hastened to the kitchens and returned carrying a tray of breakfast and tea for Lottie, whose stomach growled as she took in the delicacies awaiting her on the salver.

"I understand why the poor fellow didn't wish to leave," she admitted with a sigh of pure appreciation as she tucked into her meal.

After eating, she began her *toilette*, only to have it interrupted by another servant bringing the news that the letter-bearing lad had returned with yet another missive. It was passed to Jenkinson, who delivered the new note to Lottie.

She opened it, foolishly amused that Brandon had taken the time to send round a second communication.

Dearest Lottie,
Tea shall not suffice as remedy. There is only

one panacea my feeble constitution requires, and it is the honor of your company.

Say you will join me on a drive in Rotten Row at the fashionable hour, else I shall perish.

Yours in bilious despair,
Brandon

A CHUCKLE STOLE FROM HER. The absurd man. She ought to deny him. What good would come of being seen in his carriage by polite society? He needed a bride, and she most assuredly would not be it. What was he thinking, inviting her? Surely Lady Lavinia would make a better accompaniment.

"Will you send an answer, my lady?" Jenkinson inquired.

"I suppose I must." Huffing a small sigh, she hastened to her writing desk, dashing off her reply.

O Duke of Bilious Despair,

I should never forgive myself for denying you the cure you seek. Although I must caution that you would be better served in finding a suitable lady to join you on Rotten Row, your elegant pleading has persuaded me to accept.

Yours,
Lady Grenfell

She had finished with her *toilette* when the next note arrived.

> *My dear Lottie,*
> *There is no lady more suitable than yourself.*
> *Fear not, a new nursemaid has been procured.*
> *Pandy and her demon shan't be accompanying us.*
> *Your faithful servant,*
> *Brandon*

Lottie couldn't help but to smile as she scrawled her response.

> *Brandon,*
> *I admit that I prefer the company of Miss Pandora and her beloved spaniel to most people. Consider me gravely disappointed that she and Cat will not be joining us.*
> *Yours,*
> *Lottie*

At the last moment, she realized she had signed with her name instead of her title. A telling slip. She must gird herself against him better. For although she had been as intimate with him as a man and woman could be, she had been doing her utmost to maintain a necessary distance.

Lottie,
Would that you were mine.
Yours,
Brandon

THE LAST MISSIVE quite took her breath. She didn't know how to respond, and as it was soon time for their drive in Hyde Park, Lottie decided to maintain her silence.

∼

BRANDON DETESTED drives in the park.

He loathed Rotten Row, the fashionable hour, and the notion that he must be seen.

He couldn't abide by the simplistic courtship rituals so beloved by polite society.

But none of that mattered one whit as he drove a matched pair of Bays toward the park. Because the woman at his side made all the rest of it fall away. Of all the barouches in London she might have seated herself in this fine day, Lottie, the Countess of Grenfell, had chosen his.

A miracle.

The sun was shining—a rare occasion, indeed, and one to be celebrated, so much more for the gingery glints it brought to life in Lottie's hair. Her fiery tresses had been subdued into plaits, then confined in a knot at her nape. Curls framed her forehead and face beneath the brim of her jaunty hat.

Light reflected in her eyes, rendering them somehow an even brighter hue of blue. She was nothing short of delicious.

He wanted to devour her. He didn't want to bloody well take her on a drive like a proper swain. He *wasn't* a proper swain. He'd shagged her, and quite rudely, in a salon at a ball. And another time, equally salient, upon his study desk. It was undeniable that he had proceeded with his courtship out of the correct order.

However, he'd never been respectable. And it was too damned late to start now, anyway.

He had pressed his luck mightily today, and he had emerged the victor.

"My notes charmed you," he said, unable to keep from grinning. "Confess."

"I wouldn't say charmed so much as *obligated*," she countered in true Lottie form, her mouth unsmiling, her contralto measured and yet cutting in a way that was uniquely hers.

He transferred one of the reins to his left hand and clapped his right palm over his heart in dramatic fashion. "I am wounded, o beloved sorceress of wayward children and ragtag mongrels."

His ebullient praise earned nary the hint of a smile from her berry-pink lips. "O tolerated driver of sleek barouches, I beg you to steer our conveyance with more than one hand and whilst directing your attention to the road ahead."

"Ah, but the road ahead is so very uninteresting," he pointed out, continuing to drive one-handedly, his gaze glued to her. "What is there to be seen other than the rear of boring carriages or the arse-end of a horse?"

She bit her lip, looking as if she waged an inner war against levity and her pride. "There is the road one must navigate."

"Boring," he declared. "I'd rather ogle you."

She sputtered.

He grinned harder.

"Ogle," she spat, as if it were a foreign word, unfamiliar on her tongue. "Me?"

Surely she didn't doubt her allure. She carried herself like a woman who well understood her worth and who knew she could command it from the men permitted within her charmed circle.

"Why wouldn't I ogle you?"

"Because gentlemen don't ogle."

"And?" He waved a hand at himself in dismissive fashion. "You are aware of my reputation, are you not?"

Color crept up her throat, chasing the smattering of golden freckles on her ivory throat. Clearly, the Countess of Grenfell's spots were the most entrancing in the history of humankind. Brandon had never been similarly enthralled by another's.

"Of course I am aware," she muttered, pinning him with a grim look. "All of England is, I daresay. And perhaps farther. One never knows where you have traveled."

"To a great many countries, of course," he informed her. "Would you care to hear which ones?"

"You may keep your conquests to yourself," she said primly.

"Never say you're jealous, my dear."

"Hardly." She sniffed, as if the notion couldn't be more ludicrous.

But he didn't miss the way her spine stiffened.

"Mmm," he hummed noncommittally, transferring the reins to his other hand again as he navigated a turn.

"What does that mean?" she demanded.

He kept his gaze on the road ahead. "That you protest too much."

"Tell yourself whatever you like."

Oh yes, he had her where he wanted her. Well, not *exactly*

where he wanted her. Not physically, anyway. That would have to wait for a more opportune moment. One containing both privacy and a bed.

He smiled. "You needn't worry about past conquests, you know."

"Wonderful, because I wasn't." She diverted her attention to the road, an elegant and icy queen.

God, she was delectable. When she was cool with him, it made him want to do wicked things to her.

"Wonderful," he repeated cheerfully, allowing a silence to fall between them because he knew it would only heighten her discomfiture.

In his mind, he began to count, suspecting he wouldn't make it beyond a full minute before she surrendered to the need to speak.

Thirty.

One-and-thirty.

Two-and-thirty.

Three-and-

"Why are you so quiet all of a sudden?" she burst out.

He cast a glance in her direction, admiring the creamy column of her throat, where a dusting of coppery freckles disappeared into her bodice. "I was seeing how long you could last without speaking to me."

Her head swiveled to him, giving him a view of her entire lovely face rather than only her profile. "I beg your pardon?"

"Just over thirty seconds," he added, unable to keep a note of smugness from his voice. "I don't blame you for yearning to hear my voice."

"Perhaps I was bored," she countered. "About to expire from *ennui*. Have you considered that?"

Brandon grinned. "Not even once."

She made a small huffing sound that made him grin harder whilst he turned his attention back to the road as they approached Hyde Park. A crush of conveyances had already begun to descend upon Rotten Row. Everyone would know, and in quite short order, that the Duke of Brandon had been seen with the Countess of Grenfell.

"Only think of what the gossips shall say when they see the two of us on a drive together," she said, almost as if he had spoken his thoughts aloud. "You ought to have asked Lady Lavinia to accompany you instead."

"I'm not courting Lady Lavinia," he said, keeping his tone mild.

"You aren't?"

They were in the official procession, traveling down the bridle path as onlookers watched from the rails.

"I'm not," he affirmed.

"Who *are* you courting, then?"

You, he might have said. But again, Brandon knew the woman at his side well enough to understand that such news would not be greeted with enthusiasm. No, best to conduct his courtship covertly. To plead his case without her aware of it.

Until it was too late.

"You certainly have taken quite an interest in my romantic entanglements," he observed instead.

"I'm merely trying to help you," she countered.

He slanted a glance in her direction. "Generous of you."

She shrugged. "My mother taught me that one must perform good deeds in one's life."

"A clever woman indeed."

"Perhaps not always clever. She did encourage me to marry Grenfell, and I count my marriage as the great disaster of my life."

She didn't often speak of her marriage. Or her husband. Brandon wasn't unfamiliar with the gossip concerning her.

Grenfell had been an unabashed philanderer, both before and after their nuptials.

"Yours was an unhappy union?" he ventured.

"Vastly." She sighed, her mouth tightening as she revisited painful memories before she forced a smile—for his benefit, he knew. "Grenfell was an adulterous scoundrel."

"Only a fool would have strayed from you," he told her quietly, meaning those words to his core as he turned his attention back to the bridle way.

"Or perhaps only a fool would have believed in his avowals of love," she said, her smile fading. "Or for expecting constancy in a marriage. Faithfulness is so very bourgeois, I've learned."

"I am sorry for the pain he caused you, Lottie. You deserved far better." He looked at her, holding her gaze to show her it was not a mere platitude he offered.

He meant it sincerely. Grenfell hadn't been worthy of her, the bastard.

She nodded, her countenance softening. "Thank you for saying so. It is exceedingly rare for a man to admit that a woman has a right to something more."

"Perhaps you've been keeping company with the wrong men," he suggested gently.

Her gaze turned thoughtful. "I'm beginning to think that I have."

They spent the remainder of the drive engaged in lively conversation, deftly avoiding such weighty matters. They spoke of their reading preferences—Lottie adored mysteries. He preferred romances. They both favored the poetry of Elizabeth Barrett Browning. As they approached her town house, he found himself reluctant to part.

"Will you join me for dinner this evening?" he asked, hoping she wasn't otherwise engaged.

He needed all the time with her he could manage to beg,

borrow, or steal. If he was to plead his case—and with all haste—he needed as many of the hours in the day that she was willing to give.

"Shouldn't you be continuing your hunt for a bride?" she asked pointedly.

Damn her for her persistence on that subject. *Yes*, he thought to himself, *and continuing is exactly what I will be doing. With you.* But he kept that carefully bottled away inside.

"There comes a time when every hunter grows weary and needs to rest," he offered instead.

She frowned. "Who will be in attendance?"

"You're looking at him."

Her eyes narrowed, drawing his attention to those brilliant orbs and coppery lashes. "Just you?"

"You find me an insufficient dinner companion? I ought to be affronted."

"Hardly, but it seems an unwise decision to accept your offer."

"Unwise, how?" They had reached her dwelling now, a humbler affair than his own town house, though still fine for a widow's portion. He stayed the horses and turned to her fully, thinking her quite the loveliest—and most stubborn— woman he'd ever known.

"Because we have already..." Her gloved hand waved between the two of them. "And that portion of our association is decidedly at an end."

"Is it?" he asked mildly. "I wonder if you would think so if I were to kiss you now."

Her eyes went wide. "Kiss me? Before all of London?"

"Before all of London presently on this street." He slid nearer to her on the bench, until his thigh pressed into her voluminous skirts.

"To do so would be an invitation to disaster," she said, sounding properly scandalized.

Which was rich for a lady who had no qualms about shagging against a door at a ball.

He leaned nearer to her, tantalized by the faint scent of roses and violets. "Then you had better accept the invitation to dinner instead, my dear."

"Dinner," she conceded, looking adorably flustered. "Very well, but I'll bring my new list of prospective brides along with me since the last round didn't pass muster."

Her bloody lists. Unless she brought one with her name atop the latest version, she was wasting her time.

Brandon smiled anyway, for he had achieved yet another victory in this protracted war of theirs, albeit a small one. "I'll see you tonight at half past seven."

CHAPTER 12

To Lottie's dismay, there was no hint of Pandora or Cat upon her arrival at the Duke of Brandon's town house that evening. Instead, she was led to the drawing room where Brandon himself awaited her, cutting a dashing figure in evening black.

He bowed solemnly at her entrance, and she had to forcibly remind herself that she had not come here to be seduced. The crisp white of his shirt and necktie were in stark contrast to his mahogany hair, and his emerald eyes seemed somehow greener in the lamplight.

He grinned as he straightened, taking her hand in his and bringing it to his lips for a chaste kiss. "Good evening."

It was scarcely the whisper of his mouth upon her, and yet, he may as well have skimmed his hand over her cunny for the way her body reacted. Warmth settled low in her belly, and her nipples hardened instantly beneath the familiar shield of her corset.

"Good evening," she managed.

Lottie didn't know how she had been cozened into dinner with the Duke of Brandon. It was both foolish and reckless.

As a widow, she possessed the freedom to dine with him alone, certainly. However, he was seeking a bride. Continuing to spend time in his presence was only leading to inevitable disappointment.

Because whilst Lottie had no qualms about taking lovers, she took great care to make certain none of them was married or engaged. She would never visit that pain upon a fellow woman. It had been too late when she had learned that Grenfell had been keeping a mistress during their courtship and subsequent betrothal.

She would simply have to resist Brandon and his sensual allure. She'd come armed with her list. It was in her reticule, folded neatly in thirds. The fourth such draft, not that he needed to know that she had spent the intervening hours between their drive and her departure for dinner privately agonizing over her choices and striking lines through half a dozen ladies' names before rewriting the list.

He released her hand, his gaze searing hers. "Shall we proceed to dinner?"

"Of course." Stupidly, she had left the reticule with her wrap and hat. She would just have to remember to fetch it before she left and deliver it to him.

He brought her hand into the crook of his elbow. "I enjoyed our drive today in the park. I'm pleased you accepted my invitation to dinner."

"As I recall, I was rather blackmailed into acceptance," she couldn't help but grumble, reminded of the way he had neatly trapped her.

He chuckled. "Hardly that. More like sound persuasion than blackmail."

"How is Pandy getting on with the new nursemaid?" she asked, because she was curious and because she needed to change the subject to something safer than his kisses, potential or otherwise.

"Splendidly." He guided her from the opulent drawing room, down the carpeted hall. "Cat has yet to eat her skirts, and Miss Bennington seems to genuinely enjoy Pandy's exuberance."

"I'm glad to hear it."

"Pandy wanted me to tell you hullo, by the way. She was dreadfully disappointed that she had to retire to the nursery before you arrived."

"I'll admit that I was hoping I might get to see her. Please do tell her hullo from me and give Cat an ear scratch." She smiled with genuine warmth, thinking that Pandy and her dog were equally high-spirited. A matched pair.

He inclined his head. "I will be happy to relay your greeting. As for the ear scratch, however, I'm not sure the beast deserves one. She's managed to mangle another pair of my boots, and I'm quite peeved with her over it."

Lottie bit her lip, trying not to chuckle at the picture his words painted. They moved into the dining room, where settings had been laid and an assortment of freshly cut flowers decorated an epergne at the center of the table linen. The place settings were at an intimate proximity, which was customary for lovers sharing a meal.

Except they weren't lovers.

Not current lovers, anyway.

Past lovers. Never to be lovers again. He was getting married, and she was remaining a merry widow. That was what she wanted.

Of course it was.

"I brought my list," she announced, determined to maintain her fortitude even as his scent curled around her.

Musky citrus and something that was indefinably him. She inhaled through her mouth instead.

"Your list?" He stopped before her chair.

"My new list of prospective brides, that we spoke about

on our drive," she elaborated. "I left it in my reticule. I can fetch it now so we can review it together during dinner."

"Later, perhaps. I have no wish to discuss something as dull as debutantes over the soup course. Dullness makes me bilious."

She almost chuckled at his dramatic statement but refrained at the last moment, allowing him to seat her. "Rather a lot of things seem to make you bilious."

He sat in the chair at the head of the table, to her right. "What can I say? I have a highly sensitive disposition."

She shouldn't find his nonsense charming.

Or endearing.

Or amusing.

And yet, she did, curse him.

"When it favors you to have one," she countered wryly.

He smiled at her, and when the Duke of Brandon smiled, he smoldered, capable of sending any female within reach up in flame. Lottie was vexingly not immune.

"My dear Lady Grenfell, why should I do something that *isn't* in my favor?"

With a single motion from him, dinner officially began.

Wine goblets were filled, and a tureen of artichoke soup was delivered. Brandon discreetly dismissed the attending footman, leaving the two of them alone as he raised his glass of wine to her.

"A toast is in order, I should think," he said. "To the loveliest lady I know agreeing to accompany me for dinner."

His attention was steady upon her, and just as it had been earlier during their drive, the unwavering intensity of his stare cut through her defenses. She couldn't look away, even though she knew she would be better served to distract herself with the wine in her glass and the delicious-smelling soup awaiting in her bowl.

"To the most maddening gentleman I know," she returned with meaning, clinking her goblet against his.

He laughed, the sound deep and dark and decadent. He was somehow even more handsome when amused. Goodness, it required all the self-control she had to keep from launching herself upon the table and offering her body as the evening's feast instead of the courses his cook had planned.

They both drank.

And still, he didn't look away, holding her ensnared in his emerald gaze. She watched the way his lips molded to the rim of the glass, the bob of his Adam's apple as he drank. He was so potently masculine. She well understood how he had left a trail of conquests across England and—if his teasing earlier was to be believed—the world beyond as well. He was magnetic and intoxicating. A man who made a woman want to savor him.

She couldn't do that, however, so she settled for his wine instead. It flowed over her tongue, awakening her palate.

"This is delightful."

"Procured from one of my travels to the Continent," he said. "Fine French wine is becoming dearer and dearer, thanks to the phylloxera pestilence. It's a crime, what is happening to some of the world's best vineyards."

"I've been reading about it in *The Times*." And although she wasn't well-versed in the art of wine, she knew enough to appreciate the dire circumstances facing France, with the roots of grapevines being systematically destroyed. "It sounds perfectly dreadful."

"That is because it is," he agreed, bringing a spoonful of soup to his mouth. "Nearly half the vineyards of France have been, or are in the process of, being destroyed by it. Despite the measures being taken to stop the plague from spreading, it continues to do so."

She ruminated on his words and the soup she had just

DUKE WITH A REPUTATION

tasted. It was excellent. Apparently, the Duke of Brandon's cook was quite skilled. This didn't surprise her in the slightest. He struck her as a man who demanded the best of everything. His apparent interest in French vineyards, however, did.

"Have you visited France in your time on the Continent?" she asked.

"I have," he confirmed with uncharacteristic brevity.

Her curiosity took control of the conversation and her tongue.

"And how did you find it? I have always longed to travel to France. Not to Paris, as is so common, but to Bordeaux. To visit the grand wineries, the first-class vineyards such as *Chateau Lafitte* or *Chateau Margaux*."

He smiled with genuine warmth, displaying enthusiasm and true pleasure rather than the suave charm he so often affected. It disturbed her to realize she could discern the difference now. That she knew this man well enough.

Not just his body, as had been the way of it for her with past lovers. But his personality. The deepest, truest parts of himself. She'd learned long ago that giving one's body to another was purely a physical act. One's mind was the true source of intimacy. The rest was merely assuaging a need, like eating to dispense with hunger.

Grenfell had taught her that.

"I have an 1864 *Chateau Margaux* that is a marvel," he told her. "We must try it together. Tell me, why have you never traveled to France?"

"I was a girl when I married, only eighteen. Grenfell didn't prefer to travel abroad, for he suffered from terrible seasickness. I suppose, in hindsight, that the seasickness may have been a ruse. Likely, the true reason was because he didn't like to stray too far from his mistresses here in

London. Either way, after he died, I threw myself into the London whirl as well."

"He hurt you badly," Brandon observed, his jaw clenching.

How odd to speak about her failed marriage with a man who was her former lover. A man who had persuaded her to dinner. A man who could not be hers.

And yet, how right it felt. Surprise washed over her at the realization. She felt comfortable with the Duke of Brandon. And it had nothing to do with the physical intimacy they had shared and everything to do with the times they had simply spent in each other's company, talking.

She swallowed hard. "He did, but we needn't speak of it. That's all where it belongs now, in the past."

"Is it?" He raised a brow, his gaze searching, seeking. *Seeing.*

"Not entirely, perhaps," she allowed.

"I would love nothing more than to plant him a facer," he declared grimly. "For the grief he caused you. For failing to realize what he had in you. For being the source of the hurt I see lurking in your eyes. For everything he did and all he didn't do that he ought to have done. No man deserves a sound drubbing more."

No one had ever said that to her. Most of the members of her inner circle had been sympathetic yet firm. Keeping mistresses was the sort of thing men in their circle did. And wives looked the other way. Some of them took their own lovers after they'd done their duty of providing their husbands with the heir and spare. Everyone pretended not to care.

She didn't know what to say, how to adequately express her convoluted emotions without giving herself away. So she took up her wineglass and drained half its contents.

"Thank you," she said when she could find her voice, her silly hand trembling as she replaced the goblet on the table.

Hopefully he wouldn't take note of how deeply affected she was. She loathed speaking of her terrible marriage. Hated talking about Grenfell. It was a part of her life that she had closed away, like an awful secret locked in an attic, never again to see the light of day. Except the Duke of Brandon was resurrecting all the ghosts of her past. Shining light into the darkest corners of her soul.

She didn't like it.

And yet, she couldn't resist it.

What a strange, compelling man he was.

"You needn't thank me for stating the obvious, Lottie," Brandon said, frowning.

"Some people wouldn't think it obvious," she pointed out. "Most husbands are unfaithful to their wives. I shouldn't have been so naïve as to expect differently. It's the way of our world. Indeed, I scarcely imagine that you will be a faithful husband to your bride."

His stare was rapt upon her, trapping her as surely as if he'd caught her in an embrace, and she could not look away. "Is that what you think of me, that I intend to treat my wife as Grenfell did you?"

She didn't want to think about him in relation to his wife. His young, innocent debutante, who would be lovely and sweet, a credit to him on his arm. Perhaps he would fall in love with whomever he chose. Perhaps he *would* be faithful to his duchess. Perhaps he would never stray, and they would live happily and create a brood of bubbly children just like Pandy. Those thoughts were acid poured upon her soul.

"I'm sure it isn't my place to think about such matters," she forced out.

And yet, he refused to relent, holding her gaze, so still that he might have been a statue but for the sensual heat he radiated. "But it is, you see. I've asked the question of you."

The soup course was cooling in their bowls. Her stomach

—once eager for the delicious meal ahead—was mutinying. It wanted nothing of food, tied up in knots of envy she had no right to feel.

Lottie took another sip of wine, trying to calm her wildly vacillating emotions. Failing. She had somehow done the unthinkable. She had failed to heed her own rules for conducting herself with lovers. She wanted more from the Duke of Brandon than his body and the pleasure he could bring her.

"I think you are a rakehell with a reputation," she answered. "I think you have never proven yourself faithful. I think that when you marry, you will continue to be sought-after and desired by many women, to whom it shan't matter that you are someone else's husband. That sort of temptation can be difficult to resist."

At least, that was what Grenfell had claimed. He hadn't wanted to betray her. It had simply been his nature. He was a virile man, made to spread his seed.

Her hand trembled as she settled her wine goblet back on the snowy table linen.

"If *you* were my wife, Lottie, I would cleave unto you, and you alone," Brandon told her with an earnest intensity she could not doubt was anything other than genuine.

Something inside her quickened. His words reached a place she'd thought long inured to feeling, a place that had been hollow and numb. But that wasn't the sole effect. Heat blossomed between her thighs, an unwanted reaction she couldn't suppress. Her body was clearly a lunatic. So was her heart.

"But I shan't be your wife," she forced herself to say quietly. "I hope that such steadfast devotion will also be applied to the lady you ultimately bestow that honor upon."

"Why *are* you so unwavering in your resolve to never wed again?" he asked softly instead of speaking to whether he would be faithful to the lady he ultimately chose as his bride. "You've never explicitly stated the reasons. One can presume your unhappiness with your former husband is a concern, but surely you cannot imagine every man will treat you as he did."

The reasons were many. And deeply private. Something else occurred to her.

"You have never explained precisely *why* you need to marry,"

she countered. "I find it difficult to believe you would take a wife simply because your grandmother demanded it of you. It would seem neither of us has been entirely candid with the other."

He inclined his head. "Touché, my dear."

The soup course was whisked away and the next was laid before they could further their conversation. Although it smelled as delicious as the previous offering had, Lottie found herself loath to partake of it.

"If you must know," he began solemnly when the footmen had once again retreated and they were alone, "I must marry because my grandmother has decreed it to be so. She hails from a wealthy family, and she is a property owner in her own right. One of her properties, Wingfield Hall, is especially dear to me for many reasons. However, Grandmother recently informed me that she intends to will Wingfield Hall to a distant cousin of mine if I fail to do her bidding."

She studied his countenance and found nothing but unguarded, unvarnished truth there. The Duke of Brandon may be a rake as she had pointed out to him, but he wasn't a liar. Still, Lottie sensed there was a portion of his tale that was missing.

"Why now?" she asked curiously. "What has spurred her sudden decision?"

He winced. "I'm afraid it is the fact that my natural child

was delivered to her door after my domestics refused her mother entrance here. When my grandmother arrived to inform me of what had transpired, there was a regrettable incident with a famous opera singer, which, no doubt, did nothing to inspire Grandmother's faith in me."

"Oh my," she said, because she was so stunned that she couldn't think of anything else to say for a moment.

He sighed heavily. "I only learned of Pandy's existence from my grandmother that day when she arrived to give me a dressing down and impart the news of Wingfield Hall."

The revelation surprised Lottie, for he had seemed quite at ease with his daughter. Pandora and her father appeared to have a natural bond, even if the girl did refer to him as Duke. Lottie had supposed it was a courtesy instilled in the child, paying deference to his rank and her unfortunate position in life as an illegitimate daughter.

She found herself curious to know more. However, she knew that she didn't have the right to ask. Heavens, what they had already discussed was beyond the pale. And yet, she wanted to know. It startled her to realize the reason—that she was fond of Pandy. Fond, even, of her menace of a dog, Cat.

"Her mother no longer wished to keep her?" she asked, unable to comprehend the notion, but recalling Pandy's words at their first meeting.

She's gone on a grand adventure 'n young girls can't go on adventures. Did you know that, missus? They might fall off the ship and get drowneded.

"Her mother left for America with her most recent lover," Brandon explained, his tone and expression equally grim. "A grand adventure that didn't require the unwanted burden of a child. And lest you think me heartless, Pandy's mother never informed me that she bore my child. We had an…association. And then she disappeared from London and my life.

I presumed she had moved on with another chap. She had, of course, as I later learned, and married him. But after her husband died, she found a new lover, one who was not willing to bear the burden of a child that wasn't his own. Pandy was abandoned like an unwanted mongrel sent to the streets. I can only thank God her mother knew to try my grandmother's address before surrendering Pandy to only Christ knows what fate."

Her heart ached anew for the child to hear the desperately sad circumstances of her young life thus far. An illegitimate child, never truly accepted or belonging, then summarily abandoned by her own mother at such a tender young age. Lottie had never been terribly close to her family, but the very notion of them abandoning her was anathema.

The food before them was cooling, and it occurred to her, quite distantly, that neither of them had touched their plates.

"I'm very sorry to hear what happened to Pandy," she said softly, honestly. "And to you, Brandon. You seem, to your credit, not just tolerant of her as some men in your place would be, but adoring."

"I love her," he said, holding her gaze. "I understand that is, perhaps, irregular in our world. But the circumstances of Pandy's birth mean less than nothing to me. She is my daughter, and if I had known of her previously, I would have moved heaven and earth to see that she was, if not with me, then well provided for. I would have made certain she knew me. In the absence of the opportunity to interview her mother myself, I can only guess at her reasons for failing to apprise me of Pandy's arrival."

"That is quite honorable of you." Many aristocrats would not be so moved to acknowledge or house the children they sired on the wrong side of the blanket.

It was a dreadful offense against the children, and yet it was simply a fact. Men had children out of wedlock. Polite society turned the other way. The innocent children suffered.

The smile Brandon gave her was small, almost sad. "I'm hardly an honorable man, but I'm trying to be better for Pandy's sake."

There was no doubting his sincerity. And as she sat at the Duke of Brandon's table with him, Lottie made the most astonishing realization of all.

She hadn't just come to care for Pandy.

She cared for the Duke of Brandon as well.

CHAPTER 13

Brandon was awakened by a familiar scratch at his door, accompanied by an equally recognizable bark.

Pandy and Cat were awake.

"In a moment, Pandy girl," he called, rising from his bed to the cool air, for once grateful for the dressing gown he'd been sleeping in since her arrival at his town house.

Her new nursemaid had stressed the importance of Pandy observing boundaries and rules. Such as not running wildly about the house each morning and bounding into his bedroom unannounced and uninvited. He had given in to Miss Bennington's wisdom on the matter. Because, whilst he detested the notion of making his Pandy sad, he was more than aware that when he married, Pandy couldn't come sprinting into his bedroom with Cat at her heels.

In bare feet, he padded across the cool Axminster to the door, opening it to the sight of his beloved daughter in her dressing gown, nightgown, and cap, her hair a dark cloud spilling over her shoulders.

"Good morning, my dear." With a narrow-eyed stare, he settled upon the incorrigible pup, whose tail wagged excitedly as she regarded him, tongue lolling. "And Cat."

"Good morning, Duke!" Pandy executed a small curtsy. "May I enter?"

Progress, he reasoned. "Of course, Pandy girl. Thank you for using your manners this fine day."

She made a moue of distaste. "Miss Bennington says I must, and I don't like no manners, but I *do* want to make you proud of me. Does manners make you proud?"

Something in his chest tightened painfully. "I am incredibly proud of you, poppet, manners or no. However, it is very important to comport one's self in a mannerly fashion, as Miss Bennington so very wisely suggested." He gave her head an affectionate rustle over the nightcap. "In with you, then."

She raced over the threshold with her customary enthusiasm, Cat chasing at her heels and nearly tripping her as she rushed to his bed and launched herself into it as if she were capable of flying. Her diminutive stature and his high, large bed meant that she could only attach herself to the side, rather like a barnacle, until she climbed higher. Cat leapt with graceful ease.

"Cat, you're going to make my bed all full of fur," he said grimly.

The beast eyed him and then burrowed her face into his pillow, shoving it halfway across the mattress as she inhaled and snorted.

"Cat doesn't got no manners yet," Pandy told him, lying on her back atop the coverlets and hanging her head over the edge to regard him, upside down.

"So I see," he murmured as his pillow went sailing to the floor and Cat rolled happily on her back, burrowing herself into the bedclothes. "Pandy girl, you mustn't hang your head like that. What if you fall upon it?"

"I ain't gonna," she declared, grinning.

Her nightcap fell to the floor, joining the pillow, her hair dangling.

His daughter was as stubborn as he was, but Brandon had learned there were ways to maneuver her into doing what he wished. So he crossed the room and laid his fingers on the coverlet, wriggling them.

"What if a spider were to tickle you?" he asked with feigned portent. "Then you might fall."

Her eyes went wide. "Not the Duke spider!"

His fingers crept closer. "The Duke spider loves to tickle girls who don't listen to their papas."

It was the first time, he realized, that he had referred to himself as her papa. If Pandy took note, she didn't comment upon it, but perhaps that was because in the next moment, his fingers had reached the place under her chin where he knew she was ticklish, making a peal of giggles ring from her.

Swiftly, he scooped her up and moved her so that she was lying safely in the midst of the bed before straightening. Cat took the opportunity to bathe her face with kisses until, giggling and wriggling, Pandy freed herself from the dog's keen attentions.

"Blech," she declared, wiping her mouth with the back of her hand. "Cat, your breath smells like pig trotters. It's asgusting."

"*Disgusting*, you mean," he corrected gently, amused.

"That too," Pandy agreed, wide-eyed.

He chuckled. "No, Pandy girl. The proper pronunciation is *dis*gusting, not *as*gusting."

"Oh," she said. "Are you my papa, Duke?"

The question hit him with the force of a blow. For a moment, he couldn't speak. All the breath seemed to have leached from his lungs. He hadn't known how to address the circumstances of her birth, nor how she had come to live with him. Nor had he understood how to speak to little girls, particularly his own, whom he had only recently learned about. And so, he had held his tongue, biding his time. Waiting.

The time had come.

"Yes, Pandy girl," he answered, his voice thick with suppressed emotion. "I am your papa."

"I knowed it was you," she said solemnly, scratching Cat behind her ears.

"How did you know?"

"Your eyes." She nodded. "They're just like mine. And Mama always said I had another papa somewhere. A fancy bloke. One what was importament."

"We do share the same eyes," he agreed, a rush of tenderness sweeping over him. "And the correct pronunciation of the word is *important*, my dear, although I don't know how important I am."

Indeed, he'd never felt so until now, with his daughter's gaze upon him.

He wondered what she saw when she looked at him. Wondered if she was happy here. If she resented him for only entering her life now.

"You're the most importamentest to me, Duke," she said.

A strange tickle began at the back of his throat, accompanied by a prickle behind his eyes. His vision blurred and he blinked furiously. The Duke of Brandon didn't cry. He was stronger than that.

"That's the loveliest thing anyone has ever said to me, Pandy girl," he managed to say, still struggling to keep those tears at bay.

Pandy reached into a pocket on her night wrap and extracted a small scrap of fabric. "Here y'go."

He accepted the handkerchief from her. "Thank you."

Feeling foolish, he dabbed at the corners of his eyes.

She nodded sagely. "I only used it for my nose a time or two."

Sweet God.

He instantly held the cloth away from his face, peering at it as it dangled from his fingers. There was something suspicious and dried marring one of the corners. His stomach tightened.

"Next time, you might warn me before I use your handkerchief," he managed, holding it out for her.

She nodded, taking it back from him and stuffing it into her pocket. "Are you going to find a wife soon? That's what the frowning old lady said when she bringed me to you. Her said you need a duchess to keep you from trouble."

Ah, his grandmother. He could well imagine her response if he told her Pandora had referred to her as *the frowning old lady*.

"I am trying to find one, Pandy girl, yes," he admitted gently. "The frowning lady was not wrong. But you needn't fear that my doing so will change anything. You shall always be my very best poppet."

Cat rolled happily to her back, inviting Pandy to give her a belly rub, and the meager, remaining hopes of keeping his bed free of dog fur vanished.

Pandy obliged, but her gaze was solemn and so like his. "I like Missus Lady Grenspell."

His heart quickened. "I like her too, Pandy girl."

He thought of their dinner, which had been meaningful yet chaste. He'd been careful not to press his suit, not with Pandy in the house. Losing his head that day in the study had been risk enough. Instead, they had spent an excellent evening learning about each other's pasts, and at the end of their dinner, he had seen her to her carriage, brushing a kiss over her gloved knuckles after he handed her up into the conveyance.

Pandy nodded, looking thoughtful for a moment as she rubbed Cat's white stomach. "Duke?"

"Yes, my dear?"

"Should I call you Papa now?" she wondered.

His heart seemed to swell to twice its size. "Yes, Pandy girl. If that is what you want, then you should."

She grinned at him. "It's what I want."

This time, Brandon didn't bother to hide his tears. "I do too, poppet. I do too."

~

"Hell's bells, hell's bells," chirruped Megs from her position on Rosamund's shoulder.

"Hush," Rosamund chided, giving the parrot's head a gentle pet. "I told you to behave today."

"Behave today, what a good little parrot," Megs said. "Megs wants pistache."

Lottie bit her lip to keep from chuckling at the bird's antics. Once again, her friend and the African grey who was her beloved companion were joining her for tea. And once again, Lottie was grateful for the distraction they provided.

"Where did our dear Megs manage to obtain her interesting lexicon?" Lottie asked, seeking to divert herself even more.

Because ever since she had left the Duke of Brandon's house the evening before, she had been thinking about the way they'd parted.

A chaste kiss on her knuckles as he handed her into the carriage.

Nothing more.

Not even the slightest hint of impropriety.

To say she'd been disappointed at his lack of attempts at seduction was a vast understatement. She'd been left aching with pent-up longing and no cure, save her own attentions once she was safely abed for the night. But *thinking about* Brandon's cock deep inside her and *feeling* it fill her, stoking the flames of need ever higher, were two different things entirely.

Heat swept over her cheeks—she hoped Rosamund wouldn't take note.

Her friend sighed, happily oblivious. "I would like to claim complete innocence where her vocabulary is concerned, but I'm afraid she has learned some interesting language from my household. However, Megs belonged to someone else before she came to me. A sea captain whose own language must have been somewhat...er, salty."

That explained some of the parrot's more colorful quips.

"Salty, salty," Megs squawked, cocking her head at Lottie.

Lottie found the parrot's scrutiny a bit disconcerting. It was as if Megs could look into her soul and find her darkest secrets lurking.

"Saltier than the sea," Rosamund quipped, offering the parrot a bite of tea biscuit. "I'm afraid you'll have to make do with a biscuit, Megs. I've forgotten your pistachios at home."

Megs accepted the biscuit, chewing greedily, a shower of crumbs falling from her beak into Rosamund's lap.

"At least she will always keep the conversation lively and interesting," Lottie said with a chuckle. "No one shall ever be bored with Megs about."

"Indeed. You should hear the things she's said to Camden." Rosamund laughed too, apparently unconcerned with the African grey's lack of manners.

"Speaking of Camden," Lottie said, seizing upon that

thread of conversation, "I saw the notice of your engagement in *The Times*. You're certain, then?"

Rosamund's smile faded. "As certain as I shall ever be. Marriage is not a decision I make lightly, of course."

"Lightly, of course," chirped Megs. "Lightly, of course."

"Believe me, my dear, I understand." Lottie took a sip of her tea, trying to calm the disquiet within her that had been rising steadily ever since the Duke of Brandon had offered his unexpected proposal. "Marriage can be quite dreadful. Although I hope it is different for you than it was for me."

Speaking about marriage took her back to dinner the evening before and the surprisingly deep, meaningful discussions she had shared with Brandon. Lottie hadn't been honest with the Duke of Brandon about her reasons for wanting to avoid marriage. If she had been, she might have revealed a truth so stark and debilitating that it was impossible to comprehend. She kept it shut away, like a cursed treasure in a box, hidden and never to be opened again.

Her marriage to Grenfell had nearly destroyed her.

But like a phoenix, she had risen from the ashes. She had made herself wanted, lighthearted, amusing, desired. She had transformed herself into a lover, a merry widow, a woman who was unabashedly who she wanted to be, with no one to answer to. She had not, however, found that ever-elusive feeling she'd spent the years since Grenfell's death seeking.

Contentment.

Happiness.

Peace.

"I don't think there's any need to fret over my marriage with Camden," Rosamund reassured her. "Ours is not a love match. We are, each of us, free to carry on our lives in whatever capacity we like. There shan't be feelings involved."

"A marriage of convenience," Lottie said. "I do so wish

that was how Grenfell explained our union to me. Instead, I told him I loved him, and he returned the sentiment."

And then, on their wedding night, he had consummated their marriage quite unsatisfyingly in the dark before going to his mistress.

It had been the first time he had shattered her heart, but it hadn't been the last.

"I am so very sorry for what you endured with Grenfell, my dear," Rosamund said, her tone sympathetic. "I am quite confident in the agreement I've made with Camden. I never considered marriage a business decision, but this one is. And in truth, I understand business matters so much better than I comprehend affairs of the heart. It is far more familiar territory to me—and far less easily manipulated."

Rosamund was a shrewd businesswoman. Although she was an heiress in her own right, she had steadily built upon her family's wealth. Lottie dearly hoped her friend was taking every effort to protect her autonomy and her funds from Camden, though she was also mindful that her friend had not requested advice. Rosamund was an intelligent woman, and her decision had been made clear by the betrothal announcement.

"All I want is what's best for you, my dear," Lottie told her, refraining from voicing her fear that marriage to the Duke of Camden decidedly wasn't it.

"What's best, what's best," Megs said. "Hell's bells."

"Megs, you're being perfectly dreadful," Rosamund scolded the parrot.

"Perfectly dreadful, perfectly dreadful," Megs squawked. "Close your gob, close your gob."

"Yes," Rosamund said pointedly. "Do follow your own advice, if you please. Truly, I don't know why I ever deign to bring you along with me when you can never be a lady."

"Never a lady, never a lady," Megs said. "Show me your bubbies."

"Oh good heavens." Rosamund's face was red, her embarrassment as comical as the African grey's disreputable behavior.

Lottie chortled. "The sea captain strikes again."

Her friend offered up another bite of biscuit for the bird. "There you are, you little scamp. Eat this and be quiet."

Megs obligingly ate the biscuit, sending a new shower of crumbs falling.

"I don't suppose she'll be a guest at the wedding?" Lottie asked, biting her lip as she struggled to contain her merriment.

"She most definitely won't," Rosamund confirmed, her tone grim. "But I do hope you will be in attendance. Say you will."

As a rule, Lottie despised weddings. But she had exceptions, as in the case of her dear friend Hyacinth. For her friends, she would hold her head high and pretend as if her own marriage hadn't torn her apart, piece by piece, second by minute, hour by day by year, until there had been nothing left.

She forced a bright smile. "I'd love nothing better."

∿

A SECOND INVITATION, far more formal and yet infinitely more dangerous, arrived after Rosamund and Megs had taken their leave.

Lottie stared at the by-now-familiar masculine scrawl on the missive she'd just unfolded, her heart pounding fast.

O beloved sorceress of wayward children and ragtag mongrels,

Join me for dinner again this evening. I'll send my carriage for you at seven.

B.

ALTHOUGH HIS SALUTATION had her smiling even when she knew she shouldn't allow herself to be amused by his ridiculous charm, Lottie couldn't help but to take note that Brandon hadn't requested her presence for dinner, nor had he inquired after whether she would need the use of his carriage. Also, taking his carriage as opposed to her own felt far too intimate when she couldn't afford to allow herself to get any closer to the man.

Falling for him would be the height of folly, and from such lofty altitudes, there was so very far to fall.

She struck the smile from her face and hastened to put her own pen to paper. What was she thinking? Accepting a dinner invitation from the Duke of Brandon would be nothing short of disastrous. Her response was swift.

Your Grace,

I am not yours to command, nor shall I ever be. For future reference, presumably as it may pertain to your courtship of a bride, a lady ought to be asked. Her presence must be inquired after, not demanded.

Further, I always prefer to take my own carriage, as you quite know.
Sincerely,
Lottie, neither sorceress nor beloved

HIS RESPONSE WAS HASTY. Jenkinson brought her a new note within the hour. And although she told herself to allow the missive to sit, unopened and unread, for at least fifteen minutes, she scarcely lasted two before she tore it open.

My darling L.,
Never think you are not a sorceress, for you have surely and thoroughly bewitched me, along with my daughter and her vagabond of a hound. Forgive me for the blunt clumsiness of my previous invitation. Having been intruded upon by a slavering dog bearing a pig trotter and a wayward child playing a game of chase-chase, I had to make haste.
Allow me, I beg of you, a second opportunity to cure my mortal ailments with the elixir of your presence this evening. Will you please accompany me for dinner tonight? Also, if you please, I would prefer the discretion of my own conveyance to your John Coachman.
Yours,
B.

. . .

His dramatic flair had her chuckling despite herself. The man truly was charming when he wished to be. And for some reason, he wished to be today. With her.

Peril lies ahead, warned her mind. *Proceed at a very great risk to your own welfare.*

Experience was the truest form of authority. She knew better than to continue whatever it was between herself and Brandon. And yet...

And yet, there was another part of her that longed to be desired. To be charmed and wooed and seduced. Brandon wasn't engaged to another woman yet, after all. What could be the harm in one more dinner, perhaps another wicked interlude, before they inevitably parted ways?

She bit her lip.

Paced the floor.

Wandered to the window and looked down at the familiar sights below, vaguely aware of the jangling of tack as horses and carriages passed.

Paced some more.

And finally sat down to jot her reply.

> *Brandon,*
>
> *We shall agree to disagree on the matter of whether I am a sorceress—decidedly, I am all too woefully human—however, I will forgive you for commanding me to dinner. I will join you this evening. However, I remain quite firm on taking my own carriage.*

His next reply arrived as quickly as the previous one had.

L.,
I insist upon the carriage. I shall see you this evening.
B.

The audacity of the man. He was taking for granted that she would simply accede to his wishes. And the worst part of all was that he was correct in his assessment. She would. Because as much as he teasingly referred to her as a sorceress, he had a similar effect upon her. The man had clearly addled her mind.

"Will there be a reply, my lady?" Jenkinson asked, hovering at the periphery of Lottie's preferred salon.

"No," she decided, adding Brandon's latest missive to the stack she was already keeping, tied together neatly with a satin ribbon. "There won't be. But we do have a change of plans for this evening. I've just received an invitation to dinner. Please lay out my gold silk."

Jenkinson's brows rose only the slightest hint at her announcement. Lottie didn't know if the reaction was down to her choice of dress or her sudden reversal of schedule. Either way, her lady's maid was nothing if not loyal. She dipped into a curtsy.

"Of course, my lady."

Absently, she thanked Jenkinson, watching her bustle from the room to see about preparing her *toilette*. The gold evening gown was one she had deemed too scandalous to wear, for the almost shocking expanse of her bosom it left bare. Almost to her nipples. She had worn it precisely once, standing before her looking glass on her way to a ball, and decided it must never be worn in public, lest she wish to tear her reputation entirely asunder.

But it wasn't her reputation she was thinking of now, the slow, steady ache of anticipation beginning deep within her. Rather, it was the satisfaction of wearing the gold silk for the Duke of Brandon. For it was a gown that had been cleverly designed by one of the finest Paris houses to bring every man to his knees.

And Lottie had suddenly decided to use it for its intended purpose.

CHAPTER 14

The Countess of Grenfell was a goddess tonight. A Venus draped in diaphanous gold, her creamy breasts lifted high above a daring decolletage that left almost nothing to the imagination. Brandon took one look at her upon her arrival in the private salon of his house in St John's Wood, and his cock went instantly hard.

A primitive sense of possession surged through him, and it required all the gentlemanly self-discipline he had to keep from throwing her over his shoulder and carrying her away to the bedroom so he could devour her at once.

Not now, old chap, he thought wryly. *You'll have to wait your turn.*

Instead, he took her hand in his, bringing it to his lips for a reverent kiss as he drank her in fully. Her riotous cinnamon curls had been coaxed into Grecian plaits coiled thickly at her nape, with a spray of ringlets left free, along with a fringe of them on her high forehead. The gilded flecks of freckles adorned her nose, and her full, lush lips were the pink of a wild English rose. A sapphire necklace at her throat sparkled as a complement to the brilliant blue of her eyes.

Briefly, he wondered if Grenfell had gifted the necklace to her, and then he vowed that he would buy her a hundred necklaces with larger, costlier gems and drape them around her throat. He'd fuck her as she wore nothing else when she was well and truly his.

He cleared his throat, inhaling deeply of the rich scent of violet and rose and Lottie. "Good evening, o beloved sorceress of wayward children and ragtag mongrels."

He straightened to his full height, and she smiled at him, and he thought he could happily spend the rest of the evening just admiring her thus as her pretty Cupid's bow curved with amusement.

"Good evening, o silly duke of ridiculous imagined titles and insistence upon sending secret carriages to take me to my destination," she returned.

She was still bristling about his sending his own conveyance to her. He had done so for a very good reason. Brandon hadn't been certain if she would deign to join him here, for St John's Wood was notorious. It was where most gentlemen either discreetly engaged in affairs or settled their mistresses. Where a married man could keep his secrets and have his bed warmed beyond the watchful eye of polite society and his wife.

That wasn't why Brandon had brought her here. Rather, it was because he couldn't justify another coupling whilst his daughter was beneath the same roof. Pandy would face struggles enough because of her illegitimacy. There was no need to cause further scandal where she was concerned. When he had taken Lottie in his study, he had been overwhelmed. Overcome by a temporary madness brought on by Lottie and her steadfast devotion to his daughter.

"Your John Coachman doesn't know my address," he told Lottie lightly.

She arched a cinnamon brow. "He would have known it had I told him."

"Yes, but would you have come to me here in St John's Wood?"

"That would have depended."

He was still holding her hand in his, so he availed himself of her wrist, pressing his lips there, absorbing the steady thrum of her pulse. "Upon?"

She held his gaze, unsmiling. "Upon whether this is a home where you have previously installed your mistresses."

"This house has never been used for a mistress," he told her honestly. "Not by me, at least. My sire is another matter, but you can rest assured that I had all traces of him and whatever filthy deeds he performed here removed. Everything, from the paper hangings to the curtains and the Axminster, has been replaced."

He kissed along her inner arm until he reached the place where her glove ended and glorious, soft skin met his seeking lips. The inner curve of her elbow. Brandon couldn't help himself. He nipped her lightly there.

She shivered, then inhaled sharply, the action making her breasts rise in tempting swells, threatening to burst free of her bodice. "What have you used it for, then?"

"Various purposes," he said lightly as he straightened, for prior to choosing Wingfield Hall as the home of the Wicked Dukes Society revelries, this house had been used. "Most recently, as a discreet meeting place for Sidmouth and his new wife."

"This is the house Hyacinth spoke to me of, then," Lottie said, unsurprised by his revelation.

"She told you about it?" That rather startled him to learn, for Lady Southwick—now Lady Sidmouth, he reminded himself—hardly seemed the sort to bandy her private affairs about.

"We are dear friends. Of course she did. But she needn't have done so. I am already more than aware of your love nest. All London knows about it, I daresay."

"Love nest," he repeated, thinking maybe he had done his cause a disservice in bringing her here after all.

"Perhaps you have more than one," she mused, "given that you've just told me you never used this house for a mistress."

He shook his head. "I never know what manner of scandal broth is swirling about me, and I'm increasingly persuaded that is for the best. I can assure you that I don't have a love nest. But enough of idle gossip for now, however. Let us eat the dinner my chef has prepared for us."

It was a dinner designed to impress. Intentionally decadent. Brandon was many things, but a fool wasn't one of them. He was wooing her in every way he could.

"That sounds lovely," she said, her soft voice settling over him like a caress.

"Excellent." He offered her his arm, and together, they went into the dining room. "I've taken the liberty of having the 1864 *Chateau Margaux* brought up from the cellar and opened. I think you'll enjoy it."

The house was formal, yet intimate. He guided her to the dining room, trying to think about the meal awaiting them rather than about the stunning woman on his arm. Even if the air between them was sparking with mutual awareness, he was doing his utmost to prolong the evening. To torment them both with anticipation, until they were equally burning with need.

"Why did you choose this house for dinner?" she asked as they entered the dining room and he guided her to a seat.

By design, no footmen were about. He had given careful instructions concerning when the dinner was to commence, and they still had a few minutes until a discreet domestic would knock at the door, heralding the arrival of the first course.

"Because," he said, bending down as she sat primly in the chair he offered, so close that his lips brushed the shell of her ear as he spoke, "I wanted to be certain I could have you all to myself this evening. Where you're concerned, I'm a greedy man."

She slanted him a sultry glance beneath her extravagant gold-tipped lashes. The light caught in the burnished glints of her hair and made her eyes deepen to the mysterious blue of the sky after a torrent.

"Greedy for my company—or for something else?"

His cock pulsed.

"For both, Venus." He allowed himself a chaste kiss to her temple before rising and moving to his own seat.

"I'm hardly a Venus, Brandon."

Her modest protestations had him grinning. "You're right, of course. You're far more magnificent than Venus could ever hope to be."

She raised a brow. "You needn't woo me with flattery. I've already come here at your bidding, have I not?"

"Flattery is glib. I speak truth." He raised his glass of *Chateau Margaux* to her in toast. "To you, o goddess."

"You're absurd," she said without heat, lifting her own wine in turn. "We both know I'm all too mortal."

He sipped from his wine, savoring the depth of flavor, and she did the same, her eyes widening in the moment the excellent year must have rushed over her tongue.

"Oh my heavens," she murmured when she had swallowed, licking her lips and making his poor cock twitch. "You were not wrong about this vintage."

He winked. "I'm not wrong about most things, you'll find."

A servant gave the door a subtle knock before either of them could say more.

"Enter," he called.

The first course arrived, a French oxtail soup that they consumed over lighthearted conversation until the *filets de sole au beurre noir* arrived. He waited for the footman to once again discreetly retreat before resuming with a more salient topic.

"You never did tell me last evening about the reason you are so set against another marriage," Brandon said, keeping his tone conversational.

Lottie was quiet for so long, he feared she wouldn't answer him. But then, at last, came her mournful reply.

"Because it destroyed me."

Four words, and he felt them pierce his heart as surely and as painfully as the sharpest of blades.

"You were in love with your husband." It was a statement rather than a question.

Brandon didn't know why the realization had failed to occur to him during their previous discussions of her past. Grenfell seemed a murky figure to him, a man he knew of but scarcely recalled. And the notion of Lottie in love with another man—well, it cut him to his marrow. Jealousy blossomed, bitter and dark. Jealousy he had no right to feel. Lottie was not his now, not yet, nor had she been then.

Yet, he couldn't help the way he felt.

"I was young and hopelessly foolish when we married," she said sadly. "I thought myself very much in love with him. He was dashing and compelling in his own way, and I was too naïve to realize that he was merely toying with me. That our every interaction served a purpose—giving him what he wanted without thought for anyone else."

"And what he wanted was you," Brandon said, understanding what must have possessed Grenfell.

Lottie was like the finest, rarest wine. Priceless. A man could spend a lifetime scouring the best vineyards, sampling years and varieties, and still never find anyone as glorious as she. But to have had her, to have won her heart, and then to have dashed it to bits beneath his boot heel? A terrible, dreadful waste.

Sacrilegious, even.

She nodded. "What he wanted was me. I'll never know quite why. Oh, he told me he loved me, and perhaps he did in his own way. I don't think he was capable of loving anyone else, not even himself. Perhaps it was because I was the most sought-after of the crop of debutantes I curtseyed with."

She shrugged, her smile pained. "Either way, it hardly matters now."

"It matters to me, Lottie." He swallowed hard against a rush of raw emotion. "*You* matter to me."

But Lottie didn't only matter to him. She also mattered to Pandy. To Cat. To Lord and Lady Sidmouth, to the countless others in her charmed coterie. She mattered to so many. He hated that she hadn't mattered enough to the man she'd wed, despised Grenfell for all the hurt and damage he'd caused. He never wished ill of the dead, but it was a bloody good thing the man was buried and gone.

"I…" She hesitated, looking flustered. "I don't know what to say."

"You needn't say anything at all. Thank you for telling me about your past. It helps me to understand how you've become the woman you are."

"I wouldn't trade the woman I've become for the one I was then," she told him firmly. "Not for anything. I've worked hard to be who I am. I've wept many tears, fought bitter battles. But through it all, I've come to know myself, I think."

"And I admire the woman you are, quite thoroughly—

your wit, your spirit, your dauntless determination, every part of you." Again, it wasn't flattery. There was more he could say, more that he *wanted* to say, and yet, he felt like an awkward lummox in her presence. All the easy charm and practiced ease he had accumulated over the years had fled him in the face of stark, earnest appreciation.

The regal mask she so often kept in place shifted, and he was treated to a rare glimpse of the vulnerability hiding beneath as her face softened. "No gentleman has ever said something so kind to me before."

How astounding to realize that no man before him had ever told this glorious woman that he admired her. Not just for her beauty, but for her mind, her determination, her sensuality, for all the nuances that made her who she was.

And suddenly, it disturbed him greatly that he had not been entirely forthright with her. She deserved his candor and so much more.

"In the interest of honesty, there is something I should tell you," he said, broaching the subject of the Wicked Dukes Society for the first time. "When we spoke about my grandmother and Wingfield Hall, I wasn't entirely truthful. For the last few years, Camden, Kingham, Riverdale, Whitby, Richford, and I have been operating a secret society."

He paused, gauging her reaction, for whilst he knew why he and his friends had begun the society, he couldn't deny that it all seemed so very gauche and seedy now. Earning one's own money was bourgeois. But earning one's own money through carnal depravity was more than one shade beyond the pale.

"Go on," she said softly.

"Membership in the Society is selective and costly," he continued. "And for good reason. The revelries we host are indulgent odes to hedonism. Members are assured anonymity and privacy to do whatever they wish with whomever they desire, as long as all parties are willing."

"Do you take part in these revelries of yours?" she asked, her gaze searching.

"I have in the past," he admitted, "though the appeal is no longer there for me. The next fête is in a month's time, and I'll not be joining the revelers."

"Why do you tell me this now?"

"Because I don't want to hide the truth from you. And because I want you to know the true reason I am desperate to keep Wingfield Hall. The Society holds its revelries there. If we lose Wingfield Hall, we will have to begin anew, and the six of us have already invested a great deal of time and funds upon it that we won't be able to recoup. Not all of us can afford such a loss of investment and future funds."

He was grateful that he was in no danger of penury. But for some of his friends, the only wealth they possessed was what they earned from the Society.

"Thank you for entrusting me with your secret," Lottie told him. "You have my word that I shan't tell another soul."

He trusted her implicitly, and now that he had revealed the full truth to her, it was as if a great weight had been lifted from his chest. He felt lighter. Relieved.

"Thank you," he said simply.

The footman arrived with the next course then, mutton pie *à la Perigord*. As usual, it was delicious, redolent with the earthiness of truffles and the rich flavors of bacon and butter. But they both ate sparingly, a new anticipation burning hotly between them. Not for the next course, but for what would inevitably come after this dinner.

By the time the *blancmange* arrived, he was positively aflame.

Lottie's spoon hesitated over her plate, her gaze meeting his. "I find myself feeling quite greedy as well."

It was a return to the beginning of their dinner, and his cockstand was instant, as was his reaction. Thank God. He might have shouted his relief to the heavens, so great was his relief—he didn't give a damn about the *blancmange*.

Brandon shot from his chair, extending a hand to her. "Come here."

She didn't hesitate, settling her hand in his, the softness of her bare skin making his pulse pound harder. "Where are you taking me?"

He pulled her swiftly to her feet. "To bed. We've made use of a door and a desk thus far. I think it's more than time we tried something more comfortable."

He drew her hand into the crook of his elbow.

"I won't be your mistress, if that is what you're thinking," she cautioned as he led her from the room and up the stairs. "You'll soon be a married man, and I do not abet husbands who are unfaithful to their wives."

"I didn't ask you to be my mistress, did I?" he asked mildly. "Besides, I'm not presently a married man, and I have no one to whom I owe faithfulness."

Except you, he might have said, but he kept that to himself.

Lottie was to be handled with kid gloves. Her instinctive reaction was to flee in the face of the slightest hint of matrimony. His intentions regarding her had never changed, not from that first meeting in the emerald salon when he'd bumbled through a regretful proposal. But she didn't need to know that.

Yet.

"I suppose you haven't," she allowed. "However, it's not an unreasonable expectation. We are lovers, after all."

And he intended for them to be more than that. Much, much more than that.

"A lover is not a mistress," he pointed out.

"Fair enough." Lottie inclined her head, but the stubborn

set of her lips suggested she didn't entirely believe him. "Just so you know, it will never happen. I'm not a kept woman."

"Nor do I expect you to be one. You are a force unto yourself."

They reached the bedroom, and he stopped, gesturing for her to precede him into the chamber. Lottie released her hold on his arm, crossing the threshold, her golden silk skirts shimmering in the low gas lamps. He couldn't help but to admire the way the light shone in her cinnamon hair, the curls that were artfully arranged to fall down her nape. He longed to brush them aside and press his lips there, to know the satiny heat of her skin.

To savor her, to take his time and learn every inch of her body.

And he intended to do that.

All.

Night.

Long.

He followed her inside the bedroom, which was his alone. Even when he had granted Sidmouth and Lady Southwick the use of the house, he had made certain to keep his private space precisely that. The door closed behind him with a soft snick, and the blood rushed to his cock.

This woman was his. She didn't know it yet, but he fully intended to make it so.

She turned to him, a small smile flirting with the corners of her rose-pink mouth. "A force. A goddess. What else am I to be this evening?"

"Whatever you wish to be, darling."

She moved toward him, her silk gown playing with the light like liquid gold, and he thought he had one more to add to the list: naiad.

"The woman who brings the greatest lover in London to

his knees, I think," she told him with sultry intent, sliding her hands up his waistcoat until they locked around his neck.

"You won't even have to try, Venus." He dipped his head and claimed her mouth.

She opened instantly, her kiss eager and hot, her tongue gliding past his lips to tease. She tasted like *Chateau Margaux* and sin and decadent desire, and despite the delicacies his chef had offered up that evening, nothing had ever been so delicious. He had intended to take his time, but she was kissing him ravenously, making soft sounds of need, crushing her breasts into his chest.

His fingers found buttons and hooks. Fabric parted and spilled and fell, giving way to glorious feminine flesh. To hot skin, curves, and the sweet scent of roses and violets. He found hooks and eyes and pulled them free, her satin-and-lace corset falling with a dull thump at their feet. He had her half undressed without his mouth ever leaving hers, and she did the same for him, working his coat from his shoulders, tugging away his necktie, tearing open his waistcoat.

Her nimble fingers danced over the fall of his trousers, and that was when he finally moved, denying her what she wanted, lest she make him spill in his trousers like a callow lad touching his first woman. He ended the kiss to find her lips lush and swollen, her blue eyes glittering up at him like twin storm-tossed seas.

"I want to suck your cock," she told him.

And fucking hell, there went his ability to resist her.

He swallowed hard against a rush of desire so intense that he could scarcely think. "That isn't why I abandoned the *blancmange*."

"I know." She traced the line of buttons bisecting his shirt. "You're all I want for dessert."

Sweet, holy God. He'd give her himself. He'd give her anything. Everything. Whatever she desired. She was brazen and beautiful, her gown flung on the carpet, standing before him in nothing more than her stockings, drawers, and chemise. But her glorious curls were still confined, and there remained too many barriers between them. If she wanted to pleasure him, then he intended to savor the moment.

"Take the pins from your hair," he said. "Please. I want to see it down."

He thought she might balk at his request, but she didn't, reaching for her pins instead and plucking them from her hair, one by one. Cinnamon curls fell, framing her heart-shaped face, glinting with hints of gold in the lamplight. It was the first time he had seen her hair entirely unbound, for he had begun dismantling her coiffure that night in the emerald salon and never finished. The intimacy of the act—watching her remove each pin for him alone—made fire lick through him.

When she had finished, her curls rained down her back and over her shoulders, long and lustrous, and she laid her palmful of pins on a nearby table. "Your turn."

"What would my lady have me do?" he asked, throat gone thick with want.

Her gaze seared his. "Take off your shirt and waistcoat."

"As you like." He took off his waistcoat and then worked open the buttons of his shirt, fingers fumbling in his eagerness, heart pounding, cock as hard as marble.

"Let me help." She moved to him, chasing his useless hands, plucking buttons free until they both had him out of his shirt. "Now this." She tugged at his waistband, her forefinger grazing his bare stomach and making him inhale sharply at the simple contact.

God, how he longed for her touch. Everywhere.

His reaction to her was unlike anything he'd ever experienced, so powerful it scared the devil out of him. He had to somehow persuade her to be his wife. He couldn't lose her.

At the thought, he caught her hand in his, bringing it to his lips for fervent kisses on each knuckle before lifting his head and meeting her gaze. "I want you naked in my bed."

"With pleasure." She grasped handfuls of her chemise and hauled it over her head, revealing the milky globes of her breasts at last and hard pink nipples he couldn't wait to suck.

She undid the button on her drawers and those, too, fell away, leaving her in nothing but her silk stockings and pretty gold-ribboned garters. Better than Venus, she was a lush deity unto her own, all riotous, flaming curls and copper-flecked curves and wickedly seductive femininity.

"Leave them," he said hoarsely, knowing that watching her roll them down her legs would be a torment he couldn't withstand.

His cock was already leaking, desperate to be freed from his trousers.

A knowing smile flirted with the corners of her lips. "Now you."

He unfastened his trousers with lightning speed and, naked, guided her to the bed. He stretched alongside her, his mouth on the delicate curve of her shoulder. She was hot and soft, and she smelled so bloody good. Her hair fanned over the pillow like silken fire.

"God, you're glorious," he praised. "I've been longing to do this all dinner long."

"Why did you not, then?" she asked breathlessly. "I wouldn't have offered protest."

He kissed a path over the curve of her left breast, tracing the trail of freckles that endlessly bewitched him. Following them to her nipple, which was puckered and pink and waiting for his mouth. He flicked his tongue over the distended tip, and her back arched, a gasp tearing from her.

Lightly.

Gently.

Teasingly.

"Brandon," she said, her voice strained. "More."

He caught her nipple in his teeth and gently bit. "Like this?"

"More," she demanded again.

He liked her when she was desperate. When she was issuing orders and commanding her own pleasure. She made him ravenous.

Mindless.

Her devoted servant.

He tugged at the peak, then sucked harder while cupping her other breast in his hand, plucking at her nipple with his thumb and forefinger until she was arching into him, her body an offering he gladly accepted.

But then she flattened a palm on his chest, staying him. "On your back."

His cock twitched at the bold command. "Why, Venus, do you intend to ravish me?"

"Thoroughly."

He obliged, rolling to his back. And now it was Lottie peppering his bare skin with a dozen kisses, her sweet mouth falling hotly upon him from his collarbone to his chest, then lower, following the dark trail of hair that led to his groin as her hair spilled over his thigh. He held his breath, watching as she kissed his hip bone.

Another sultry smile curved her lips, her stormy eyes flicking to his. "I want you to come in my mouth."

He clenched his jaw against a stinging rush of desire so potent that it robbed him of the ability to think for a moment. It took all the control he had to keep from rolling her onto her back and sinking his cock deep inside her now.

His grasp of the English language slowly returned as she kissed his navel, teasingly avoiding his aching prick, which was jutting upward, thick and ruddy and ready for her.

"Already on my proverbial knees now, darling," he managed.

She sent him a Siren's smile. "Good."

Gripping the base of his shaft, she lowered her head and flicked her tongue over him. He moaned helplessly, wondering how he had gone from seducer to seduced with such haste and ease. She laved him, swirling around his cock head, then licking along the underside of his erection.

His hips pumped. He abandoned his hold on the bedclothes in favor of her beautiful hair, threading his fingers through those vibrant curls that were smoother than the finest silk. And then she took him in her mouth. Just the tip at first, then more, as half his rigid prick was engulfed in wet heat.

A strangled sound fled him. He wanted nothing more than for her to take him as deeply as she could. To fuck her mouth until he came and she swallowed every drop of him. But he also wanted inside her cunny just as badly. She sucked him and his ballocks tightened. She lowered her head, bringing him to the back of her throat until she withdrew, leaving his cock glistening with her saliva, her lips wrapped around him.

He wanted to tell her how beautiful she looked, taking his cock this way. But words were elusive. And when she slid back down his shaft, there was no chance for thoughts. There was only the roar of his body's demands, urging more, more, more. His hips worked in time with her pretty mouth, his heart pounding ever faster. Her hand worked his cock with the same rhythm, and within seconds, he was there, on the razor's edge of complete release.

"If you don't stop, I'm going to spend," he warned.

She made a low sound in response, her mouth never leaving him as her pace increased. Faster, faster, now. She truly wanted to undo him. And heaven help him, he wanted to be undone.

By her.

By Lottie.

Only, always, forever her.

The realization was as jarring as his release, both so potent and magnificent that blood thundered in his ears and black stars speckled his vision. A groan of pleasure tore from his throat as he spurted on her tongue. He felt her swallowing around him, felt the hot flood of his seed coating his cock, felt her sucking and draining him dry until there was nothing left but his sated body and a sudden, shocking recognition.

He had fallen in love with this woman.

CHAPTER 15

Lottie still tasted Brandon on her lips as he rolled her to her back and nudged her legs wide, his palms branding her inner thighs as he urged her to open to him. His heated emerald gaze was on her cunny, and it occurred to her that no lover had ever studied her thus, with the lamps blazing. Likely, she should feel at least a hint of embarrassment. Their previous couplings had been frantic, and they had remained clothed. This was the first time they were naked—save her stockings, of course—and in a bed together, but it all felt intimate and wonderful.

There was no embarrassment now. There was only desire, raw and wild and unfettered. Sucking his cock, knowing she had the power to make him lose himself completely, had proven a potent aphrodisiac. She was aching for him.

"You're so wet," he praised. "You liked taking my cock down your throat, didn't you?"

"Mmm." She spread her legs wider, shameless, taking her breasts in her hands and toying with her nipples. "I loved it."

The truth. Perhaps she was a wanton, but she didn't care.

She had spent her marriage wallowing in self-loathing, thinking herself insufficient. But she had come a long way from the naïve young bride who had married Grenfell. She was a woman now, and she was in control of her body, her desires. She had learned that she *was* enough, damn it. And she would seize what she wanted with both hands.

All further thought abandoned her when he spoke again.

"You've had your dessert, and now I must have mine." He lowered his dark head, and he lapped lightly at her swollen clitoris.

The breath fled her in a rush, her head falling back against the pillow. No more words now. They were beyond her. She could only feel. And oh, what she felt. He wasted no time in thoroughly devouring her using his lips and tongue and teeth, laving and sucking and licking. Now, it was her turn to be helpless, awash in the pleasure he bestowed upon her.

He slipped a long finger inside her as he worked her pearl with his mouth, and she planted her feet on the mattress, arching to bring him deeper. Her breaths were ragged, her eyes closed as she surrendered to him. This night, she was his. She would forget all else. Tomorrow and whatever it brought was far away, and she had until the early morning hours to savor him.

A second finger joined the first, pumping in and out as he licked and sucked. Lottie's hips swiveled, seeking more. Her orgasm, when it hit her, was swift and powerful. She clenched on him, feeling as if a part of her splintered into a thousand jagged shards. He stayed with her as she rode out the waves of pleasure on his tongue and fingers, and when the last ripple of bliss ebbed, he rolled her onto her stomach.

He brushed her curls to one side and kissed her nape, his breath fanning hotly over her bare skin. And then his mouth moved lower, following the line of her spine all the way

DUKE WITH A REPUTATION

down until he reached the base. She knew the sharp pressure of his teeth as he bit her right cheek, then kissed the sting away.

"On your hands and knees," he commanded, his voice a hoarse rasp, roughened with the force of his own need.

Her limbs felt leaden, her entire body sated. It took her a moment to do as he asked, lifting herself onto her forearms and knees. He was positioned behind her, and she turned her head, watching him over her shoulder as he caressed her bottom with one hand and stroked his rapidly thickening cock with the other.

"You're ready again?" she asked, equal parts amazed and amused.

But then he slicked his rigid shaft up and down her wet folds, and her levity instantly died a swift death.

"You tell me, Venus. What does it feel like?"

His grin was potently male as he continued rubbing the blunt head through her, until the tip prodded her entrance.

She inhaled sharply and exhaled on a moan of helpless need. "It feels like you are."

"For you, I'm ready all day. Every day. All night, too." One thrust, and he was planted deep, the angle so exquisite that a strangled sound emerged from her that she scarcely recognized as hers. "I want you to come on my cock the way you did on my tongue."

And she wanted it too. Wanted him so much it frightened her, for the knowledge that this arrangement of theirs would necessarily end soon was never far.

He withdrew almost completely, only to glide into her again.

"Oh," she gasped, her cunny shuddering convulsively around his length in the precursor to another climax.

It was building already, a fire he was cleverly, expertly stoking as he thrust in and out of her, his hips slamming into her bottom, his ballocks swinging against her in a rhythm that grew increasingly frantic. Faster, deeper, harder.

Her entire world consisted of nothing more than pleasure. Pure and holy, raw and rude, animalistic and unabashed. The mindless bliss of it all was almost too much. She grasped the bedclothes, panting now, needing every thrust he gave her, pushing back to get him closer. As if the weight of his own need became too much, he collapsed against her, his chest to her back, his mouth on her nape, her ear, as he thrust and thrust and thrust, his motions growing jerky, his hands holding tightly to her hips.

She was his in this moment, so completely and thoroughly taken by him, their skin slick from perspiration, their breaths ragged in the stillness of the room, the sounds of their bodies colliding beautifully obscene.

"Come for me, Venus."

She didn't know if she'd been waiting for his permission or if the low, velvet sound of his baritone was what pushed her over the edge. It didn't matter, because in the next second, she reached her pinnacle again, quaking and quivering from the force of her release, screaming his name into the pillow.

"That's it. Come all over me." His movements grew jerky, and she knew he was close.

Another few pumps, and the hot spurt of his seed filled her along with his cock, and she whimpered at the indescribable joy of it. The rightness and the ecstasy. The full force of his weight was on her now, pinning her to the mattress, his heart thumping wildly against her back in a pattern that resembled her own.

He kissed her nape again, her temple, her shoulder, murmuring things she could scarcely hear over the rushing in her ears. And as she lay there beneath him, reluctant for him to move and sever their connection, Lottie thought once more that it was a very good thing that her heart was safe and she hadn't fallen in love with the Duke of Brandon.

BRANDON SIFTED glorious strands of cinnamon-gold through his fingers, an immense feeling of immeasurable contentment pervading. If not for Pandy at home, he would never leave this room. He'd stay here, basking in Lottie, happily losing himself in her sinful curves, for the rest of his days. The world went on beyond the four walls sheltering them, but for this charmed space in time, how easy it was to pretend that this idyll need never end.

If he had his way, it wouldn't. He wanted to wake up every morning with her in his arms, in his bed, where she belonged. To kiss her awake. To make love to her whenever he desired, rather than in furtive coupling sessions.

"There is something I've been meaning to ask you," Lottie said into the comfortable hush that had lulled between them, looking mussed and lovely and as if she had been thoroughly bedded.

Because she had.

Brandon couldn't contain his self-satisfied grin as he gazed down at her. "You can ask me anything."

They had dozed for a time after making love, Lottie curled against his side, his arm wrapped around her waist. He had awoken before her, content to lie there with her, listening to the soft, even sound of each breath she took, pleased beyond measure. Plotting any conceivable means he could conspire to persuade her to marry him.

Because he loved her. He had to acknowledge it, if only to himself. The feeling was still there, not at all faded now that they had made love and slept. If anything, it had taken root and was growing already, quite akin to a shoot in a garden.

"The chair," she said, jolting him from his maudlin thoughts.

He blinked at her, bemused, wondering what the devil she was talking about. "What chair?"

"Surely you're aware of the rumor circling concerning a certain chair you had fashioned specifically to facilitate… sexual congress."

Ah.

Heat licked up the back of his neck, making his ears prickle. "That chair."

Her eyebrows rose. "So there *is* a chair, then?"

"There is indeed a chair, but it isn't mine."

"I *knew* there was a chair," she pronounced, as if she had just solved some grand mystery of the ages. "But whose is it, then, if not yours?"

"Kingham's, I suppose. It was a crude joke he orchestrated. King is quite a genius when it comes to inventing things, whether it be elixirs or chairs or God knows what. It was meant to be used for…er, pleasuring two women at once."

Her eyes widened. "Oh."

He swallowed hard. "Now, it's at Wingfield Hall. I've never personally made use of it, though I suppose some Society revelers may have."

"I didn't realize that Kingham was so talented," she said idly. "I don't know him very well, of course."

"He's a genius. More often than not, an evil one." He kissed the tip of her nose, an odd sensation welling up inside his chest. "But enough about that devil. I'd prefer for him to stay out of our bed, if you don't mind."

A teasing grin curved her lush mouth, her blue eyes dancing with laughter. "Never say the great Duke of Brandon is jealous of the Duke of Kingham."

"Of course not," he scoffed.

Her lips twitched. "Methinks you doth protest too much."

Maybe he had been hasty in his reply. And he couldn't deny that the mere thought of King touching Lottie or kissing her or—God forbid—more made him want to throw her over his shoulder and carry her away like some marauding Viking of old.

"Guilty," he allowed with a rueful smile, kissing her cheek, her jaw. "I must admit, I want you all to myself."

He lifted his head, and the levity fled both of them as their gazes held.

She cupped his jaw. "You do have me all to yourself for tonight."

"For tonight," he repeated, unable to keep the bitterness from his voice.

He wanted more from her than stolen moments. Wanted more than secret meetings and shagging in the shadows against a door. He wanted to be her husband. Wanted to be at her side.

"When I said I didn't know Kingham well, I meant it," she said softly, perhaps sensing his tumultuous mood. "He and I have never been intimately acquainted."

He had no right to feel the primitive rush of relief coursing over him. It was certainly no business of his to know whom she had taken as a lover in the past. Christ knew he had more than his fair share of lovers in his own murky history.

"You needn't tell me that," he said gruffly. "It wouldn't matter to me if you had. Our pasts bear no hold over our present or our future."

Future—a dangerous word. He knew it the moment that she stiffened at its utterance. She was so determined there could be none for them. Lovemaking was all she would countenance.

And so he distracted her in the best way he knew how.

He took her mouth with his, kissing her slowly. Tenderly. Patiently. Showing her with deeds rather than words that he would woo her, take care of her. That he would allow her to take control and choose what she wanted from him, whether it be pleasure or something infinitely more.

She softened, the tension easing from her as she wrapped her arms around his neck and rolled against him, her pebbled nipples and rounded breasts crushed against his chest. He gave her his tongue, and she made a low sound of surrender. His cock rose to attention, prodding her belly. He wanted her again. Couldn't get his fill of her.

Fortunately, Lottie was similarly voracious. She hooked a bare leg over his hip beneath the bedclothes, bringing her slick, hot cunny into contact with his groin. Beneath the coverlet and sheet, his fingers unerringly found her center, tracing over her seam to swirl over her clitoris. She moaned into his kiss, feeding him her tongue now, twining her fingers in his hair as she pumped her hips into his hand, seeking.

He grasped his cock, dragging it up and down her folds before sliding into her with one deep thrust. She was wet and welcoming, tightening on him instantly, and it was pure bliss as he began a rhythm, gliding in and out of her. Not just bliss. Perfection. Her body had been made for his.

Their tongues tangled, their kiss growing more frantic. He intended to shag her senseless this night. As many times as he could. To fill her with his spend. The thought made him harder, his cock even more determined as he drove into Lottie's sweetly pulsing cunny. He teased her bud, and she cried out, clamping down on him as she came.

He tore his lips from hers, raining kisses down her throat, over her breast. Taking a nipple in his mouth, he sucked hard as he thrust into her again and again. He was close. So close.

He rolled to his back, pulling her astride him, his cock still gloved inside her velvet heat. "Ride me, Venus."

She was atop him, all curves and copper-flecked cream and wild-rose pink, from her pussy to her nipples to her lips. Her hair was a riotous halo of cinnamon curls, her breasts full and high. A goddess, a conqueror. She undulated against him, her palms planted on his shoulders as she fucked him.

He watched, mesmerized by the sight of his harsh, ruddy cock impaling her pretty feminine flesh again and again, trying to stave off his own release for as long as possible. But she felt so good, so slick, a mixture of her desire and his own seed coating them both, and he thought he might happily die from the sheer pleasure of it—being inside her, watching her ride him and take what she needed, a marauding Venus intent upon finding her own climax. He leaned up and caught her other nipple in his mouth as she rocked down on him, taking him deep.

She moaned his name, head tilted back, eyes closed, and continued her rhythm. He was moving too now, helping her, his hips leaving the mattress to thrust upward as she received him. A symphony of sounds swirled around them—skin colliding, ragged breaths, soft moans, the creaking of the bed as their lovemaking became more frenzied and desperate.

Suddenly, she seized on him, crying out as her back bowed and a new rush of wetness bathed his cock, spasms of her cunny bringing him swiftly to the edge. He couldn't last. Clasping her waist, he guided her up and down his length once, twice, thrice more, and then he surged upward a final time, filling her with the hot burst of his seed.

His heart galloping, he released her nipple and sank back against the bed, more certain than ever of one thing.

Whether she liked it or not, Lottie was his.

CHAPTER 16

She had broken the cardinal rule of taking a lover.

Lottie stared at the missive on her writing desk, overwhelmed by the cloying grasp of dread. The masculine scrawl was familiar. The tone was teasing, intimate, and she had been awaiting it from the moment she had risen that morning, beset by an acute sense of eagerness she hadn't been able to shake, despite how very much she *didn't* want to feel it.

The note itself was nothing extraordinary. An invitation to tea with himself, Pandy, and Cat. It was also one she couldn't—mustn't—accept. The time had finally come to face what could be avoided no longer.

There was no doubt that Lottie was going to have to put an end to her affair with the Duke of Brandon. A fortnight had passed since that glorious night of lovemaking at Brandon's house in St John's Wood. Fourteen precious days and nights which had passed in a blur of pleasure. They had met most evenings. At his love nest, in his carriage, in an alcove at a ball, in her own bedroom where she had not previously allowed another lover.

And in all this time, she had never, not once tired of him. She woke, counting the minutes and hours until she could see him again. Their lovemaking had grown, their knowledge of each other's bodies rendering each assignation better than the last. Frantic coupling or all-evening seduction, it didn't matter. Their every interaction left her longing for him even more.

It was a grievous mistake. One she knew too well. She had allowed Brandon past her defenses. But now, the time had come to resurrect the wall she'd built around her shattered heart. Before it was too late. Caring for him was one thing. What she was beginning to feel now was so much more, which was why it had to be stopped.

One never developed too much tender sentiment for a lover. Because doing so inevitably led to peril. Heartbreak, disappointment, disillusionment. She had suffered once, and she would not do so again.

It was settled.

Putting pen to paper, she composed her answer to Brandon's invitation, and for the first time in a fortnight, she declined.

"Jenkinson," she called to her lady's maid, who was across the chamber, busying herself with her duties for the morning.

"Yes, my lady?"

"See that this note is sent to His Grace, the Duke of Brandon, if you please," she said, holding the folded missive out for her lady's maid to take. "And have my carriage readied as well. I'm going to pay a call to some friends today."

A call to all her friends. Every friend she could find. Anything to keep her from giving in to the desire to see Brandon again.

"Of course, Lady Grenfell," said the ever-efficient Jenkinson. "Shall I prepare a promenade dress?"

Oh, how she longed to don a tea dress and join Brandon, Pandy, and Cat. She adored Pandy, and she was inordinately fond of Cat. But she had fallen into the same pattern each day of vowing she would not spend more time with the duke before swiftly giving in.

"A promenade dress would be just the thing," she answered, forcing a smile she didn't feel.

It was for the best, she told herself. She had known from the start their affair could not last. Best to draw the blood now and then find the time to heal. Already, she knew she could not bear the day when she would inevitably see the notice of his engagement in *The Times*.

This had to stop.

Distraction was what she needed. Distraction and distance.

A great deal of both.

Her first stop was a call upon Rosamund, who received her in the drawing room, Megs not far on a perch, presiding over the call like a regal, feathered queen.

"Lady, lady," chirped Megs. "Landlubber."

"I didn't expect you today," Rosamund said without censure. "I've scarcely seen you over the past fortnight. Where have you been?"

Heat crept up her cheeks. She couldn't precisely say she'd been in the Duke of Brandon's bed, could she?

"I've been quite busy," she offered brightly instead, hoping her friend couldn't read the discomfiture that was likely written all over her face.

"Busy?" Rosamund gave her a knowing look. "That sounds rather intriguing. Do tell me what you have been doing whilst I have been dreading my impending nuptials."

"Dreading, dreading," said Megs. "Gormless shite."

"Megs," Rosamund chastised, giving the African grey a

hard look. "No pistachios for you if you're going to misbehave again."

"Pistache," the parrot chirped, then made a trilling sound followed by a whistle, her head cocked. "Megs wants pistache."

"Then hush," Rosamund ordered sternly, "and you shall have your pistachios."

Megs made a kissing sound and ruffled her feathers.

"Perhaps you should tell me why you're dreading your marriage to Camden first," Lottie said, not wanting to talk about herself.

"Gormless shite," Megs repeated.

Rosamund wagged her finger at the bird before sighing. "I suppose it is common enough to have misgivings before such a tremendous undertaking. Is it not?"

"Of course it is, dearest," she reassured her friend. "Particularly when one is entering a marriage of convenience."

"Were you nervous before you married Grenfell?" Rosamund asked and then winced. "Forgive me for asking. I shouldn't have done so."

"You need not apologize. I don't mind speaking of it, particularly if it proves helpful to a friend."

Besides, she was grateful for anything that would keep her mind from Brandon.

Blast it, there she went again, thinking of *him*.

"I was nervous, as I recall," she added, forcing herself to return to the subject at hand. "I was hopelessly in love and terribly naïve. I didn't know the first thing about being a wife. Tell me, is it that you fear you'll prove incompatible with Camden after you marry?"

That had never been a consideration of Lottie's, and she had suffered for it. Being trapped in a loveless, joyless, hopeless marriage had been its own form of hell.

"Kissing," Megs declared, making an exaggerated sound that corresponded to the word. "Fucking, fucking. Show me your bubbies, luv."

"Er, rather the opposite, I fear," Rosamund confessed, color in her cheeks.

Lottie wouldn't have been more surprised if Rosamund had announced her intention to leap headfirst from the window. She reeled for a moment, taking in the implications of what her friend had just revealed.

"So you're saying that you and the Duke of Camden have…been intimate together?" she asked, uncertain of what, if anything, she should say in such a moment. It had simply never occurred to her that Rosamund and Camden would have been engaged in anything of a scandalous nature.

They didn't even like each other, for heaven's sake.

Did they?

Her gaze narrowed on her friend, who was looking suspiciously uncomfortable.

"That, er…ah," Rosamund began, shifting uncomfortably on her seat, "I suppose you might…that is to say…we never… we wouldn't. We absolutely wouldn't."

But Lottie was no fool. She knew a lie when she heard one, and she also knew her friend well enough to understand that she was prevaricating.

Lottie pressed a hand over her mouth, shocked. "I don't believe it," she murmured quietly, lest her voice carry to the servants moving silently through the halls beyond. "You have *bedded* the Duke of Camden."

Rosamund said nothing, her cheeks flaming, a telltale giveaway.

"How?" she asked, then shook her head, her mind suddenly a vast jungle from which there seemed no escape. "When?"

"In the customary way, I suppose," Rosamund said quietly, biting her lower lip as if something deep within her pained her greatly. "As for when, it matters not, does it?"

Megs chirruped and then whistled. "Matters not. Bedded Camden."

"Megs," Rosamund gasped, eyes going wide. "You must not repeat that."

"Gormless shite," Megs said, blinking.

Lottie bit her lip to stifle her chuckle. "Is Megs speaking about the duke, perchance?"

"She isn't Camden's greatest devotee, I'm afraid."

Megs fluffed her feathers as if in affirmation but remained where she was on her perch.

It occurred to Lottie with sudden clarity that both she and Rosamund were experiencing the same misgiving. Just as Lottie feared she had begun to like Brandon too much, Rosamund feared she could grow to care for Camden. They were both scared of becoming too vulnerable. Of having their hearts broken.

But unlike Rosamund, Lottie would be spared that fate, because she wasn't marrying Brandon. Someone else was.

As she and her friend continued their tea, Lottie decided that the odd heaviness in her chest was caused by relief. Nothing more.

∼

"Why have I yet to see a betrothal announcement in *The Times*, Brandon?" Grandmother demanded without preamble.

"My dearest darling Grandmama, it is lovely to see you as well," he drawled, bowing over her proffered hand.

She looked august as usual this afternoon in black silk,

her countenance pinched into an omnipresent expression of displeasure, as if all the world around her and everyone in it was a source of great disappointment. He had been thoroughly nettled by Lottie's refusal of his invitation to tea this afternoon, and the unexpected arrival of his grandmother meant that his day was going from dreadful to worse.

"Do you dare to mock me?" she demanded coolly.

"Never, dear lady." He tucked her gloved hand into the crook of his elbow and guided her to a nearby settee, noting that she had brought a gilded cane with her and she was leaning more heavily upon it than she ordinarily did whenever her arthritis particularly pained her.

She favored her left leg, using him for support as well as the cane. "Don't lie to me, Brandon. I'll box your ears."

He didn't doubt she would.

"I wouldn't dream of lying to you," he prevaricated, tongue in cheek.

She seated herself on the settee with a harrumph that told him she hadn't believed his protest for a moment. "Where is the girl child?"

"Pandy?" He was surprised that his grandmother asked after her, for despite her family's lineage, she was a stickler for propriety. He hadn't known whether Grandmother would ever even mention Pandora again.

Grandmother's silvery eyebrows snapped together. "You've a pet name for her now?"

He seated himself with ease opposite her, intentionally beyond reach of any ear-boxing he might receive. "Pandy suits her best, I believe."

His grandmother's eyes narrowed shrewdly. "You haven't sent her away, then?"

The very notion of sending his Pandy girl anywhere else made his chest tighten. "Naturally not. I am her father. She belongs with me."

"Not if you are to find a bride, she doesn't." Grandmother frowned, thumping her cane on the floor for emphasis. "No gently bred young lady will come to live in a house where you are keeping your bastard. The scandal would be far too great."

He tensed, not liking the impersonal way his grandmother spoke of Pandy. "I'll thank you not to refer to Pandy thus. And if any lady wants to marry me, then living in a house with my daughter is the price she will have to pay. I'm not sending my daughter away as if she's a shameful secret."

Grandmother's lips thinned. "She *is* a shameful secret, Brandon. By her very birth, she is a tremendous scandal, and no woman of virtue is going to countenance her presence here in your household."

He clenched his jaw, gripping the gilt arms of his chair so tightly he feared they might snap. "Pandy is not responsible for the circumstances of her birth, and I'll not allow her to be punished for them. She is to remain here, with me. I refuse to send her away."

"Little wonder you have yet to find a bride," Grandmother lamented. "Your time grows thin, Brandon, and with this nonsensical insistence upon keeping your natural child in your household, I expect to hand the keys of Wingfield Hall over to your cousin Horace soon."

"I am courting a lady I would very much like to make my duchess," he ground out, frustrated, "a woman who will be pleased to share a household with an innocent child who deserves a loving home, having been ruthlessly abandoned by her own mother mere months ago."

Not that one could aptly name what he had been doing with Lottie as courting. Their present relationship was complicated. They were lovers in secret, polite acquaintances in public. As far as she or the rest of London knew, he might be courting any of the young debutantes he had obligingly danced with at balls. But that was all a ruse to hide his true aim, not just from polite society, but from Lottie herself.

He didn't wish to frighten her off until he was sure he could persuade her that marrying him would be nothing like marrying Grenfell had been.

The sudden cacophony of excited barking interrupted his tête-à-tête with Grandmother, heralding the arrival of Cat and, perchance, Pandy too. At least, he thought rather wryly to himself, the interruption during this visit with his grandmother would be caused by his daughter and not a naked opera singer wearing his dressing gown.

"What in heaven's name is that commotion?" Grandmother asked, frowning.

Before Brandon could answer, the doors to the drawing room burst open to reveal a grinning Pandy racing into the room, the barking spaniel at her heels.

"Sweet angels, child, what is that you're holding?" Grandmother demanded of Pandy, sounding horrified.

That was when he realized his daughter was clutching a pig trotter in one grimy hand as if it were the greatest prize she had ever obtained. Also, likely, the reason for Cat's frenzied barking.

"Me and Cat is playing chase-chase," Pandy declared proudly. "She hided the trotter in the garden, and I dugged it up."

Grandmother extracted a handkerchief from her reticule and held it to her nose, looking ashen. "What *is* that wretched smell?"

"Likely the pig trotter," Brandon guessed, eyeing the dirt-encrusted trotter, which was quite pungent now that a whiff had reached him. "Pandy, how long has that trotter been buried in the garden?"

"I dunno," she said, shrugging dramatically.

Cat barked, clearly unhappy with being kept from what

she wanted most in the world. Brandon could empathize. Only, it wasn't a rotten old pig trotter buried in the garden that he longed for. Rather, it was a stubborn, beautiful goddess who had been so badly hurt by her scoundrel of a husband that she was determined never to marry or love again.

Brandon took in the spectacle unfolding before him. There was the eager spaniel, who continued to shift restlessly and bark, her eyes fastened upon the trotter Pandy held out of reach. Then there was his daughter, her cheeks flushed from her madcap dash from the garden with Cat on her heels, oblivious to the dirt streaking her hands as she wielded her prize aloft. And last, his grandmother, handkerchief pressed to her nose, eyes wide, the pallor of her skin ominous. He couldn't blame her. The trotter did smell quite terrible.

"Pandy girl, where is Miss Bennington?" he inquired lightly. "Was she not watching you in the garden?"

"I'm faster'n Miss Bennington, and so's Cat," Pandy pronounced. "Her couldn't catch us."

Dear Lord. He could only imagine the poor woman racing through the maze, frantically trying to find a fleeing dog and a small child.

As if on cue, Miss Bennington appeared at the threshold to the drawing room, dashing into a quick curtsy.

"Your Grace, madam," she greeted breathlessly, looking shamefaced. "Forgive me for the interruption. Miss Pandora, please accompany me to the nursery at once."

"What 'bout this?" Frowning, Pandy waved the trotter about.

A piece of something fell to the Axminster, and Cat promptly ate it with a delighted chomp.

Grandmother groaned.

"Oh my goodness, whatever can that be?" Miss

Bennington asked, peering at the dirty trotter. "And what is that horrid scent?"

"It's the pig trotter," Brandon offered.

The nursemaid's eyebrows went up. "Oh dear. I am so sorry, Your Grace. Miss Pandora is not usually so spirited at this time in the afternoon. I thought to take a turn in the gardens, that fresh air would prove a boon, and Cat was sitting at the door…"

Grandmother made another choked sound.

Idly, he wondered if she was going to cast up her accounts. That would certainly complete the ridiculous display, which seemed rather indicative of his life. How had he gone from being a rakish bachelor, unencumbered by anyone else, to a father, a man in love, who now had so many to answer to?

"You needn't explain further, Miss Bennington," he said reassuringly. "If, however, you would kindly see that the trotter is taken away with the rubbish before you lead Pandy back to the nursery?"

"Of course, Your Grace." Miss Bennington curtseyed, clearly flustered. "Thank you, Your Grace. Once again, my deepest apologies for the interruption. It won't happen again, will it, Miss Pandora?"

Pandy's nose crinkled. "What's a 'rupption?"

"What you have just done, child," Grandmother informed her from behind the handkerchief. "A lady never goes running about halls or digging through dirt. She is to be clean and presentable and mild-mannered at all times."

His daughter shook her head. "Then I don't wanna be no lady."

Brandon couldn't contain his shout of laughter at Pandy's response. Nor could he blame her. His daughter grinned at him, her green gaze twinkling. Cat barked. Miss Bennington looked as if she didn't know whether to weep or flee from the room, and Grandmother continued to look bilious.

He rose from his chair and ventured to where Pandy stood, dubious pig trotter still in hand, and sank to his haunches so that they were at eye level. "You'll make a fine lady one day, Pandy girl. But for now, you're to do as Miss Bennington says. You mustn't run off with Cat or play chase-chase indoors. Do you understand?"

She nodded, looking a bit crestfallen. "Yes, Papa."

There was that word, the one that was by far the greatest title he'd worn, the mantle that made him feel like a goddamned king. Papa.

He ruffled her curls affectionately. "Good. And if you discover any pig trotters Cat has buried in the garden, you're to tell Shilling, who will see that they're properly removed by a footman."

Her expression grew mulish. "But Cat loves 'em."

"Cat also loves to scoot her bum on the carpets," he explained patiently. "That doesn't mean she ought to do so."

"Brandon!" protested his grandmother over his shoulder, her tone scandalized.

"That was a rather indelicate matter for me to discuss," he conceded, giving Pandy a wink. "You see? None of us is perfect. We are, each one of us, a book that's still being written. From now on, Cat is only to have fresh trotters from the kitchens, no running about, and mind Miss Bennington."

She nodded solemnly. "Yes, Papa."

He bussed a kiss over her crown, love for her bubbling up in his heart, more than he had ever known possible. "Now run along, Pandy girl, and do see that you give the trotter to one of the footmen. It's making Great-Grandmama gag."

"I would never do something as indecorous as that," his grandmother protested, her voice muffled from behind the handkerchief.

He gave Pandy another wink and patted her lightly on the head.

Cat barked, still miffed that she was being kept away from her stinky prize. Brandon gave her a thorough scratch between her ears as well. "Off you go, Pandy girl. And Cat, too."

Cat barked, her tongue lolling. Pandy dipped into a passable enough curtsy, and then she hastened toward her waiting nursemaid, thankfully taking the trail of stench along with her. Cat followed in her wake, ever hopeful that she might get a second mouthful of rotten pig trotter.

Miss Bennington curtseyed. "Thank you, Your Grace, madam. It won't happen again. You have my word."

He inclined his head. "Thank you, Miss Bennington."

Brandon waited until the unlikely trio filed from the drawing room, rotten pig trotter and all, before returning to his chair. In the absence of the source of the smell, Grandmother lowered her handkerchief, eyeing him warily.

"The child called you Papa, Brandon."

"I am her father, am I not? What else should she call me?" he asked evenly, holding her stare without flinching.

She was silent for a moment, taking stock of him, perhaps the way some might a horse one was intending to purchase. "You truly intend to keep her here," she said at last, breaking the silence.

"It's where she belongs," he repeated firmly. "I'll not lock her away like a shameful secret. The woman I intend to wed will need to accept my position on the matter, and that is final."

She thumped her cane on the floor with another harrumph. "Well, you had better wed the girl quickly, because you're running out of time, and I remain firm in my determination that Horace will receive Wingfield Hall and the rest of my fortune if you refuse to marry."

"I assure you, Grandmama, that I have already chosen my bride. Cousin Horace won't be setting so much as one foot upon Wingfield Hall if I have anything to say about it."

Because Brandon was going to marry Lottie, damn it.

All he had to do was convince her to give him a chance first.

CHAPTER 17

By the fourth day of avoiding Brandon, Lottie was miserable.

She had dismissed every invitation he issued with a litany of excuses. She was too busy. She had calls to pay. She had stubbed her toe and couldn't be imposed upon to dance at a ball. And last, the refusal that had made her stomach feel leaden with guilt—she was abed, too ill to leave her sickroom.

To make matters worse, Brandon had come to her upon hearing she was unwell.

She'd been forced to have her butler turn him away.

Now, seated in the small library of the town house that had been Grenfell's gift to her in death—a home of her own instead of relying upon the alms of family or her widow's portion—she was hopelessly listless. The book in her lap didn't hold her interest. The crackling fire in the grate offered warmth but no comfort. And she'd eaten her last chocolate and been forced to ring for Jenkinson in the hopes that her lady's maid could procure more.

The door to the library opened at her back, but Lottie

didn't bother to look over her shoulder. "Jenkinson dearest, I've eaten all the chocolates. Could you have one of the footmen run and fetch me some more?"

She had a feeling she was going to need them. Either chocolates or good French wine. But French wine would only make her think of Brandon, and thinking of Brandon made her miss him and his sinful lips and his verdant eyes that made her melt and his knowing hands and clever tongue... No, she didn't dare have any wine at all. Chocolate it was.

"Too ill to venture from your sickroom, are you?"

The deep, masculine drawl thieved a gasp from her as she cast a wild look over her shoulder to find Brandon standing at the threshold instead of her lady's maid. He was tall, handsome, and potently male. If she hadn't been seated in the chair, she might have been tempted to launch herself at him like a stone loaded into a catapult and unceremoniously flung.

"What are you doing here?" she demanded, and then instantly wondered if she had chocolate smeared in the corners of her lips.

Her tongue darted out to catch any lingering traces of the sweet she had been consuming in a fruitless attempt at diversion.

"I was worried about you," he explained, striding deeper into the room, his emerald eyes burning into her, rendering her incapable of looking anywhere else. "When I was turned away and told how ill you were, I was determined to see you myself, regardless of what your damned butler said."

Heat crept up her throat.

She'd been caught.

Lottie gripped the arms of her chair, refusing to relent. "Are you playing house cracksman now, Brandon?"

He stopped perilously near, towering over her, and it

occurred to Lottie that he was still wearing his hat, gloves, and coat. The scent of rain melded with musk, citrus, and leather. She tried to quell the stinging surge of lust that arced through her at his proximity.

He cocked his head, looking down at her with an unreadable expression. "No, I'm playing concerned suitor. Why did you lie to me?"

"You're not my suitor," she hedged, snapping her book closed in her lap and wishing he hadn't effectively trapped her in her chair.

He was so blasted tall, and she had to crane her neck to hold his gaze. As if he possessed all the time in the world, he removed his hat with a calm, efficient motion, depositing it on a nearby table. His hair was all mahogany waves beneath.

"What am I, then?" He planted his hands on the arms of her chair, leaning down. "Hmm, Lottie? What am I to you?"

"You *were* my lover," she corrected airily. "Now, you are once more my acquaintance. A friend of a mutual friend."

"Ah, is that the way of it, then? You have decided to cry off our agreement, and you are too much of a coward to tell me. I thought better of you, darling."

Lottie resented being called a coward. However, she *could* inwardly acknowledge that her actions were hardly brave. She had been hiding from him, and there was no denying it. Because resisting the man was so deuced impossible. It was a form of self-preservation, really. If she never saw him again, she might have a hope of remaining impervious to his charms.

"We didn't have an agreement," she pointed out instead of saying aloud any of the wayward thoughts running through her head.

His dark brows both hiked upward. "What would you term spending almost every night in my bed for a fortnight, then?"

She wished that he weren't so close. That he weren't so handsome. That she weren't so damned tempted to kiss him.

That she could resist this man. Her defenses were disintegrating by the second.

"A man and a woman seeking mutual pleasure," she told him curtly. "You needn't act as if I were your mistress. What we shared is…"

"Incredible," he finished for her.

"Over," she said in the same moment.

"Over," he repeated, staring at her. "That's what you think? That we're over?"

Oh God, she wanted to kiss him. She wanted to kiss his sulky mouth more than she wanted to see another day.

I can resist him, she thought sternly.

"Yes, Brandon," she said slowly. "That is what I think. That we are over. It was lovely whilst it lasted. However, the time has come for us to part ways. You are marrying a debutante, and I am going about living my life as I wish."

"I see." He nodded, holding her gaze.

For a moment, she believed she had won their battle of wits and words.

"Good," she forced out, feeling numb. "I'm glad."

"Tell me something first, if you please." He leaned forward, impossibly near now, his scent wrapping around her and comforting her, the same way a lullaby soothed a child.

She licked her lips, tasting sweetness. "What would you have me tell you?"

Perhaps if she held her breath, she might better resist.

His head dipped, his lips brushing her cheek in a light, tender kiss. "Does this feel like we're over?"

Lottie was still holding her breath, and she told herself that was why she didn't answer him.

Apparently, he took her silence as acquiescence. Because

his mouth brushed her temple next. "Does this feel like we're over, Lottie?"

She swallowed, her heart pounding. Soon, she would need air. But she bit her lip, delaying the inevitable.

He laid a hot, gentle kiss on her jaw. "What of this?"

Her throat was next, and she inhaled, her lungs feeling as if they might explode. But that was no good, because he was all she could smell, that glorious, irresistible blend of man and musk and citrus mingled with the crispness of rain and the earthiness of leather and the faint, clean hint of shaving soap too.

"Answer me, Venus."

Not his pet name for her. How could she withstand such torture? She couldn't, and he knew it. Just as she hadn't been able to face him to put an end to their affair. Because she didn't want to end it. She wanted it to go on and on. She wanted to spend every night in his bed, in his arms, to kiss him whenever she wished. She wanted him to be hers and hers alone, and that terrified her more than words could possibly convey.

He kissed the hollow behind her ear, and she shivered. "Does this feel like we're over?"

"Brandon," she protested, unable to lie with him so near, his tender, sensual onslaught bringing her to her knees more swiftly than the most passionate seduction ever could.

"How about this?" He feathered a kiss over her brow next.

"How did you get in here?" she muttered, trying to think of anything other than what he was doing to her and the effect his reverent, carefully placed kisses were having on her. "Whoever allowed it is sacked."

"I let myself in through the servants' stair," he said, amusement lacing his voice as he kissed the bridge of her nose. "But enough of that. You're meant to be telling me if it feels as if we're over to you."

His lips found the corner of hers, and a strangled sound of longing emerged from her before she could stop it.

She gripped the book in her lap so tightly that her fingers ached. "Are you trying to torment me, damn you?"

"No." He lifted his head, his gaze tangling with hers once more. "I'm trying to prove to you that we very much *aren't* over. That we're far from it, in fact."

She heaved a sigh of frustration. "You know as well as I that we cannot continue in this vein. You need to marry, and I will never wed again. To carry on as if our futures were otherwise is nothing short of pure folly."

"And yet, you can't tell me that we're over," he pointed out, more than a trifle smug. "You can't say the words. Perhaps you should show me, then. Kiss me and convince me you feel nothing."

Lottie inhaled, bringing the heady scent of him into her lungs, trapping it there as if she could somehow keep this part of him forever. Because that was what she wanted, even if she only dared admitting it to herself. She wanted the Duke of Brandon selfishly and foolishly. She wanted him to be all hers, only hers. *Always* hers. She felt dizzied from the maddening combination of his nearness and his mouth. She could not kiss him and remain unmoved. She knew it, and she did not doubt that he did too.

"I'm not playing games with you," she told him.

He cupped her cheek, his leather glove cool on her heated skin, and she wished that his hand was bare so that she could feel him without encumbrance, this trapping of civility removed. "Yes, you are. And they must stop. Just as you must stop lying to the both of us that you don't want me. That you want to put an end to what's between us. It's as much a prevarication as every one of your excuses these last four days."

He was not wrong, curse his stubborn, beautiful hide.

What had she been thinking, allowing this man close? Rakes were like flames. Venture too near, and one was inevitably bound to be burned.

She held his stare defiantly. "Very well. I want you. It is only natural. I'm a woman with needs, and you're a reasonably handsome man. You're also skilled in the bedchamber."

He chuckled, his breath falling over her lips. "Only *reasonably* handsome, darling? I would have thought you could do better than that."

"Vain wretch," she complained without heat. "You know how despicably gorgeous you are."

"Perhaps I like to hear you admit it."

Silence fell between them again, their gazes locked. "You know why we cannot continue, Brandon. Why are you still here?"

"For the same reason you have yet to tell me that it feels like we're over."

Another moment of heavy, heated silence descended. A quickening began, deep within her. A physical acknowledgment of the effect he had on her. Her nipples were hard beneath the stiff boning of her corset. And between her legs, she was embarrassingly wet. There was no question she desired him. That had never been her fear. Passion and lust were raw, elemental. They were physical aches like hunger, easily enough placated.

But the heart—that was what she truly feared most. Because she knew from experience that it could not be governed. The heart, that restless, foolish enemy. And hers knew what it wanted too well.

This man, it whispered insidiously. *Him.*

"Brandon," she began, not certain of what she intended to say, only that she had to fill the quiet with something, that she had to protest before she did something truly dangerous and—no, she wasn't going to—oh heavens, yes, she was...

She acted without thought, wrapping her arms suddenly around his neck and pulling him to her, pressing her mouth to his. The kiss was so sudden and ferocious that it was almost painful. Her teeth were mashed against her tender inner lips. It didn't matter. In the next breath, his tongue demanded entry, and she surrendered without hesitation.

Somehow, he performed the feat of gathering her from the chair and into his arms. Her book went sailing, landing with a thump on the floor. The world spun, their lips chasing each other's hungrily, tongues writhing, and then he had whirled them about so that he was in the chair she had occupied and she was in his lap.

He broke the kiss for but a moment, rearing back to sear her with his potent stare. "We're not over, Lottie."

She swallowed, still reluctant to make the concession aloud, even if every part of her body and soul and all her stupid heart had already made the decision for her. Even if she knew to her core that they would never be over, that though they might travel far, and he would wed another, her body would always ache for his. She would forever want him.

A strange prickling sensation burned the backs of her eyes then. She refused to believe it was tears until she felt the hot, wet glide on both cheeks and her vision blurred. And though she blinked furiously to clear them away, he saw them.

Of course he did.

He caught them with his lips, drying each drop where it fell. Then he kissed her again, and as she tasted the sweet bitterness of chocolate and the salt of her own tears, she knew that the last of her defenses had shattered. Nothing remained. Not even pride.

And all the while, he kissed her as he had not kissed her before. Slowly, tenderly, but worshipfully too, as if she were indeed the goddess he had proclaimed her to be, and he a mere mortal at her feet. Lingeringly, patiently, as if he had all the time in the world to hold her thus, cradling her as if she were fashioned of finest crystal instead of weak flesh and bone. He made her feel revered in a way no one ever had. Not just desired, but needed too.

And that scared her.

Badly.

But she was too far gone for him to stop it now.

He kissed her and kissed her and kissed her. And though they had engaged in sexual congress many times before, his lips on hers somehow felt far more intimate than any other act. More intimate, even, than his cock in her mouth and his spend shooting down her throat. Because this was different. It transcended physical desire. He took his time, his hands caressing her with soothing motions, almost as if she were a horse easily spooked. And he made no move to undress her.

He touched nary a button nor a hook nor a tape. Her hem stayed where it was, her bustle crushed at an awkward angle beneath her bottom, his length buried somewhere under the layers separating them. All he did was ravish her mouth. Again and again and again until she felt delicate and new, as if one false move might destroy her.

No one had ever made her feel like this.

She cradled his face in both hands, holding him to her, returning his kisses, accepting his tongue, giving him hers. Until finally, they were both breathless, her lips swollen, and he gently tipped her head back, severing the connection.

"Tell me that felt like we're over to you," he rasped.

She stared at him, struggling to gather a comprehension of the English language. She felt like a forest that had been burned to the ground, and now that the flames had died, she must find new life again.

"It doesn't feel like we're over," she admitted quietly.

To him. But, perhaps, most importantly, to herself.

"Good." He leaned into her, pressing his mouth to hers in a surprisingly chaste kiss before breaking away. "I'll send my carriage for you tomorrow after luncheon. Come and spend the afternoon with me and Pandy."

She gawped. This was not what she had expected him to say or do. An invitation to bed. A crude shag in the chair, yes. Chaste kisses followed by a request to share the day with him and his daughter? Decidedly not.

"I… Brandon…"

"Cat too," he added, grinning and making her heart beat faster. "We cannot forget our favorite rotten-pig-trotter-loving mongrel."

"Rotten pig trotter?"

She had been reduced to repeating his words. But she was lost. Confused. Adrift at sea, trying to find any piece of flotsam to which she might cling.

He chuckled, the sound low and pleasant as silk drawn over her bare skin. "A long story. One I will share with you. Tomorrow."

With that, he rose, the two of them moving as one until he settled her gently on her feet. Her knees threatened to buckle, her legs like those of a newborn foal.

"Please, o beloved sorceress of wayward children and ragtag mongrels. Say you will join us."

Lottie shook her head, amused by him. Entranced by him. Falling further for him despite herself.

What was wrong with her? How had her plan to avoid him gone so amiss?

"My coachman will deliver me," she said, feeling as if she must at least retain some manner of control.

"You and your bloody coachman," he grumbled.

"John Coachman knows my secrets."

A muscle worked in his jaw. "I never thought to see the

day I'd be jealous of a coachman."

Was this more of his dramatic flair? Surely he couldn't be serious.

She searched his gaze. "Why should you be jealous of him?"

"Because I want to be the keeper of your secrets. I want to be the man you entrust yourself to, Lottie."

The earnestness in his voice made her breath catch. Before she could form a response, he stepped away from her, retrieving his hat in one elegant motion and placing it atop his head.

"Tomorrow," he repeated. "Bring your own carriage if you must."

With a bow, he started for the door. She watched him, feeling oddly bereft.

"Brandon," she called.

He stopped, cocking his head toward her.

"No need to use the servants' entrance when you leave," she said, feeling foolish because she hadn't wanted him to go, and she had been grasping at any means she could think of to stay him.

He inclined his head. "Through the front door like a proper suitor, it is."

And then he was gone, and her heart was still beating wildly. Belatedly, it occurred to her that she hadn't bothered to correct him when he had declared himself a suitor. She wasn't certain why.

∾

Tick, tick, tick went the mantel clock.

From his vigil at the fireplace, Brandon tried not to count the seconds that had passed as he waited. Instead, he concentrated on sounds.

DUKE WITH A REPUTATION

Thump, thump, thump went his daughter's feet on the Axminster.

Bark, bark went her silly hound.

He had been waiting for Lottie's arrival one quarter hour, but it felt more like a century had passed. Likely, his interminable pause wasn't helped by Pandy's enthusiastic and boundless energy. She was like a watch spring, too tightly wound and then suddenly set free.

Brandon watched with mild amusement as his daughter galloped in a circle around the drawing room, Cat trailing happily at her heels, occasionally offering a cheerful bark. Likely, he ought to take her to task. Tell her to seat herself like a lady and calmly await their guest's arrival.

But he didn't have the heart to chastise her. He'd leave that duty for Miss Bennington.

"Pandy girl, you shall wear yourself out before Lady Grenfell even arrives," he cautioned as she made another gleeful circumnavigation of the chamber.

"I'm assited for her to visit," Pandy explained unapologetically.

"*Ex*cited, my dear," he corrected out of sheer habit.

Her vocabulary was large for a girl just approaching five years of age. However, her elocution was decidedly lacking.

"*Ass-ited*," Pandy repeated, still mispronouncing the word, although she did so with painstaking care.

Oh well. He had tried, hadn't he?

"Quite." He smiled at her as she breezed by yet again, her cheeks tinged pink from her exertion.

"Do you think she'll wanna play hide 'n seek?" Pandy called over her shoulder.

Cat barked.

He watched their procession, a swell of love rising in his chest, making his throat go tight. It was difficult to fathom he'd once had a life without his precious daughter and her ragtag spaniel in it.

Brandon cleared his throat. "I'm not certain Lady Grenfell will be in the mood to play games today, Pandy girl."

Hell, he hadn't the slightest notion of whether she would even deign to call. She had spent the last few days in a campaign of avoidance, fabricating all manner of excuses to keep him at bay. He knew why—she was stubborn and determined, and her disastrous marriage with that arsehole Grenfell had left her feeling that she should never trust a man again.

But he was every bit as resolute. He would prove to her that he was nothing like that bastard. Slowly. Carefully. He didn't want to send her fleeing in the opposite direction, and he had no doubt that if he pressed his suit too far, she would. Lottie was beginning to feel something for him. Recognition had flared within him when he had looked into her eyes yesterday. And it had been those tender emotions that had sent her into hiding.

Pandy raced past him again. Was it her thirteenth or fourteenth lap of the room? He'd lost count, trapped in his own ruminations.

Just then, Shilling appeared at the door, dour and unsmiling. "The Countess of Grenfell to see Your Grace."

"Missus Lady Grenspell!" Pandy shrieked, clapping her hands in delight.

Cat barked uproariously.

Brandon winced at the din. "See her in, if you please, Shilling."

"Of course, Your Grace," his butler said, displaying an astonishing ability to show no reaction whatsoever to the commotion in the drawing room.

He felt some of the tension ease from his shoulders as Lottie sailed over the threshold wearing a violet gown that made her glorious hair appear even more vibrant. Although the bodice was modest, her delicious curves were on full display, from her waist to her bountiful breasts.

Pandy rushed toward her, so eager that she scaled a settee that was in her way, fearlessly launching herself over the gilt-edged backrest.

"Pandy, you mustn't climb the furniture," he chided, watching as Cat followed suit, landing on all four paws with a soft thud before scrambling toward Lottie.

Brandon couldn't fault them for their enthusiasm. He felt much the same at seeing her. For a wild moment, he wondered what his hard-hearted countess would do were he to rush toward her as well.

Instead of giving in to such a maudlin flight of fancy, however, he offered her a bow, remaining where he stood by the mantel and its steadily ticking clock. "Lady Grenfell, you are looking remarkably lovely this afternoon."

"Thank you, Your Grace," she said softly, with equal formality.

Pandy bounded into her, throwing her arms around Lottie's skirts and nearly sending her to the floor. Cat, who had been remarkably well-behaved in recent days when it came to attempts at eating gowns, took a mouthful of her hems and began tugging.

"Cat," he scolded. "You are to leave Lady Grenfell's skirts alone."

Cat pulled again, gleefully ignoring him.

His house resembled nothing so much as a wayward menagerie at the moment. He hastened forward as Lottie laughed, returning Pandy's embrace.

"I've missed you, Pandy," she told his daughter.

Her patience and acceptance made him love her even more.

"Cat," he said sternly as he reached the trio, pointing a finger at the naughty beast. "Stop. Bad dog."

"Cat, no," Pandy added, frowning down at her hound. "No eating Missus Lady Grenspell's dress."

"Perhaps this is Cat's way of saying she's happy to see me." Smiling, Lottie reached into her reticule, extracting what appeared to be a small hunk of cheese that had been wrapped in a cloth. "Or perhaps she knows I've brought a treat for her."

Cat's ears twitched, and she immediately released her mouthful of silk, retreating to her bottom, her dark-brown gaze rapt.

"Would you like some cheese, Cat?" Lottie asked.

The dog barked.

"Then you must have manners," Lottie informed the spaniel.

Brandon felt a keen kinship with the dog in that moment. He wondered if he watched her with the same longing expression of undivided adoration. Likely so.

Lottie gave Cat a small bite of cheese, which the dog didn't even bother to chew. Then she turned to Pandy. "Would you like to give Cat some cheese as well?"

"Oh yes!" Pandy grinned. "Please."

Manners? Brandon was astounded. Perhaps some of Miss Bennington's edicts had worn off on the child after all, despite the furniture climbing.

"Here you are." Lottie placed the remainder of the cheese in his daughter's outstretched hand. "But you must command her first. Tell her to sit. Let her know that you are in charge and she must behave."

Pandy's fingers closed around the cheese, and she turned her attention to Cat, who had risen at the first bite of cheese, her entire body wiggling with the movement of her tail. "Are you bein' have?"

"Behaving," he corrected gently. "The word is *behaving*, Pandy girl."

"Sit, Cat," Pandy ordered the dog.

Miraculously, Cat sat, eyes firmly pinned to Pandy's hand and the promise of more cheese.

"Good Cat," his daughter praised, then opened her fingers, allowing the cheese to fall.

The spaniel caught it effortlessly and swallowed it down, licking her chops.

"Excellent work, Pandy," Lottie said, smiling down at her. "You see? You can persuade Cat to learn her manners by offering her a reward."

"What is my reward for displaying manners?" he couldn't resist asking, clasping his hands behind his back to keep from reaching for her.

Lottie smiled at him, and it was as if he'd been hit in the gut, the force of it. "I'm afraid I'm out of cheese, and besides, I'm not certain I would call you mannerly."

She wasn't wrong there. He wasn't the politest fellow in the world.

"Oh, but I would beg to differ," he countered. "I have been working quite hard on being a gentleman. I will accept all forms of bribery from you, regardless of whether it involves cheese."

"What's briarby?" Pandy asked, her nose crinkling as she struggled to repeat the word.

"Bribery, Pandy girl," Brandon and Lottie corrected in unison.

Their gazes met and held, a becoming tinge of pink creeping over Lottie's copper-dusted cheeks.

Her affection for his daughter was plain. And he loved her for it.

"Bribery," Pandy repeated, slowly dragging out the syllables.

"There you have it," he said, tearing his eyes from Lottie and smiling down at his daughter.

"But what's it mean?" she wanted to know next, curious poppet that she was.

"It means persuading someone to do something you want them to do by offering them something they dearly love in return," Lottie answered for him. "Such as persuading Cat to sit by offering her cheese."

"What do you love, Papa?" Pandy asked him, looking at him with wide eyes so like his own. "So's I can ribe you."

"*B*ribe," Lottie corrected gently.

Surely it was wrong to teach an impressionable child how to bribe someone, he thought, trying not to laugh.

"You needn't bribe me," he told his daughter. "You've already managed to twist me around your pinkie and do your bidding."

She shook her head stubbornly. "Not true."

"No? How so?"

"You didn't let me put a dress on Cat."

She wasn't wrong. Given the hound's penchant for eating fabric, he'd deemed it ill-advised to do so.

A noise stole from Lottie, and he glanced back at her to find her attempting to suppress her laughter and failing. *God*, she was beautiful when she was amused. She was beautiful always, actually. But her smile. the husky sound of her chuckle, the way her sky-blue eyes danced with levity—it was almost more than a man could endure.

He wanted to kiss her.

But, of course, he couldn't do that. Not in front of Pandy.

"I pray you can forgive me, Pandy girl," he said solemnly. "However, I think it was a reasonable enough denial, since Cat likes to make dresses her supper."

"It wasn't suppertime," Pandy pouted.

He sighed. "You know what I mean, dearest. Now, enough

talk of bribery. It looks as if the rain is holding off. Why don't we all take a stroll about the gardens? Unless Lady Grenfell objects?" He glanced at Lottie, waiting.

"Some fresh air would be just the thing."

"Hope Cat don't find no more pig trotters," Pandy grumbled.

Lottie raised an eyebrow, giving him a searching glance, and Brandon launched into his tale of the infamous rotten trotter. By the time he was done, tears of laughter were sparkling in the corners of her eyes, they were crunching down the gravel path past blooming roses, and he didn't think he'd ever known a moment of such complete and utter happiness in all his life.

CHAPTER 18

Lottie woke to the early traces of dawn being painted across the London sky. A heavy, masculine arm was wrapped around her waist, and the hot brand of a strong chest was at her back. Beneath the counterpane, she was naked. And there was no mistaking the rigid length prodding the cleft of her buttocks.

It took her a moment to blink the slumber from her eyes and recognize her surroundings. She was in Brandon's bedroom at his love nest in St John's Wood, where they had decamped for dinner following an afternoon with Pandy and Cat.

Against her better judgment, she had accepted his invitation.

And against all ration and reason, she had allowed him to take her hand and lead her to this room where he had systematically stripped her bare and made slow, sensual, deliberate love to her. Not just once, but twice.

The hand that had been splayed over her stomach shifted, gliding upward to land on her breast. She glanced down at his hand, taking a moment to admire the long, elegant fingers, the signet ring he wore on his pinkie, the smattering of dark hair on his skin, so very masculine, so much larger than her own.

His hand shifted, his thumb grazing over her already hard nipple, which was separated from his touch only by two thin layers of bedclothes. Her breath caught, sensation pulsing to life. She wanted him again.

But she would not give in, she told herself. She would roll away from him gently to keep from waking him. And then she would slip from the bed and gather her garments, dressing in the semi-light before he rose. Before he made her forget all the reasons she must not linger with him. Why she must not continue sharing his bed. Why she must not allow the tender feelings threatening to blossom like a summer rose.

His thumb stroked over her nipple again, and all her stern warnings to herself fled. Lips fluttered over her nape, then found their way to her shoulder. He was awake. The state of his cock and those teasing caresses to her nipple ought to have told her so.

"Good morning, Venus."

His voice was a low, delicious rasp. She wanted to hear it every morning. Wanted to fall asleep to it as she had last night.

"Good morning," she said carefully, reminding herself that what she wanted and what she needed to do were two entirely different things.

"I recognize that tone." He nipped the side of her throat.

"What tone?" Despite herself, she craned her neck, giving him more space to tantalize her.

He kissed her ear. "The one that says you are already thinking of leaving me."

"Already? I spent the night here. As it is, poor John Coachman has likely spent a very uncomfortable evening in the alleyway behind your house."

"I sent him home with instructions to return at dawn. He'll not have passed the night without the comfort of his own bed."

He sounded pleased with himself. She'd had no notion he had been so high-handed.

Lottie cast an arch glance in his direction, trying to summon outrage and finding it difficult indeed. "Sure of yourself, weren't you?"

He smiled, looking not at all slumberous, but rather like a big, menacing jungle cat stalking his prey. "I reckon I was rather confident I might persuade you to remain."

His confidence hadn't been misplaced either. For he had convinced her with ease. A few expert kisses, a few knowing caresses, and she had been clay ready to be molded in his hands. He had found a place on her inner elbow that was absurdly sensitive. When he kissed her there, it was impossible to remember her name. It was silly, and yet it was true. Languid warmth pooled between her thighs at the reminder of his mouth roaming hungrily over her body the night before.

She tried to banish the needy sensation, and yet it lingered, not helped by his body pressed to hers, his cock prodding her bottom, his scent tangled around her.

"You persuaded me well enough," she allowed. "But now, I truly must go. I dare not linger and risk discovery."

"Or," he said, drawing out the lone word as he kissed her spine, "you could remain with me for a few moments more. What could be the harm?"

The harm could be significant. To both of them, of course. He had to marry. She wished to hold her head high in polite society. Her affairs had always been kept private. One needed to attend to propriety in such matters, or at least observe the pretense.

"I don't dare," she said, but there was precious little protest in her voice or in her body.

He kissed lower and then moved, rolling her to her back as he glided beneath the covers. Kisses rained over her breasts, down her stomach, to her navel. How novel, not being able to see him, only to *feel* his mouth whispering over her bare skin. She was even wetter now, curse the man. But then his lips landed there, at the apex of her thighs, and he kissed her aching clitoris before taking her into his mouth and suckling.

Perhaps a few minutes more, then.

She arched her back, a gusty sigh leaving her as she surrendered to pleasure, legs widening to accommodate his broad shoulders as he wedged himself more firmly between her thighs. Her eyes fluttered closed as his tongue swirled over her, followed by the nip of his teeth. She cried out, bowing from the bed, grasping twin handfuls of the bedclothes.

How could she already be so far gone, on the edge of reaching her pinnacle? It defied reason. He'd had her up half the night satisfying her, wearing them both out until they had fallen into a sated slumber together.

He lapped at her languorously now, as if he had all morning to lazily bring her to her peak. She writhed beneath him, eager, needing more. And when his tongue sank inside her, she hooked her knee over his shoulder, crying out his name.

So close.

She was so close.

He strummed his thumb over her pearl, playing her as if he were a maestro and she his instrument, knowing just where to touch, how much pressure, the perfect pace as he dipped his tongue into her.

She couldn't withstand another second. Her crescendo burst over her like the sun appearing abruptly after a summer storm. She quaked beneath him, hips pumping, seeking, as he pleasured her to near madness. When the last ripple of bliss had been wrung from her, he lowered her leg gently and emerged from beneath the bedclothes, his mouth dark and glistening.

She was still struggling to catch her breath, thinking him the most handsome man she'd ever beheld when he spoke.

"Marry me."

Her heart was yet pounding in her ears from the force of her orgasm. She was sure she had misheard him.

"I beg your pardon?" she managed weakly.

His emerald gaze locked on hers, his hair tousled and falling at a rakish angle over his brow. "Marry me, Lottie."

And just like that, the pleasure drained away like used bathwater from a tub.

She sat up, the bedclothes falling to her lap, her hair a wild tangle that would have to be thoroughly brushed and combed out, but that was a worry for later. "You cannot be serious."

But he wasn't smiling, propping himself up on a forearm, unmoving and unrelenting. "I am being serious. Deadly so."

Lottie stared at him, uncertain of what she should say, her chest tightening, her foolish heart rejoicing. Something deep inside her said this was what she wanted—a husband, a family, Brandon and Pandy. But that was a lie, she reminded herself firmly. That was what the old Lottie would have wanted, the Lottie who had existed before Grenfell. The Lottie who had been naïve and trusting, who had worn her heart on her sleeve. And it had all been for naught.

"You know I cannot," she told him. "I'll never marry again."

Brandon's nostrils flared in a rare show of ire. "I'm not him. You understand that, do you not?"

The vehemence in his tone startled her.

She drew the bedclothes over her breasts, feeling exposed to him in a way that had nothing to do with her own nudity, and yet the act felt like a comfort, however small. "Of course I am aware of who and what you are. Good heavens, do you think that makes it any better? You are a bigger rakehell than Grenfell ever was."

It was the truth. Grenfell had been a philanderer, but his conquests had been few rather than legion. His paramours had been lasting. He'd only had four during the course of their marriage that she'd known of, each one a dagger in her heart.

Brandon's jaw was as tense as she'd ever seen it. Naked and powerful, the bedclothes pooled at his waist, he straightened his spine. "I am nothing like that bastard, Lottie, and you know it."

Part of her said he was different from her husband. And the other part of her said he was worse—he was beautiful where Grenfell had been harsh-looking though compelling. Brandon had a rumored phalanx of conquests. Grenfell had fallen in love with few by comparison.

And yet, there was the side of Brandon that had melted her inner ice—the doting father who patiently listened to Pandy and tended to Cat. The handsome lover who always attended to her pleasure first instead of assuaging his own lust. The man who treated her opinions as if they were of value, who made her laugh with his dramatics, who reiterated tales about rotten pig trotters.

She was a torn mess of head and heart, common sense and emotion. She didn't know which part of herself she ought to trust more. She was astonished to realize she *wanted* to believe Brandon was earnest in his proposal. And yet, she also knew he made it out of necessity rather than as a man who was in love with her, one who wanted to marry her, who needed her not just in his bed, but by his side.

It would never work.

He needed a wife, any wife, and he had clearly decided that she would do for convenience's sake.

She shook her head. "Brandon, we've been through this before. A marriage between the two of us cannot—*will not*—happen."

He flicked the hair from his brow, studying her with an intensity that was as disconcerting as it was rousing. "It seems a sensible enough solution to me. We are well suited to each other. Why do you refuse me?"

If only she could render herself impervious to him. To his charm, his masculine beauty, to his wicked seduction. Well. Grenfell had taught her rather a great deal about how to feign invulnerability.

She eyed Brandon calmly. "It seems like a terrible idea, which is why I've already told you that I have no intention of wedding anyone."

He resembled nothing so much as a young lad who had just been informed that he could no longer have his favorite toy.

"Why?" he repeated, sounding hurt.

She swallowed against an unwanted rush of sentiment. "There are many reasons."

He took her hand in his, lacing his fingers through hers. "Tell me them."

The gesture shook her. She wanted to tug her hand away, and yet she found herself oddly reluctant to do so, to sever the contact.

Lottie bit her lip, summoning her reserve. "You won't change my mind."

He brought her hand to his lips for a fervent kiss. "I have better means of persuasion than words."

She knew. Oh, how she knew. Had he not just demonstrated them, after all? And still, her body stirred at the sensual intent in his green eyes. But Lottie also was cognizant of the fact that she needed to remain stalwart. To not allow the protective walls she'd rebuilt around herself to crumble.

Suddenly, it occurred to her that perhaps he thought he could wield pleasure against her as a means of persuasion. Heavens, he likely thought her little better than Cat being swayed by a lump of warm cheese.

She tugged her hand away. "You can't bed me into marrying you, Brandon."

He shrugged. "Perhaps not. Or perhaps I can."

Her eyes narrowed. "There is no *perhaps*, you rogue. Nothing you can do shall alter my opinion on the matter."

He tossed the bedclothes away. "Don't marry me, then. I'll marry Lady Lavinia and breed her until she gives me an heir and a spare."

His words were cold. Cutting. But it wasn't just that. They burrowed beneath her skin. Found a tender, raw place inside Lottie she'd no longer believed was vulnerable. For a moment, it felt as if her very breath were frozen in her lungs.

Oh dear God.

When had she come to care for him so deeply? When had she so thoroughly devastated her own rule that she must never develop feelings for a lover?

She tried not to look at Brandon, but it was impossible. He was so virile, so potent, so beautifully formed, all lean muscle and masculine strength.

"You *should* marry her," she forced herself to say, injecting a contrived lack of concern into her voice. "Lady Lavinia would make a perfect duchess, and I'm certain she would bear you all the children you require."

All the sweet languor from their earlier lovemaking had fled, chased by the grim reality that their continued association was not just unwise, but impossible. She was losing the jagged shards of her heart to Brandon, and she could not bear to suffer beneath the agony of a one-sided marriage again. He'd not spoken a word of tender sentiment. *Marry me*, he said, as if it were as simple as blinking her eyes.

No, she couldn't do that. And she couldn't remain here either. The sun drew higher in the sky by the moment. She threw down the bedclothes and slipped from the bed, cool morning air drifting around her as she hastily retrieved her flung garments from the night before.

"I don't want to marry Lady Lavinia," he said quietly from the bed.

A part of her rejoiced, but she tamped it ruthlessly down.

"She is young and beautiful," she said, priding herself for the coolness in her voice as she discovered her drawers hanging from the edge of a table. "She is everything you would want or need in a bride. All your problems will be solved."

Lottie snatched up the drawers and stuffed her right leg inside.

"What are you doing?" he wanted to know, his voice a low, dark growl as the bedclothes rustled, indicating he was getting up.

Don't look at him, she told herself. *Do not look.*

"Dressing so that I can leave. What does it look like?"

She kept her back to him as she muttered the question, slipping her left leg into the other half of the garment and hastily gliding it up over her knees, thighs, and hips.

"It looks like I've angered you with my own stupidity."

His voice was low. And close.

Too close.

But Lottie wasn't quick enough. Long arms banded around her waist and hauled her into a hard chest. His bare skin against hers was all she required for that infernal yearning to start building deep within her once more.

"Brandon, let me go," she gritted, her hands falling on his arms in an attempt to extricate herself.

But the action was futile. He was too strong. And besides, when her hands had been placed over the inviting warmth of his forearms, her ability to resist him eroded precipitously. His chest was a brand at her back, and his lips, when they grazed over her ear in a tender kiss, sent a frisson down her spine.

"Please, Venus."

She huffed a sigh, hating her heart for the way it reacted to his ridiculous pet name for her. "I've told you again and again, I'm no goddess. I'm a widow who is thirty years old. I'm bitter and jaded, and the only thing I want from a man is the pleasure he can give me, not his name."

But even as she made the protestation, it fell weakly from her. Brandon's mouth was on her throat now, kissing softly. Her resistance was melting faster than a candle thrown into a blazing fire.

He lifted his head, storms swirling in his eyes. "I'm three-and-thirty, which makes me three years your senior. I'm also bitter and jaded, and until recently, the only thing I wanted from a woman was the pleasure she could give me. But that has changed. Perhaps *I've* even changed."

No, no, no. This was not what she wanted to hear. She didn't want tender kisses or sweet protestations. She didn't want him to stay her. She wanted him to let her flee.

"Brandon."

"Lottie."

Another sigh left her, so deep this time that the undersides of her breasts grazed his arms. "You know what I'm telling you. What do you have to gain by keeping me here? You'll not persuade me to marry you."

"Because you're running from me, damn you, and I don't accept that." His words were urgent, practically vibrating with undeniable feeling that caused an ache deep inside her. "I've thoroughly enjoyed your company these last few weeks."

"You've enjoyed my body," she countered grimly. "You'll find another woman to warm your bed with ease. Never fear."

"Yes, but she won't be you, damn it."

He spun her about suddenly so that she faced him, trapped in the circle of his arms, her bare breasts pinned to him, her nipples crushed into a wall of muscle, her hands settling on his broad shoulders. But it was not his finely honed body alone that made a curious tingling pass through her. Rather, it was the way he was looking down at her, such raw tenderness in his eyes, in the relaxed lines of his countenance.

She swallowed hard, trying not to think about Brandon with another woman as he inevitably would be—future lovers, his bride, sharing his bed, knowing him as intimately as she did. How she loathed the notion.

"Whomever you choose as your wife," Lottie forced out, "she will be better than me."

He shook his head, ever stubborn, his jaw tightening. "No one can be better than you."

Was that his charm talking? He couldn't truly believe that no other woman would make him a better wife. She was too bitter, too old. She had known too much of the disappointments life inevitably had in store, and she didn't want any more.

"Your grandmother is holding your feet to the fire with an impending marriage, else you'll lose Wingfield Hall," she continued, determined to reason with him. "Surely you cannot believe she would be satisfied with you marrying a jaded widow of my advanced age, and one with a noted reputation for taking lovers of her own."

"She cannot choose my bride," he vowed. "I would sooner see my odious cousin walk away with the estate."

"If he did that, there would be no reason for you to wed," she pointed out quietly.

"But why must *I* settle?" His emerald gaze searched hers, seeking answers she didn't want to give. "Why can I not have the wife I desire and the estate that is rightfully mine both?"

"Spoken like a man," she said. "A duke who has never known a moment of being denied what he wanted, when he wanted it. I'm not an estate, Brandon. I'm a woman. You cannot keep me. Your spoiled tantrums shan't work on me."

He worked his jaw some more. "So you mean to tell me that everything we've shared has meant less than nothing to you? Is that what you expect me to believe? That you only wanted me for my cock?"

She bit her lip at his crudeness, unsure of what to say.

They were already hurting each other, and she hated it.

"Don't you see?" She shook her head. "This is what I seek to avoid."

"What?" he asked. "Feeling? I hate to tell you, darling, but life is all about feeling. You cannot exist for a second on this earth without feeling something. It's a sheer impossibility that defies all logic and reason."

"Perhaps I'm mad, then. But I should like to keep myself free of all such encumbrance."

"You think emotion an encumbrance?"

She closed her eyes as hot tears stung them. "I think it a mistake. A weapon that can be wielded against me. I'll not allow it to happen. Not ever again." Her voice was shaking, her hands trembling.

"I hate that bastard for hurting you," he growled.

Lottie opened her eyes, still trying to keep those foolish tears where they belonged. "Neither of us can change the past. It's made me who I am. I'm sorry, but this is all I can give you."

"You refuse to marry me," he repeated, his mouth drawn in a taut, harsh line.

"It's for the best. I vowed I would never marry again, and I meant it."

"What if you're carrying my child?"

Her heart tripped over itself. Not that she hadn't thought of the possibility, but it had seemed so very farfetched until he'd uttered it aloud. But she didn't dare allow him to see the effect it had upon her.

She raised a brow, martialing her countenance into one of complete serenity. "Then I'm carrying your child."

His jaw tensed. "Lottie."

"Brandon, I'm likely barren," she said quietly. "There was no issue in the years of my marriage to Grenfell."

"It doesn't matter to me if you are."

"But it should. You'll want an heir, surely."

"I would far prefer to have you."

Those stupid tears pricked her eyes again, but this time, it wasn't sorrow for herself she felt. It was an incredible depth of emotion for the man holding her in his arms as if she were precious to him. As if he couldn't bear to part from her. It was sadness over what might have been, but what could never be.

"You can't have me," she told him softly, painfully. "Find a suitable bride. You're running out of time."

They stared at each other, at an impasse.

And then he released her so abruptly she swayed on her

feet, bereft without his heat and his strength. She had finally convinced him to surrender to defeat. She felt no joy in knowing she had won this particular battle. There was only a tremendous sense of mourning.

Without uttering another word, Brandon helped her to dress.

Lottie waited until she was in her carriage, John Coachman taking her home, before she allowed herself to weep.

CHAPTER 19

Kidnapping was out of the question.

Forcing her to marry him by causing a scandal was as well.

Persuading her with lovemaking hadn't worked.

No amount of reason or pleading his cause had made her waver from her determination to remain unwed.

Brandon faced a dearth of time and options. Who knew that the business of convincing a woman to marry him would be so bloody difficult?

"You're looking Friday-faced," King observed shrewdly, breaking through his ruminations.

They were playing billiards, which was ordinarily a game Brandon thoroughly enjoyed. However, he had been preoccupied by thoughts of Lottie, and he had been soundly trounced twice already.

"I'm feeling Friday-faced as well," he said, grim. "I don't suppose you've one of your potions handy, do you?"

The urge for oblivion was strong.

King grinned, aiming his cue stick for another shot. "Not

today, I'm afraid. All I have is brandy and Scotch whisky. Would you care for a dram of either?"

"To hell with a dram. I'll likely need the whole damned bottle," he grumbled, gripping his cue stick tightly.

"That bad, is it? I wondered why you were losing so pathetically."

He glared at his friend. "I'd hardly call it pathetic. Perhaps I was being charitable, allowing you a rare victory."

King chortled. "Ha! Charitable. Tell me another, if you please. This billiards game is deadly dull, and I'm in need of amusement."

Brandon sighed. "I have a problem."

"I know." King gestured at him airily. "Only just look at that waistcoat."

Frowning, he glanced down at the satin waistcoat he was wearing. "What's wrong with it?"

"It's purple."

"And?"

King shuddered. "And it looks like something more suited to a Georgian chap than a modern gentleman."

"Pandy chose the color for me," he admitted.

He had taken her shopping, and she had found a bolt of satin at his tailor's that had struck her fancy.

"Ah, a child is responsible for that monstrosity," King said. "I feel ever so much better now."

Brandon scowled. "Why do I like you?"

His friend grinned. "I haven't an inkling."

"That makes two of us," he grumbled.

"Will you take your turn, or are you intending to glower at me for the rest of the evening?" King wanted to know.

Blast.

He hadn't been paying attention to the game.

"Glowering at you might yield a better result," he pointed out. "It looks as if I'm about to lose to you for a third time."

"It does indeed." King made no effort to hide his glee. "I'll not lie. Defeating you at billiards is one of my favorite pastimes."

"You're only winning because I'm too distracted," he said, taking aim.

"And what are you distracted about? Your impending nuptials? You never did say who you'd settled upon as a bride. Whitby and I have a bet, and the only thing better than triumphing over you at billiards would be collecting fifty pounds from him."

Brandon's shot was woefully amiss. "You're betting over me, now? *Et tu, Brute?*" He straightened to his full height. "Who did you choose?"

"Lady Lavinia," King said. "Whitby was persuaded that it's Lady Grenfell. Didn't think widows were to your taste, however."

He swallowed hard against a rush of longing at the mentioning of Lottie. "One widow in particular."

"Oh Christ." King stared at him. "Never say you've fallen under the Countess of Grenfell's spell."

Her spell? *Damn it.* Accurate words. She had ensorcelled him quite neatly, and he hadn't even realized it until it had been too late.

"I'm not sure I like the way you've phrased that, King."

"How else to phrase it?" King shrugged. "It's been said she has a magical—"

"Finish that sentence, and I'll break this cue stick over your bloody head," he bit out, interrupting before his friend said something they would both regret. "That's the woman I love that you're talking about."

He hadn't meant to blurt it out like that, and he felt his ears and neck growing hot beneath his friend's steady regard.

King whistled, propping his hip against the billiards table and leaning on his cue stick. "The mighty Duke of Brandon, felled by a feminine sword. I never thought I'd live to see the day our fearless leader would find himself at the mercy of any woman, let alone Lottie Grenfell. When is the wedding, old chap?"

"That's the problem," he ground out, his grim mood returning, chasing his ire. "There isn't going to be one."

"But you need to marry to appease your grandmother."

"Yes."

"And you're—" King paused, making an exaggerated moue of distaste before resuming "—in love."

He raised a brow. "Yes."

"Vomitus."

"King," he cautioned. "You are sorely testing both my patience for you and the previously formidable bonds of our friendship."

"The very thought of marriage makes me queasy," King said with an unapologetic shrug. "I cannot help it."

"Try harder to control yourself."

King sighed. "I shall try, on account of our old and treasured friendship. However, I don't understand. You're in love with Lady Grenfell, you need to marry with all haste, and yet you're not marrying the countess. Why the devil not? It sounds as if you've discovered the answer to our Wingfield Hall problem."

"Because she won't marry me."

King's brows rose. "She won't marry you?"

"No. That bastard Grenfell hurt her badly, and she's vowed never to wed again because of it."

"Well, hell."

He inclined his head. "Precisely."

"Have you considered kidnapping her?" King asked.

"Kingham."

"It was a joke," his friend protested quite unconvincingly.

"Have you thought about blackmail or bribery? Or perhaps slipping something into her wine…"

"Are you suggesting I drug the woman I love to dupe her into marrying me?"

"Odd how neither blackmail nor bribery elicited as strong a response," King observed.

"You are a Machiavellian menace," he said without heat.

His friend grinned. "I pride myself upon it. You've told her you love her already, so it isn't as if you could make inroads that way."

"I haven't, actually."

"There you are." King made a dramatic flourish in the air. "Your problem is solved. Run along and tell the lady that you love her. Women apparently adore that sort of claptrap."

He had considered revealing his feelings to her. But the notion terrified him. Her rejection of his proposals was one thing, but if she were to reject his love altogether… No, he wouldn't even contemplate it. There was also the matter of his ineptitude at knowing how to build a proper relationship with a woman, one that relied on love and trust rather than base lust.

"I haven't the slightest idea of how to properly make such a revelation," he admitted.

King scoffed. "Well, don't look to me for advice. I've never been in love."

His claim had Brandon pinning him with a pointed look. "Not even with Miss Townsend?"

King's expression hardened. "Especially not with her."

Brandon didn't believe him for a moment. "If you say so."

"I do." A muscle twitched in King's jaw. "Ask a woman how you ought to proceed."

"The only woman I know well enough to ask is Lottie," he said dejectedly, for conversing with any of his past paramours on the matter of securing a wife was decidedly *de trop*. "Or Pandy."

King winced. "Yes, but she's a child, and she approved of that godforsaken waistcoat. Is there no one else?"

Brandon thought for a moment. "Grandmother, I suppose."

"There you have it." King beamed. "Ask your grandmother. I've no doubt she'll be pleased to see you married off and obeying her edict. Two birds, one stone, et cetera."

It occurred to him then, with sudden, painful, almost dizzying clarity, that it wasn't advice he needed to seek from his grandmother. Rather, it was surrender.

Because he'd spent the last few weeks determined to keep from losing Wingfield Hall, only to realize what mattered most. Not an estate. Not funds. Not the Society. But Lottie and Pandy. They were who mattered to Brandon more than anyone and anything else in all the world.

But if he wanted to win Lottie's hand, he was going to have to prove that to her.

∼

"I'm afraid that I don't understand, Brandon."

He was seated opposite his grandmother in her opulent drawing room, which was laden with so many *objets d'art*, plants, and pieces of furniture that it made a man feel as if he were suffocating just looking at all the *bric-à-brac*. He tried to ignore the three-foot-tall monk sculpture that was eyeing him steadily at his left and the cloying fronds of a potted palm at his right.

"You may give Wingfield Hall to Horrible Horace," he repeated, more than aware that he was being churlish.

He couldn't help it. He'd never liked the oafish clodpoll. He liked him even less now. Somehow, Brandon would have to make amends to his friends for the loss of Wingfield Hall. If he had to dig into his own coffers to do so, he would. Because he refused to marry anyone but Lottie. And she didn't seem any more inclined to wed him now than she had when he had first proposed.

"That is a most unkind sobriquet," his grandmother chastised, frowning as she stroked the pug curled in her lap.

Idly, he wondered how many dogs Grandmother had collected. He'd counted no fewer than eight during his brief call already.

"It is an accurate one," he pointed out, unapologetic.

"You've chosen not to marry, then?" she asked in a tone that dripped with disapproval.

"On the contrary. I intend to marry. However, the lady in question is reluctant to wed. I very much doubt I'll be able to persuade her to marry me in less than a month's time. Therefore, I felt it pertinent to inform you."

It pained him to admit it. Failure was a novel sensation for Brandon. But he could swallow his pride. He could forfeit that which was rightfully his. He could survive the loss of Wingfield Hall.

What he couldn't fathom was losing Lottie.

"Is the lady's reluctance regarding the institution of marriage in general or is it down to marrying you in particular, Brandon?" Grandmother wanted to know.

"Marriage in general, I believe. Having endured an unhappy union, she is deeply hesitant to entrust herself to a marriage again."

The acknowledgment was not without an accompanying surge of fury for Grenfell, that blighter. The man had been too selfish and stupid to appreciate her. Worse, he had hurt her. And Brandon couldn't lie—he absolutely despised that the bastard had broken her heart.

"A widow," Grandmother said, raising a winged silvery brow.

"The Countess of Grenfell," he confirmed.

"That explains the lady's reticence." Grandmother harrumphed, thumping her cane for emphasis. "The earl was a horse's ass."

Brandon's lips twitched at her unexpectedly blunt pronouncement. "On that, we are in agreement, madam."

"Why Lady Grenfell?" Grandmother asked shrewdly, studying him in a way that made Brandon want to shift in his uncomfortable chair.

Something was tickling his right ear, and he realized it was a bloody palm frond. He felt a nudge at his foot and looked down to find another pug nosing at his boot.

"She cares for Pandy. She laughs at Cat's antics. She looks at me, and it's as if all the world stops around us." He did squirm in his chair then, realizing he sounded maudlin, and cleared his throat. "And many other reasons as well."

"Do you love her?" she asked quietly.

"Yes," he admitted. "I do. I'm quite hopelessly, disgustingly besotted with the woman, and there is no one I want to spend the rest of my life with other than her."

Grandmother's stern mouth turned upward into a small smile. "Do you know who else was a horse's ass, Brandon?"

"Myself, on innumerable occasions," he admitted wryly, preparing himself for a richly deserved scold.

Christ knew he had earned his rakish reputation. He wasn't proud of it now, but he wasn't precisely ashamed either. His past had made him the man he was, and that man was a far cry from the wild, reckless youth he'd once been.

"I shan't argue with you on that account," Grandmother said. "However, there is a greater horse's ass I am thinking of presently, and your admittedly ill-advised foibles pale in comparison to his sins."

Brandon clenched his jaw. "I believe I know to whom you refer."

"Your father," his grandmother confirmed. "He was incapable of knowing the treasure he held in his grasp. He was arrogant and cold, and his first and only concern was for himself. Your mother fell in love with him when she was a girl newly come out. He wanted her for her youthful beauty and family fortune, of course. I knew it then, for our bloodlines yet remain too close to the stink of trade. Watching her give her heart to a man so undeserving, one who slowly, day by day, crushed not just her love for him, but also her spirit, was one of the most painful tragedies I have witnessed."

Brandon swallowed against a rush of emotion and grief. His memories of his mother were precious but indistinct. Her perfume, her smile, her arms wrapped around him, soothing him after he had fallen off a horse once, just before his father had stormed into the room, telling him that men didn't cry like puling girls. They had argued that day, his mother's voice rising until there had been the stinging sound of a slap. Brandon had hidden his face in his mother's voluminous skirts, and he'd been too afraid to look.

But he had known. Even as a lad, he'd understood that his father was a violent brute. He wondered if his grandmother knew the full extent of his sire's viciousness.

"He did her violence," he said hoarsely. "Did you know it?"

His grandmother's nostrils flared. "I suspected. Diana would never confirm when I asked her. She hid a great deal from me, some of which I only learned after her death. It is one of my greatest regrets that I didn't try harder to dissuade her from marrying Brandon."

His gut clenched. He hadn't allowed himself to think about his mother or what she had endured at the brutal hands of his sire for some time now. He wished that he had been older, stronger. That he might have protected her instead of her protecting him.

"I always hated him," he managed past the emotion tightening his throat. "He was cruel and he was a bully, but it wasn't until the day I heard him slap her that I realized the true depths of his cruelty."

He understood now why his father had been so hell-bent upon keeping him away from his mother's family for so many years, the void that had been driven between them.

"He was a vile man," Grandmother agreed. "And I feared he had made you in his mold."

"Never," he vowed. "I am nothing like him. I would not raise my hand against a woman."

She nodded, still stroking the sleeping pug in her lap. "I can see that now. Fortunately, you've far more of my darling Diana in you than you do of your father. I think that becoming a father yourself has brought out the very best in you, Brandon."

The pug at his feet licked his boots, so he bent down and offered the fellow a scratch between the ears before straightening in his seat. "Thank you for bringing her to me that day."

She gave him a pointed look. "I trust there are no opera singers beneath your roof now?"

He winced. "No."

Grandmother nodded. "Good. Is there something else you would like to tell me? Anything about Wingfield Hall, perchance?"

The last thing he wanted to do was reveal the truth of Wingfield Hall to her. But there was freedom in honesty, and if the last few weeks had taught him anything, it was that he was ready to relinquish his position as the unofficial leader of the Wicked Dukes Society.

"I suppose you know about the Society," he said.

"As I told you before, I know something of it from those dreadful whispers, though I don't wish to know all." His grandmother frowned. "I also know what you've been doing with the funds you earn from it."

"How?" he asked.

She gave him a secretive smile. "I have my ways. I don't approve of what you've been doing beneath my nose, mind you." She punctuated her words with a regal thump of her cane.

"Of course not." The pug at his feet placed his front paws on Brandon's knee, gazing up at him adoringly, his tongue lolling. "I must beg your forgiveness."

"Yes," his grandmother said archly. "You must. However, I have decided to reconsider my decision concerning Wingfield Hall and your cousin Horace."

"You have?"

She nodded, a faint smile reappearing. "I have. I'll be giving Wingfield Hall to you instead of your cousin Horace, and I'll begin the process at once. It's past time I did so, really. I have been holding on to it as if your grandfather were still there, but returning to Wingfield Hall reminded me that he isn't, and the memories will always remain in my heart."

He wasn't certain how to feel about her revelation. He had come here, having already accepted that Wingfield Hall would no longer be his.

"Did you love my grandfather?" he asked, though he suspected he already knew the answer.

"Very much so." Grandmother sniffed, her green eyes sparkling with unshed tears. "Now then, I find myself weary and in need of a nap. Thank you for paying me a call, Brandon. I hope you might do so again soon, and you may as well bring young Pandora with you."

The invitation made him smile. "Of course. I think Pandy would like that."

She would also adore the overfilled drawing room—the chance to see and touch and potentially knock over so many objects would be a potent lure.

"The mutt, however," his grandmother warned sharply, "must remain. She isn't civilized enough to meet my beloved pugs. I'm still suffering nightmares about the scent of that wretched trotter."

He chuckled. "As you like."

"And Brandon?"

He gave the pug a pat on the head. "Yes?"

"I wish you luck with Lady Grenfell."

He inclined his head. "Thank you."

He feared he was going to need it.

CHAPTER 20

"You have a caller, my lady."

Lottie started at the unexpected pronouncement of her butler. For a moment, her heart seized. Had Brandon come? They had not spoken since they had parted in silence at dawn days ago. He hadn't sent her a missive, nor had he appeared at her house. She had supposed, at first, that he was angry with her for refusing his proposal of marriage yet again. As time continued to pass, however, she had begun to fear that he had decided to sever their association. That he was indeed courting Lady Lavinia as she had told him he ought.

The butler approached her with a silver salver bearing a calling card, which was decidedly not Brandon's ordinary mode of announcing himself. She retrieved the card, and no, it was not Brandon who was awaiting her. Rather, it was his august grandmother. She knew of the widowed Mrs. Carrington-Smythe, but they had never spoken.

Lottie frowned, wondering what the woman could possibly want from her. "See her in, if you please," she directed her butler, deciding it would be too impolite to refuse Mrs. Carrington-Smythe, even if Lottie harbored some misgivings about the reason for that lady's call. "And send in a tray of tea as well."

Brandon's grandmother crossed the threshold with the grace of any queen, though she relied heavily upon a gilt-handled cane, thanks to her arthritic gait. She was dressed primly in black silk trimmed with navy lace, quite as if she were in mourning. She greeted Lottie with cool civility and a shrewd gaze that was the same emerald green as her grandson's.

They exchanged pleasantries and seated themselves as the tray of tea arrived. The maid had scarcely taken her leave of the room when Mrs. Carrington-Smythe spoke.

"I hope you can forgive me for paying you an unexpected call, Lady Grenfell."

Her forthrightness was unexpected, but Lottie appreciated it, nonetheless. "You need not ask forgiveness from me, Mrs. Carrington-Smythe."

Briefly, she wondered if somehow Brandon's grandmother had learned of their affair and had come to take her to task. Heavens, she hoped not. How mortifying.

Brandon's grandmother gave her a small, unreadable smile. "You needn't look so ill at ease, my dear. I haven't come here to browbeat you, but to speak with you, privately and without the potential for curious ears to overhear our discourse."

Had her worries been so easily read on her face? Apparently so.

She took a sip of her tea, fortifying herself for the unknowns that lay ahead. "I am relieved to hear it, madam. Though I do hope you might enlighten me as to what you would like to speak about."

Mrs. Carrington-Smythe inclined her silver head. "Fair enough. I've come to speak with you about Brandon."

Everything inside her seized at his name, her body tensing. "Is something amiss with His Grace?" she asked quickly, tea sloshing over the rim of her cup as she jolted, fear lacing through her.

"Brandon is well."

"Pandy?" she asked next, belatedly realizing the familiarity she displayed in referring to his daughter by her pet name.

"As far as I know, Pandora is well, as is the dreadful mongrel she insists upon calling Cat." Mrs. Carrington-Smythe shuddered.

Relief washed over her. Lottie rolled her lips inward to suppress a chuckle at the other woman's clear dislike of poor, misunderstood Cat. She was sure the rotten pig trotter experience was the source of Mrs. Carrington-Smythe's displeasure.

"That is a relief to hear," Lottie said mildly, keeping her opinion on the matter to herself.

"Do you care for Brandon?" the elder woman blurted abruptly.

Did she care for him? Of course she did. And despite her every intention to keep their relationship limited to mere physical alone. But she didn't know how to answer Mrs. Carrington-Smythe's query. It felt dangerous.

"He is a kind man," she said, evading the question as she forced a bright smile.

The other woman's green eyes narrowed upon her. "May I speak plainly, Lady Grenfell?"

Lottie clutched her tea in a tight grip. "Please, Mrs. Carrington-Smythe. I do so appreciate candor."

Brandon's grandmother nodded. "I know your husband was a rotter."

Her blunt statement took Lottie by surprise. "You'll not hear argument from me on the matter."

"Grenfell was a selfish, arrogant oaf, not unlike the last Duke of Brandon. I watched the duke break my daughter's heart and crush her spirit, and I was powerless to stop it. Even worse, he raised his hand to her. I've only just learned for certain from my grandson, though I had suspected, being no fool. I noticed a bruise on her cheek once that she'd failed to conceal properly with pearl powder, and on another occasion, I saw what looked like fingerprints beneath her sleeve."

Brandon's father had done his mother violence. Lottie's heart ached at the revelation. He hadn't spoken of his parents with her. But then, she supposed she hadn't spoken of her parents either. Her relationship with her mother and father had been cordial, but they had been more concerned with her making a good match than her happiness. She missed them, but she had never been close to them. Her relationship with her elder sister Caro was little different—their paths rarely crossed, Caro having been happily married for years, seemingly always with child, sending the odd letter here or there when it suited her.

Still, none of her family members had ever physically hurt her.

"I am so very sorry to hear that, Mrs. Carrington-Smythe," she said earnestly.

"As am I." The older woman blinked, her eyes glittering for a moment with what may have been tears before she sternly overcame them. "However, I did not relay the sordid secrets of my family's past to garner your sympathy."

"Why did you then, madam?" Lottie asked.

"Because my grandson paid me a visit this morning, and Brandon never makes morning calls. Heavens, I cannot even remember the last time he visited me of his own volition. I am always the one who must unceremoniously arrive at his town house, demanding an audience, oftentimes refused. I have become quite adept over the years at coercing his butler, Shilling, into doing my bidding, however."

Lottie wasn't at all shocked to hear that Mrs. Carrington-Smythe had managed to circumvent Brandon. The woman was formidable.

"I'm glad to hear Brandon did his familial duty in calling upon you," she offered, still perplexed.

Mrs. Carrington-Smythe's conversation was meandering along a confounding path.

"I love all my grandchildren, Lady Grenfell, but Brandon has always been especially beloved to me." Mrs. Carrington-Smythe's voice was undeniably tender now, fondness evident in the softened lines of her haughty face. "He may have been born the future Duke of Brandon, but in many ways, his life was far more difficult than the lives of his cousins. I suspect it is my affection for him that caused me to ignore the fact that he was using my family's estate to host some manner of illicit society engaged in heaven knows what sort of wickedness."

Lottie stared.

"You didn't think I knew, my dear?" Brandon's grandmother shook her head. "He didn't either until recently. But of course, I did. Though, for years I did my best to pretend as if I hadn't an inkling that Brandon has been collecting exorbitant sums from the members of polite society to attend his house parties at my estate. I may be old, but I'm not a fool."

"Of course not, Mrs. Carrington-Smythe," she agreed.

"Has he told you what he has been doing with his portion of the Society's earnings?" the older woman asked.

Yet again, Lottie found herself perplexed. "It is hardly my business, madam."

"As I thought." Brandon's grandmother nodded. "I shall tell you myself, then, my dear. Brandon has been sending his allotment of the funds to an orphanage that was important to my daughter. Quietly, anonymously, he has gifted them with nothing short of a small fortune that has provided hearty meals and new clothing and shoes—and even instruments for the children to learn to play."

The revelation warmed her heart. "How generous of him."

"He is a good man."

Emotion made Lottie's throat go tight. "Yes, he is."

"Do you love my grandson, Lady Grenfell?"

The question shocked her. She gawped at Mrs. Carrington-Smythe, uncertain of what to say.

Because the answer terrified her.

"I… Mrs. Carrington-Smythe…" she stumbled. "I don't know how to respond to such a query."

A silvery brow winged upward as shrewd emerald eyes met hers. "I think you do, Lady Grenfell. And if there is one thing that I have learned in the many years of my life, it is that love is stronger and more powerful than anything else. Be brave enough to listen to your heart, my dear." She thumped her cane and then rose from her seat slowly. "I bid you good day."

Lottie watched Brandon's grandmother leave the room in a swish of black and navy skirts, the gold head of her cane glinting in the lamplight.

And as the door to her drawing room closed, leaving Lottie alone with a cup of cooling tea, the truth that she had been stubbornly refusing to acknowledge fell upon her like an avalanche of snow sliding down a mountain slope.

Somehow, she had fallen in love with the Duke of Brandon.

What in heaven's name was she going to do about it?

BRANDON WAS at his desk in his study, perusing a letter from the director of the orphanage thanking him for the latest funds he had sent and cataloging what they would be used for, including training for apprenticeships and education efforts for the children. The muffled barks of Cat, followed by Pandy's delighted laughter and the telltale thump of her feet down the hall, punctuated the silence, making him smile. Grandmother's unexpected change of heart meant that the Society could continue hosting revelries at Wingfield Hall, and in turn, he would continue diverting funds to the orphanage. His friends would receive their portions. And all was right in his world.

All except for the glaring absence of the woman he loved.

How would he persuade her to marry him?

A knock sounded at the study door, startling him from his musings.

"Enter," he called.

Shilling opened the door. A blur of fur raced past him in the hallway behind, but to his credit, the butler didn't even flinch.

"Cat!" Pandy cried, enthusiastically racing after the spaniel. "Come back here!"

"Is Miss Pandora playing chase-chase again?" he asked Shilling, unable to keep from grinning.

"Yes, Your Grace. Miss Bennington gave Miss Pandora a break from the nursery for one quarter hour."

And his Pandy girl was using her freedom wisely.

"I see. Was there something you required of me, Shilling?"

"There is a caller to see you, Your Grace," Shilling said. "Lady Grenfell."

Lottie.

Lottie was here?

Lottie was here.

He shot from his seat as if it were fashioned of hot coals. "Send her in, if you please."

Brandon glanced down at his clothes. No stains on his shirt. His waistcoat was a staid shade of gray rather than the purple King had despaired over. His trousers were a bit wrinkled. No hope for it. He hadn't time to change. He raked a hand through his hair, hoping he was presentable. Ink smudged his fingers. *Blast.*

He extracted a handkerchief and hastily wiped them before recalling that he'd given the handkerchief to Pandy earlier, and she'd used it to wipe the white mucus from Cat's eyes when she had awoken that morning. Now he had sticky dog eye mucus *and* ink on his fingers.

"Fuck," he muttered, frantically trying to find a square of linen that was unsullied.

"I hope you don't curse like that around Pandy."

He looked up, and there she was, crossing the threshold of his study, wearing a blue afternoon dress that hugged her figure and brought out the brilliance of her eyes and hair. Blonde lace lined her decolletage and peeked from her sleeves, and she was so bloody beautiful that it was all he could do to keep from rushing to her and taking her in his arms.

Belatedly, it occurred to him that she had chastised him and that he was still holding the besmirched handkerchief like an idiot. He stuffed it into his pocket again.

"Of course I don't curse around Pandy," he said, offering her a bow. "At least, not often. To what do I owe the unexpected honor of your presence this afternoon?"

She crossed the chamber to him, not stopping until she was close enough to touch, her sweet perfume tempting him as surely as her presence did. "I've decided to call in the favor you owe me."

Brandon blinked. "The favor?"

"Yes." A hesitant, small smile curved her kissable pink lips. "The favor you owe me for the day I entertained Pandy for you. You do remember it, do you not?"

"Of course." He curled his fingers into fists at his sides to keep from touching her.

They had last parted in silence and hurt disappointment, and he didn't know where he stood with her.

"It took me a long time to settle upon the favor I most wanted to ask of you," she said softly, her dulcet voice making his cock twitch to attention.

"Is it wrong of me to hope that the favor is a lewd one?" he asked, half serious, half in jest.

She chuckled, the sound husky. "Not wrong, perhaps, but I'm afraid if you have your hopes set upon a lewd favor, you are doomed to disappointment."

Well, blast. He hoped she hadn't come armed with more lists of prospective brides.

"If you want me to consider any additional listings of debutantes I might court, I'm afraid it's a favor I cannot honor," he warned. "I'll pitch them into the fire first."

Her smile fled, and she took a deep breath, looking suddenly nervous. "It isn't that either."

"Well, what is it, then?" He didn't mean to sound impatient, but the suspense was as painful as standing before her and keeping himself from taking her into his arms.

"Your grandmother paid a call upon me earlier today."

At the mention of his grandmother, Brandon's rampant prick wilted a bit. "I cannot think why she would have done so."

"Can you not?" She tilted her head, gazing at him shrewdly with her storm-tossed-sea eyes. "I do believe she came to plead your case."

"Fucking hell," he muttered.

"Brandon, there is that dreadful language again," she chastised with mock solemnity.

"Forgive me. Thinking about Grandmother pleading anything on my behalf makes me bilious."

"Ah, your sensitive disposition," she teased.

"What did she say to you?" he blurted, needing to know.

By God, if Grandmother had done anything to ruin his chances with Lottie…

"She told me that you've been sending the funds you earn from the Society to an orphanage that was a favored cause of your mother's."

"Oh." His ears went hot at her persistent regard.

"She also told me that Grenfell was a rotter."

He inclined his head. "She's not wrong, though I would describe the bastard in far less complimentary terms."

"And she said that I should be brave enough to trust my heart," Lottie said.

Longing he was too afraid to feel licked up his spine. "She did?"

Bless his grandmother. Her advice thus far had been sound.

"She did." Lottie nodded, her dimpled chin tipping up. "I decided that she was right. For too long, I've been a coward, too afraid that I will be hurt again instead of being brave. That is why I decided upon the favor you owe me."

His breath felt as if it had seized in his chest. The tenderness in her countenance was raw and unguarded in a way he had yet to see. He couldn't help himself then. He reached for her hands, lacing their fingers together.

"What's the favor, Lottie?"

Her fingers tightened over his, her eyes searing him with twin blue flames. "I was wondering if you might ask me to marry you again."

He didn't hesitate. "Will you marry me?"

"Nothing has changed since the last time you asked me," she said. "I'm still terrified of what you make me feel. I may not be able to have your children. I can't compare to young and beautiful debutantes—"

"The devil you can't," he interrupted.

Lottie smiled. "I'm grateful you think so, but I'm well aware that I'm all too flawed and imperfect."

He brought her hands to his lips for a reverent kiss, one on each. "Have you met me? I'm the definition of flawed and imperfect."

"Then perhaps we might be flawed and imperfect together. Two jagged halves that together become one."

"Say it," he begged hoarsely. "Tell me."

"I love you," she said. "I love you, and it frightens me how much I do."

"Thank God." He tugged her into his chest, wrapping his arms around her. "I love you too, Venus."

"Brandon, I'm not a goddess." She was smiling up at him, quite disproving herself.

Because she *was* beautiful. Entrancing. Nothing short of magnificent. And she was *his*.

"Yes, you are," he told her, surrendering to the need to feel her lips beneath his and taking her mouth in a swift, fierce, all-too-brief kiss. "You're *my* goddess, damn it. And I won't hear a word otherwise. Now, give me your answer, if you please. I cannot exist another moment more without hearing it."

"I'll marry you." She cupped his cheek in one hand. "Yes, I'll marry you."

"You'll be my wife?" He was grinning at her stupidly, almost afraid to believe what he was hearing.

Because after fighting to win her for so long, her capitulation was almost painfully easy. He refused to give Grandmother all the credit for it, however. The curmudgeon would never let him hear the end of it.

"I'll be your wife," Lottie affirmed.

He lifted her from the floor and spun her in a circle, her silk skirts floating behind her like a bell. They were both breathless and laughing when he returned her to her feet, and then he covered her mouth with his and kissed this woman he loved, kissed her with all the longing and gratitude and raw emotion coursing through him. Kissed her until the door to the study burst open, and he reluctantly tore his lips from hers to find Cat and Pandy racing across the room in a cacophony of barks and girlish giggles.

"Papa! What are you doing with Missus Lady Grenspell?" Pandy demanded, out of breath from her relentless game of chase-chase.

"I'm marrying her," Brandon told his daughter, smiling down at her and ruffling her dark curls.

"Huzzah!" Pandy launched herself at them, throwing one arm around Lottie's skirts and the other around his leg.

Not to be left out, Cat joined her, bounding on her hind legs, tongue lolling as she gave an excited bark.

"Welcome to the family," Brandon told Lottie wryly above the din.

And his beautiful goddess just laughed, her eyes dancing with merriment and love. "Thank you. I do believe I've finally found the place where I belong."

CHAPTER 21

*I*t was her wedding night.

Her second wedding night, so different from her first.

This time, Lottie was not naïve and eighteen, inexperienced and woefully unprepared for the future looming before her. Instead, she was thirty, experienced, and more than that, she was prepared for the life awaiting her with a husband she loved and who loved her in return, along with their sweet, silly daughter and her furniture-nibbling spaniel.

"Will you be needing anything else this evening, Your Grace?" Jenkinson asked politely.

Your Grace.

A reminder that she was married now. A duchess. Brandon's wife.

She smiled at her lady's maid. "That will be all, thank you."

Jenkinson quietly exited the chamber, leaving Lottie alone to anticipate her new husband. She wore a wrapper over a gold silk nightgown that had been designed by the famed Mrs. Loveton specifically for the occasion. It was wispy and transparent, and she had no doubt that Brandon was going to love her in it. Her hair was unbound, trailing over her shoulders and all the way down her back. And she couldn't lie—she felt just a bit like the goddess her husband insisted she was.

A tap sounded at the door separating their chambers, and she called for him to enter. They had spent the day in a flurry of activity. First, the wedding with hundreds of guests, the church festooned in flowers of her choosing. Next, the wedding breakfast with all their friends and family, including a beaming Mrs. Carrington-Smythe. Cat had managed to find her way into the celebration, stealing nearly a plateful of Bayonne ham until a footman had caught her and sent her off to the nursery. Pandy had been on her best behavior, and there hadn't even been a hint of a rotten pig trotter.

The day had been wondrous and exhausting, but now it was time for Lottie and Brandon to be blissfully alone at last.

The door opened to reveal him, handsome in bare feet and a black silk dressing gown, a swath of his chest visible beneath, his wavy, dark hair tousled rakishly over his brow. She took one look at him, and her heart thudded, a rush of heat flooding her.

"Alone at last," he said, a sensual smile curving his lips.

"And not a moment too soon." Returning his smile, she reached for the belt on her wrapper, shrugging it to the floor.

His smoldering stare devoured her as his long strides ate up the distance separating them. "I thought you were beautiful in your wedding gown earlier, but my God, Lottie. You're perfection."

He pulled her into his tall, hard form, and she felt the rigid thickness of his cock prodding her belly as she looped her arms around his waist. "Do you like my nightgown? I had it made just for you and this evening."

"Like it? I love it. I want to tear it off you with my teeth."

She chuckled at his vehemence. "No tearing it, if you please. It was far too dear for that."

He pressed a kiss to her throat. "Mmm, you smell so bloody good."

She had applied some of her scent there and to her inner wrists, knowing too well the effect it had on him.

Lottie inhaled deeply, rubbing her breasts against his chest subtly as she did so. "You smell good too."

"No thanks to Cat," he grumbled. "The imp leapt on me and licked my face and neck while I was taking off my boots."

She laughed, envisioning the spaniel attacking him with her lolling tongue, and brushed her lips over his temple. "I hope you rinsed off her slobber."

He kissed his way to her ear. "Of course I did. Which reminds me, I discovered a frog in my wash basin. I suspect Pandy found him in the gardens. I'll need to have a word with her about bringing creatures into the house again." He caught her earlobe in his teeth and tugged. "I did warn you that you were joining a menagerie."

"And I told you there was nowhere else I would rather be," she reminded him, finding the buttons on his dressing gown and plucking them free, one by one.

He cupped her breast through the fine fabric of her nightgown, swirling his thumb over her hard nipple. "I love that you're here." He caught her nipple between his thumb and forefinger, pinching it lightly and sending a rush of molten desire through her. "I love that you're my wife." His mouth trailed a path of hot kisses along her collarbone. "I love *you*."

"And I love you." She opened the last button of his dressing gown, leaving it parted, and stepped back to admire him.

His cock protruded thickly from between the parted ends of fabric, calling for her attention. She wanted to lavish pleasure upon him. To show him with deeds rather than words how much he had come to mean to her. Against her will, she had fallen beneath this beautiful rake's spell, and she wouldn't change a moment of it. Not one single second. Because he was hers, she was his, and their love had proven stronger than the obstacles between them.

She lowered herself to her knees.

"Lottie," he protested.

"My love," she countered and grasped the base of his shaft, his skin hot and smooth and soft, stretched taut.

She brought the tip of him past her lips. Her tongue lashed over the crown, teasing him, taunting him, tasting the salty essence of him. He made a low sound of suppressed need, one of his hands landing on the back of her head, lightly cradling. And she was already wet between her legs, her own sex heavy and pulsing with uncontrollable need.

Because she wanted to watch, she tilted her head back slightly, looking up the muscular angles and planes of his body to meet his burning emerald gaze.

Still holding his stare, she took his cock deeper.

A strangled growl fled him, his fingers sifting through her hair. She concentrated on him, his eyes, his length, the taste of him, struggling to keep from reflexively gagging as his crown found the back of her throat. And then she withdrew, allowing him to glide past her wet lips, almost releasing him before taking him again. More and more, slowly at first, but then with increased speed as his hips chased her mouth and his fingers wrapped in her hair. She inhaled through her nose, loving the scent of him—male, musky, heady.

He was hers, and she reveled in it. In the taste of him, the feeling of him.

"Venus," he said raggedly. "My Venus. If you don't stop, I'll come in your mouth, and that isn't how I intended for this night to proceed."

His warning made her wetter still and more determined to bring him to release. She wanted him to lose control. Wanted his seed on her tongue, wanted to swallow him down, to take this part of him, wanted his helpless pleasure.

He moaned again as she continued, lavishing long sucks and slow, teasing licks on the vein at the underside of his shaft when she needed a breath. And still, she held his gaze all the while. Held his gaze until his long, dark lashes fanned over those brilliant green orbs and his head fell back, his lips parting, his Adam's apple on prominent display, his chest heaving with the force of his need.

"God, Lottie. Your mouth I'm going to spill. Final warning."

His voice was low and decadent like his French wine and soft as velvet. She loved the helpless need lacing it, loved knowing she was responsible for his loss of control. That she was the one who was about to bring him to completion, the one to force his surrender.

She withdrew, stroking over his slick cock with her hand to keep him primed, and said, "I want you to come in my mouth. On my tongue. I want to swallow your seed."

Filthy words. These were not the words a sweet, virginal debutante would ever give the man she married. But she was neither sweet, nor virginal. She had embraced her sensual nature, her needs and desires. And she had learned not to be ashamed but to be proud of who she was, the goddess he imagined her. The woman he had chosen.

She took his beautiful cock back into her mouth, giving him what they both wanted.

"Fuck," he groaned, his hips pumping wildly now, his cock hitting the back of her throat again.

And then there was the hot flood of him down her throat, over her tongue. So much that her mouth was filled with him, and she swallowed and swallowed, taking every last drop of him as hers.

∼

"My turn," Brandon told Lottie when he had caught his breath and regained his wits after she had drained him dry.

He had her on the bed in an instant, her gossamer nightgown stripped away. For a moment, he admired her, naked and glorious, all creamy skin and coppery flecks, her hair a fiery ripple on the pillow, her blue eyes dark with desire, her mouth glistening and swollen from taking his cock between her lips.

But he was voracious, so he didn't look long before he settled between her thighs. "Open for me, Venus."

And she did, spreading her legs, cupping her bare breasts as she watched, toying with her pert pink nipples. The sight was enough to have his limp prick filling again, the rush of need returning with a vengeance. Her cunny beckoned, glistening and pretty as a blossoming flower.

He bent, licking her seam, savoring the taste of her on his tongue, pleased to find she was already wet from sucking him. He licked into her then, filling her as he would soon with his cock, stroking her pearl lightly as he did so. Her hips danced beneath him. She was all he could breathe, all he could feel, his tongue darting in and out of her hot cunny, fucking her, driving them both wild. And then he pulled back her folds, revealing the swollen, sleek nub of her sex, before he latched on to it, sucking hard as he sank a finger deep inside her tight, wet depths.

She came apart in his hands, against his lips, her cunny

clenching hard on him. And he stayed there with her, licking and sucking, devouring her, worshiping her as she had him, until he could not withstand another moment. His cock was hard again, ready for more.

At last, he tore his mouth away, lips wet with her dew, and rose, taking himself in hand and rubbing the head of his cock along her slippery pussy.

"More," she commanded.

And he gave her more. With one thrust, he filled her, her sheath contracting deliciously around him as the pulses of her release fluttered through her. He glanced down to where they were joined, watching as he fucked her, his ruddy cock sinking into the hot, velvet depths of her cunny, then gliding out and in again.

"I love you," he told her, bending to take the peak of one breast in his mouth and suckling as he continued his pace.

"And I love you," she gasped, her fingernails raking down his shoulders, her hips undulating to meet him thrust for thrust.

She was his wife.

Almost impossible to believe that this woman was his forever.

They moved together, their rhythm faster, harder. He took her lips with his, kissing her deeply, giving her his tongue. She sucked on it, threading her fingers through his hair, and then she came again, her cunny pulsing around him deliciously as she moaned into his mouth. Another pump of his hips, and he followed her, the hot rush of his spend jetting from him and into her.

She held him to her, their hearts hammering like a blacksmith on an anvil, and he buried his face in her throat, breathing deeply of Lottie, of the scent of the two of them intertwined. For the first time, neither of them would leave at dawn, and the knowledge that he would fall asleep with her and wake alongside her filled him with a deep, sweet contentment.

In two days' time, they would be leaving for France with Pandy on their honeymoon. Brandon intended to show Lottie the wineries she had dreamt of seeing. Their life together was just beginning.

EPILOGUE

ONE YEAR LATER

"Gently, Pandy girl," Lottie said as she placed the swaddled baby in a seated Pandy's waiting arms. "You must support his head and take care not to move, or you will disturb him."

"Oh, Mama," Pandy said, her voice hushed. "Albert's hands is so small."

"His hands *are* small," Lottie corrected, smiling down at the two children who, though they had not been born of her womb, were hers.

It had taken time to earn that place in Pandy's eyes and in her heart, but slowly, surely, they had bonded. And when one day, Pandy had burst into tears over a skinned knee after she'd been skipping on the garden's gravel path and had rushed to Lottie for comfort, calling her Mama for the first time, Lottie herself had been moved to tears.

"Are small," Pandy repeated, gazing in wonder at her new brother. "He's sleeping."

A recent arrival at the orphanage, Albert had been left by a young mother who was already overburdened with too many mouths to feed. Lottie had been taking tea with the orphanage director, Mr. Slatkin, when the baby had arrived. And something within her had simply known that she was meant to be his mother.

"Babies sleep a great deal when they are small," Lottie told Pandy. "They need their strength to grow big."

"Big like me," Pandy said, puffing up her shoulders importantly.

"Big like you," Lottie agreed, smiling as she straightened at last, aware she had been hovering over little Albert.

The way Pandy was positioned on the settee, a pillow at her side, meant that the baby was in no danger of sliding from his sister's lap. As Lottie watched the two of them together, she had to blink furiously to clear away the prickle of tears.

"I'm biggerer 'n Jane," Pandy declared.

"You ain't," declared her five-year-old sister as she dashed into the room, Cat trailing happily at her heels.

Behind her came Brandon, grinning at the antics of their other daughter, whom they had also brought home from the orphanage. She and Pandy had made fast friends, and they shared a true sisterly bond that extended to rivalries, arguing, and the occasional bit of naughty antics, from pepper on each other's pillows to tying together the laces of each other's boots.

"I'm older'n you," Pandy pointed out quietly, displaying a remarkable restraint Lottie hadn't been certain the spirited child possessed. "That means I'm biggerer."

Jane harrumphed—likely the result of spending too much time with Brandon's grandmother—and flounced onto the settee at Pandy's side. "I'm tallerer."

"I'm the tallerest," Pandy countered.

Albert shifted, beginning to make sounds of protest.

"Hush, you two," Brandon cautioned tenderly. "You're disturbing your brother. You can argue over which of you is tallest later."

Cat settled on the carpet at the foot of the settee, curling up with a contented sigh. With two girls to play chase-chase with her, Cat now no longer had quite the surfeit of enthusiasm she had a year ago. Lottie bent and gave the spaniel's silken head a fond scratch as Brandon reached her, placing an arm around her waist and pulling her into his side.

"I've missed you," he murmured, pressing a chaste kiss to her cheek for the benefit of the children.

"You were only gone in the gardens with Jane and Cat for one quarter hour," she said, grinning at her handsome husband, love for him beating strong and firm in her heart.

"It felt like an eternity without you." He winked.

"What's a turnity?" Jane asked.

"It's a pudding, silly," Pandy answered before either Lottie or Brandon could. "And not a very good one, neither."

They shared an amused glance.

"Eternity is something without end," Brandon said then, holding her gaze. "Like the love I have for your mama and for all of you, my family."

And her heart, already bursting with an abundance of love, filled just a bit more.

∽

One year later

SOMETHING MIRACULOUS HAD HAPPENED.

Lottie didn't know quite how to tell Brandon. Their family had grown and blossomed over the two years of their marriage. Pandy, Jane, Albert, Cat, and a new furred addition as well—ironically, a gray-and-white cat who had aptly been named Dog by Jane. Lottie had reveled in being a mother, in embracing that part of herself that she had thought she would never know.

Each day was one of new challenges and triumphs, of love and laughter and fur and barking and meowing and the occasional game of chase-chase and tears and sniffles and tricks and games of hide-and-go-seek. It was crumbs and spills, mayhem and peace, all wrapped in family and home.

Lottie had the happiness, the family, and the husband she had once only dreamt of having. And now, their family was going to grow just a bit more.

When she had first begun feeling dizzied in the morning and then sick to her stomach, she had thought she had contracted some manner of illness. But then she had spoken with her friends Hyacinth and Rosamund, who had realized what was amiss when she had nearly swooned during tea.

Lottie was with child.

Yet again, something she had never thought possible for her. Two years had passed without Lottie becoming *enceinte*, and her old suspicions had proven true. She was barren.

But she had been wrong.

This morning, the doctor had confirmed her suspicions.

It was time to tell her husband.

Lottie stopped at his study door and knocked. He spent mornings tending to business affairs in the sanctity of his study and shared the afternoons and evenings with her and the children. Her news could not wait until afternoon, however.

"Enter," he called.

And with a deep breath, she did, reminded of that day over two years before when she had crossed this same threshold, coming to him to ask him to marry her. He had told her every day since, in word and deed, what her previous husband had not—that she, Lottie, was enough, that she was worthy. That he appreciated her and loved her, and that there was no other woman in the world whom he would rather have at his side, as his wife.

~

BRANDON LOOKED up from the correspondence he had been poring over when his magnificent wife swept into the room. He stood, half ready to carry her to his chamber and make love to her for the rest of the morning. She was wearing his favorite shade of blue, the one that matched her eyes.

"Did you miss me?" he teased, for they had only breakfasted some three hours before.

"Every moment I'm not with you," she said with a small, tender smile.

There was something different about her this morning, something that had been absent at breakfast, he thought. A seriousness.

"Is something amiss, Lottie?" He rounded his desk and went to her, admiring the way the sunlight shone in the window and caught in her cinnamon curls.

"Nothing is wrong," she said, "but perhaps we ought to sit down."

He didn't think he liked the sound of that. "The last time you wanted me to sit down, it was to tell me that Pandy had thrown a pig trotter through the library window."

Lottie winced. "That was because I feared you would be cross with her, and it truly was an accident."

Pandy had been playing a game of fetch-and-carry with Cat, and she had tossed the pig trotter in question with just a trifle too much force, shattering the library window in the process. Brandon had been nettled by her carelessness, but

Pandy was Pandy, and that meant that, generally speaking, wherever she went, mischief inevitably followed.

"Are all the windows intact?" he asked.

"As far as I am aware." She reached for his hand, twining her fingers through his. "Come with me, my love."

He clasped her hand, allowing her to guide him to a pair of wingback chairs by the hearth. Lottie seated herself primly in one, and he sank into the other.

"Well, darling? What is it that you need to tell me?"

She stared at him for a moment, eyes wide, and then she blinked. "How would you like for our family to grow a bit larger?"

Instantly, he thought of the dog and the cat who were forever chasing each other about, up and down the halls of their town house. "I'm not certain I can bear to add one more furred creature to the mix. These two are bedlam enough. Unless you're considering a bird? Perhaps a dove or a parrot, even. Something more contained."

"Or a child," she said.

They had already taken in two children from the orphanage in two years. Little Albert had just begun to toddle about. Pandy and Jane were growing like weeds. The thought of another child joining their family was both wonderful and daunting.

"Perhaps we might wait just a bit," he cautioned. "Albert is yet young, and Jane and Pandy have only just begun to calm in their mischievous rivalries."

Lottie licked her lips, and he found himself momentarily distracted by the hint of that talented pink tongue, wanting to kiss her. "I'm afraid we may not be able to wait for longer than early summer."

He frowned at her. "Early summer is months away."

She nodded. "Approximately six months."

Brandon still didn't understand. "So, you would like to add another child to our family, but in six months?"

"Yes."

"Well, then I reckon we shall have ample time to ponder the notion and to see what the children think before we make our decision."

"I'm afraid not," she said, biting her lip.

"There's something you're trying to tell me, isn't there, Venus?" he asked, using his sobriquet for her as he did often when they were alone.

So often that she didn't even bother to correct him any longer with nonsense protestations that she wasn't a goddess. Just as well. They both knew she was, and Brandon wouldn't accept arguments to the contrary.

"What I'm trying to tell you is that I am having a baby in early summer," Lottie said.

He blinked, thinking he must have misheard. But no, his beautiful wife was still staring at him in expectation, the gentle rays of morning sun bringing to life the golden hues hidden in her glorious hair.

"You're having a baby," he said, his voice sounding rusty.

Feeling rusty, too.

"Yes."

"But you... I thought that we couldn't..."

He spluttered, trying to make sense of everything she had said. It had never mattered to him that they might be incapable of physically having children. They had built a family of their own together, one filled with love. He hadn't considered that her becoming with child was even a possibility.

The notion now seemed astonishing for how very foreign —and terrifying—it was.

"I thought so as well," she said gently. "But I have missed my courses, and the doctor assures me that I'm going to have a baby come summer."

"We're going to have another baby," he said in wonder.

"Four children in less than three years," she agreed. "Do you think that's too many?"

"I think that our family is perfect." He reached for her hand again, bringing it to his lips for a reverent kiss. "*You're* perfect. I'm petrified at the very thought of you enduring what you must for this. But you're perfect, my love, just as you've always been."

"You will be brave for me," she said, her eyes glittering with unshed tears.

"You've been brave enough for the both of us," he countered, cupping her face and catching a tear as it fell with his thumb. "What's this, my love? Tears of sadness?"

"No." She pressed a kiss to his palm. "Tears of happiness. I never thought I would find such contentment, such joy, as I have with you and our children. And yes, even our cat and dog."

"I remain firm on no more furred creatures," he said, feeling the prickle of answering tears in his own eyes. "Cat and Dog are quite enough for the moment. I shudder to think of what will be next. A fox named Hen? A canary named Duck?"

"I suppose it could be anything," Lottie said, smiling. "Only think of what shall happen when Albert is old enough to make friends in the garden. Or this little one."

She patted her midriff.

Brandon couldn't remain where he was a moment more. He stood and, in one graceful move, scooped Lottie into his arms. "For the moment, there's only one thing I want to think about, and it hasn't a thing to do with creatures or gardens or our children."

"Oh?" Her smile turned knowing.

He kissed her swiftly, softly, tenderly before lifting his head again. "It's making love to my wife."

She cupped his cheek, love shining in her eyes. "I wholeheartedly approve."

~

THANK you so very much for reading *Duke with a Reputation*! When I first wrote Lottie and the Duke of Brandon years ago, I had no idea how many readers would reach out to me, asking for their story, and I thank you all for caring so much about these two and wanting their story to be told. Giving them their happily ever after at last, along with their children and mischievous pets, was a true delight for me. I hope you loved them all. Do read on for a sneak peek of *Duke with a Debt* (Wicked Dukes Society Book 2), featuring Miss Rosamund Payne and the Duke of Camden. (And we can't forget Megs, of course.) Theirs is an enemies-to-lovers marriage of convenience tale you won't want to miss, filled with revenge, betrayal, mystery, and steam. And if you're looking for Hyacinth and Viscount Sidmouth's happily ever after, you can find it in *Her Virtuous Viscount*.

Please stay in touch! The only way to be sure you'll know what's next from me is to sign up for my newsletter here: http://eepurl.com/dyJSar. Please join my reader group for early excerpts, cover reveals, and more here: https://www.facebook.com/groups/scarlettscotreaders. And if you're in the mood to chat all things steamy historical romance and read a different book together each month, join my book club, Dukes Do It Hotter right here: https://www.facebook.com/groups/hotdukes because we're having a whole lot of fun!

Now, do read on for that sneak peek of *Duke with a Debt* I promised!

Duke with a Debt

DUKE WITH A REPUTATION

Wicked Dukes Society
Book 2

Stuart Gilden, the arrogant and cold Duke of Camden, is suffocating beneath a mountain of debt caused by his wastrel father and gambling brother. To make matters worse, he's being blackmailed by a mysterious enemy who has threatened to destroy him. Enter Miss Rosamund Payne, London's greatest heiress, who has the wealth Camden so desperately needs. There's just one problem: she's his scoundrel brother's former fiancée.

For years, the unassuming Rosamund has been plagued by fortune hunters, but one hurt her more grievously than the rest. When that rogue's brother comes to her with a shocking proposition, she's cautiously intrigued. Soon, Rosamund finds herself exchanging venomous barbs and searing kisses with the insufferable duke, lured by the prospect of revenge and the undeniable heat smoldering between them.

With their marriage of convenience secured, Camden's problems should be at an end. But in truth, they've just begun. Because his enemy has only grown bolder and more dangerous. And the once unwanted wife beneath his roof is proving a maddening temptation he can't resist, no matter the cost.

Chapter One

THE AFRICAN GREY parrot balanced calmly on its perch was glaring at him.

"Gormless shite," the bird pronounced, flapping its wings as if to punctuate its words.

Stuart Gilden, Duke of Camden, glared back at the feathered creature who had just paid him insult, walking slowly toward it, hands clasped behind his back. He stopped before the parrot, cocking his head and holding its unique silvery stare.

"Do you know," he said pleasantly, "I could wring your neck with one hand?"

"Landlubber," the parrot squawked. "Pistols at dawn."

His eyes narrowed. "Did you just challenge me to a duel?"

Incredulousness rose within him. This was indeed the strangest bird he had ever met. Intelligent, complex, and just a touch mad. Rather like its owner, whose presence he was awaiting.

"Megs want a biscuit," the parrot told him.

"I haven't a biscuit," he said. "And to be perfectly candid, if I had one, I'm not sure I'd share it with you. You've been rather rude thus far, haven't you?"

"Gormless shite," the parrot said, extending its wings again.

"Megs, my love, I've told you about your language."

The familiar, feminine voice had Stuart turning away from the feathered menace to find Miss Rosamund Payne gliding toward him. It had been some time since their paths had crossed, for their circles had only overlapped thanks to Wesley. But little had changed since he had seen her last.

Her hair was the same, indistinct shade of neither gold nor red, but an odd color all its own. Her eyes were sharp and dark in her pale face. Her chin was stubborn and pointed, her forehead high. She still had the mouth of a courtesan, the only overtly sensual feature she possessed and quite incongruous with her unassuming spinsterish air. Her figure was trim and not overly curvaceous as he preferred, her breasts small and hidden in her modest silk bodice, her height slightly taller than most ladies' and yet still no match for his. No one could ever call Miss Rosamund Payne a great beauty.

Still, there was something compelling about her. He had always found her presence magnetic in a painfully unwanted way. She had been meant to be his sister, and it hadn't been his place to notice her. Yet, notice her, he had.

But she scarcely seemed to notice Stuart now as she bustled past him to her infernal parrot.

"Do be a good parrot, and I'll give you a pistachio," she purred in a tone that would have been better suited to a lover than a feathered beast.

"Megs want pistache," the African grey declared.

Stuart stepped to the side, granting Rosamund and her bustle more room, trying not to take note of her perfume, which also had not changed—a decadent blend of rose, violet, bergamot, and ambergris that was rich and alluring.

"Will Megs behave?" she asked the parrot, holding up a small pouch.

"Megs behave," the bird chirped, then whistled.

Rosamund carefully removed one small oval nut and offered it to the parrot, who gleefully took the object in its beak. Stuart was distinctly aware that he was being ignored, and the novel sensation wasn't a pleasant one.

Rosamund trailed an elegant finger over the bird's head. "Good parrot, Megs."

And then, at last, ever so slowly, she turned the full force of her attention upon him, her dark stare burning into his. "Good afternoon, Camden. I cannot think of a single reason you would have for paying a call upon me."

No curtsy. Nary a smile. Not a *Your Grace*, and most definitely not a hint of welcome. Stuart wasn't certain what he had expected.

"Rosamund," he greeted in turn, offering a slight bow. "It is good to see you."

She arched a brow. "Is it?"

Heat crept up his throat.

"Of course," he fibbed.

She pursed her lips. "I suppose we should sit. Comfort is important when one is being lied to, I find."

Her observation was sharper than any blade.

But he was at her mercy, and far more than she yet realized.

He inclined his head. "As you wish, madam."

"I've called for a tray of tea as well," she said coolly before swishing past him.

She moved to the seating area across the room and gingerly settled on a settee, smoothing her seafoam-green skirts. He followed, folding his taller frame into a narrow chair nearby, sparing her his proximity on her seat even as part of him was tempted to do otherwise. Belatedly, it occurred to him that her navy bodice bore the outline of gold scales as if she were a mermaid, the entire affair accented with seafoam ribbon on the sleeves and decolletage.

The fanciful dress, so incongruous with what he knew of her, took him by surprise.

"I must thank you for accepting my call," he forced himself to say, though they were both more than aware that she had kept him waiting, in the presence of the insult-wielding parrot, for half an hour.

"It was unexpected." She watched him, unsmiling, so very poised. "And not entirely pleasant, if I am honest."

Her forthright nature was something he recalled well. But what disturbed him now was that he also remembered her tears, the accusation in her sharp, dark eyes. He remembered how shattered she had looked, like a hand mirror that had been dropped upon a stone hearth.

Stuart brushed aside the memory as he winced. "I'll admit that I had harbored some hope that the intervening years might have rendered you more amenable to a tête-à-tête with me."

She laughed then, the sound throaty and pleasant and full, before her levity faded, and she continued regarding him with her unnerving gaze. "I regret to report that they have not."

God. She would not make this easy on him, then. Why had he supposed she would?

He gripped the arms of his chair. "I am sorry for that, Rosamund."

"As am I," she said, unsmiling. "Actually, I'm sorry for a great many things."

"A great many things," the parrot chimed in, apparently having finished with its pistachio.

Rosamund's searing stare made his necktie feel more like a noose. He turned his attention to the African grey for a moment to find the bird was watching him as closely as its mistress was.

"Gormless shite," the bird repeated, before issuing another whistle.

He clenched his jaw and snapped his attention back to Rosamund. "It would seem the bird has made his opinion of me quite clear."

"*Her* opinion," Rosamund corrected. "Megs is a female parrot. She was also quite bonded to her former master, who was a sea captain, hence some of her more...colorful vocabulary."

He was suddenly dying to know how an heiress dressed as a mermaid had acquired a sea captain's foul-mouthed parrot, but the question would have to wait. He had far more pressing matters to attend at the moment, none of which were pleasant.

"I beg your pardon. I assumed the creature was male."

"Naturally." She gave him a pained smile that was more of

a taunt than aught else, those full lips that would have been better served on a courtesan distracting him.

Her one-word response felt like an insult, and Stuart knew he ought to let the matter go, but he was as obstinate as she, and he couldn't.

"Why do you say that?" he asked.

"Because it is very much like a man to assume that every creature in his path must also be male, in his mold," she said.

"Your opinion of my sex is clearly poor."

Again, her brow arched upward. "Can I be blamed?"

The past lay unspoken, a heavy burden. They stared at each other, two unsmiling enemies—Rosamund with her shrewd gaze and the airs of a queen and Stuart with his swallowed pride and a disgust for his scoundrel of a brother that surely rivaled hers.

"Of course not," he relented. "What my brother did to you was unconscionable."

Her smile was serene. "What he did made me stronger and wiser."

She was utterly unflappable, and this was new. He did not remember such self-possession in her, the ability to flay a man with nothing more than her eyes and tongue. The line of buttons bisecting her bodice drew his attention as she inhaled, the urge to undo them, to muss her irritating perfection perversely rising from nowhere.

"I am relieved to hear it," he forced out.

A tap at the door heralded the arrival of the tea tray. They were silent as a servant bustled in, laying the tray on the table separating them before excusing herself with a curtsy. The dishes of tea which had been laid out looked as if they were antiques, fashioned of fine porcelain lined with gold and decorated with enamel Libra scales on the cup and a water carrier on the saucer. He watched as she prepared his tea precisely as he had always liked it: a splash of milk first, followed by tea and two lumps of sugar.

She had remembered.

Her attention to detail felt somehow strangely intimate, particularly when their fingers brushed as she handed him his tea. The sweet bergamot of Earl Grey rose from the steaming cup.

"Thank you," he said, deciding the fine porcelain he held was likely Meissen.

He wondered if Rosamund had purchased the cups and saucers herself or if they had belonged to her mother, whose eccentricities and affinity for collections had been rather notorious.

She finished preparing her own tea. "You are most welcome. To the tea if not at my home."

The reminder that they were bitterest enemies was pointed. She would serve him tea and recall precisely how he liked it made, but she drew the line at false pleasantries.

"Megs want a tea cake," the parrot called from across the room, reminding him of her presence.

Well, at least she hadn't called him a gormless shite again. Progress.

"You shall have one in a few minutes, darling," Rosamund returned, her voice gentling as she responded to the bird.

And Stuart found himself suddenly, irritatingly envious of the feathered menace still glaring at him from her perch.

"Now then," Rosamund said suddenly, returning the full, disconcerting force of her attention upon him. "I don't imagine you came here for idle conversation or tea. What is it that brought you to me, Camden?"

His heart thumped hard. Here was his opportunity. And yet, the words felt thick and heavy and improperly formed. His tongue was stuck, his mouth dry. He, who had faced death and destruction and the hells of war, was terrified of four little words that, taken separately, were all rather inconsequential save one.

He could do this.

He *had* to do this.

The contents of the letter he had received yesterday was still burned upon his soul.

Stuart took a deep, steadying breath, holding Rosamund's dark stare. "Will you marry me?"

Want more? Get *Duke with a Debt* now!

DON'T MISS SCARLETT'S OTHER ROMANCES!

Complete Book List
HISTORICAL ROMANCE

Heart's Temptation
A Mad Passion (Book One)
Rebel Love (Book Two)
Reckless Need (Book Three)
Sweet Scandal (Book Four)
Restless Rake (Book Five)
Darling Duke (Book Six)
The Night Before Scandal (Book Seven)

Wicked Husbands
Her Errant Earl (Book One)
Her Lovestruck Lord (Book Two)
Her Reformed Rake (Book Three)
Her Deceptive Duke (Book Four)
Her Missing Marquess (Book Five)
Her Virtuous Viscount (Book Six)

DON'T MISS SCARLETT'S OTHER ROMANCES!

Wicked Dukes Society
Duke with a Reputation (Book One)
Duke with a Debt (Book Two)

Christmas Dukes
The Duke Who Despised Christmas (Book One)

League of Dukes
Nobody's Duke (Book One)
Heartless Duke (Book Two)
Dangerous Duke (Book Three)
Shameless Duke (Book Four)
Scandalous Duke (Book Five)
Fearless Duke (Book Six)

Notorious Ladies of London
Lady Ruthless (Book One)
Lady Wallflower (Book Two)
Lady Reckless (Book Three)
Lady Wicked (Book Four)
Lady Lawless (Book Five)
Lady Brazen (Book 6)

Unexpected Lords
The Detective Duke (Book One)
The Playboy Peer (Book Two)
The Millionaire Marquess (Book Three)
The Goodbye Governess (Book Four)

Dukes Most Wanted
Forever Her Duke (Book One)
Forever Her Marquess (Book Two)
Forever Her Rake (Book Three)
Forever Her Earl (Book Four)

DON'T MISS SCARLETT'S OTHER ROMANCES!

Forever Her Viscount (Book Five)
Forever Her Scot (Book Six)

The Wicked Winters
Wicked in Winter (Book One)
Wedded in Winter (Book Two)
Wanton in Winter (Book Three)
Wishes in Winter (Book 3.5)
Willful in Winter (Book Four)
Wagered in Winter (Book Five)
Wild in Winter (Book Six)
Wooed in Winter (Book Seven)
Winter's Wallflower (Book Eight)
Winter's Woman (Book Nine)
Winter's Whispers (Book Ten)
Winter's Waltz (Book Eleven)
Winter's Widow (Book Twelve)
Winter's Warrior (Book Thirteen)
A Merry Wicked Winter (Book Fourteen)

The Sinful Suttons
Sutton's Spinster (Book One)
Sutton's Sins (Book Two)
Sutton's Surrender (Book Three)
Sutton's Seduction (Book Four)
Sutton's Scoundrel (Book Five)
Sutton's Scandal (Book Six)
Sutton's Secrets (Book Seven)

Rogue's Guild
Her Ruthless Duke (Book One)
Her Dangerous Beast (Book Two)
Her Wicked Rogue (Book 3)

DON'T MISS SCARLETT'S OTHER ROMANCES!

Royals and Renegades
How to Love a Dangerous Rogue (Book One)
How to Tame a Dissolute Prince (Book Two)

Sins and Scoundrels
Duke of Depravity
Prince of Persuasion
Marquess of Mayhem
Sarah
Earl of Every Sin
Duke of Debauchery
Viscount of Villainy

Sins and Scoundrels Box Set Collections
Volume 1
Volume 2

The Wicked Winters Box Set Collections
Collection 1
Collection 2
Collection 3
Collection 4

Wicked Husbands Box Set Collections
Volume 1
Volume 2

Notorious Ladies of London Box Set Collections
Volume 1

The Sinful Suttons Box Set Collections
Volume 1

Stand-alone Novella

DON'T MISS SCARLETT'S OTHER ROMANCES!

Lord of Pirates

CONTEMPORARY ROMANCE
Love's Second Chance
Reprieve (Book One)
Perfect Persuasion (Book Two)
Win My Love (Book Three)

Coastal Heat
Loved Up (Book One)

ABOUT THE AUTHOR

USA Today and Amazon bestselling author Scarlett Scott writes steamy Victorian and Regency romance with strong, intelligent heroines and sexy alpha heroes. She lives in Pennsylvania and Maryland with her Canadian husband, their adorable identical twins, a demanding diva of a dog, and a zany cat who showed up one summer and never left.

A self-professed literary junkie and nerd, she loves reading anything, but especially romance novels and poetry. Catch up with her on her website https://scarlettscottauthor.com. Hearing from readers never fails to make her day.

Scarlett's complete book list and information about upcoming releases can be found at https://scarlettscottauthor.com.

Connect with Scarlett! You can find her here:
 Join Scarlett Scott's reader group on Facebook for early excerpts, giveaways, and a whole lot of fun!
 Sign up for her newsletter here
 https://www.tiktok.com/@authorscarlettscott

- facebook.com/AuthorScarlettScott
- x.com/scarscoromance
- instagram.com/scarlettscottauthor
- bookbub.com/authors/scarlett-scott
- amazon.com/Scarlett-Scott/e/B004NW8N2I
- pinterest.com/scarlettscott

Printed in Great Britain
by Amazon